T0154720

GIVE UP
THE DEAD

Also by Joe Clifford

The Jay Porter Novels

Lamentation

December Boys

Broken Ground

Nonseries

Wake the Undertaker

Memoir

Junkie Love

Anthologies

Choice Cuts

Trouble in the Heartland (editor)

GIVE UP THE DEAD

A JAY PORTER NOVEL

JOE CLIFFORD

OCEANVIEW ((PUBLISHING
SARASOTA, FLORIDA

Copyright © 2017 Joe Clifford

All rights reserved. No part of this book may be reproduced in any form or by any electronic or mechanical means, including information storage and retrieval systems, without permission in writing from the publisher, except by a reviewer who may quote brief passages in a review.

This book is a work of fiction. Names, characters, businesses, organizations, places, and incidents either are the products of the author's imagination or are used fictitiously. Any resemblance to actual events, businesses, locales, or persons living or dead, is entirely coincidental.

ISBN 978-1-60809-296-3

Published in the United States of America by Oceanview Publishing
Sarasota, Florida
www.oceanviewpub.com

10 9 8 7 6 5 4 3 2

PRINTED IN THE UNITED STATES OF AMERICA

For Troy
Brother, I miss you like hell . . .

GIVE UP
THE DEAD

CHAPTER ONE

DINNER WAS NICE. Not the meal so much. The only restaurant we could find open on Thanksgiving was Denny's, and you never walk out of Denny's saying, "That was a good decision." But spending time with my wife and son, just the three of us, the way it's supposed to be—the way it used to be—at least for an hour or so, I was happy, content, at peace. Then her new husband picked them up in his nicer car, and I had to say goodbye to my family in an overcast parking lot as the cold November winds blew.

I tried to rub feeling back in my leg. The nerve damage from an accident three years ago always hurt worse in winter. The pain radiated down my calf, shot into my ribs, jabbing my heart. I dropped my plastic bag of turkey leftovers, lit a cigarette, and tried to forget where it all went wrong.

I was failing miserably when my boss, Tom Gable, called.

"Will you be able to make an auction tonight?"

"Tonight?"

"Hate to ask on Thanksgiving. But I got the wife and in-laws at the house, and Freddie is crawling up my ass. This fella, Keith Mortenson, flew in from North Carolina. He's clearing out the family estate. Old money. Real antsy to get back. If we don't host, he'll go to Owen Eaton, and we lose the commission. Supposed to be some bargains."

Wasn't often we got asked to auction on a holiday. In fact I couldn't remember having done one before. And I'd been clearing estates for Tom Gable since high school.

"Besides your usual percentage," Tom said, "how's three hundred sound?"

Sounded pretty fucking good. I was hurting for cash, and I needed something to do with my evening. All I had waiting for me at home was a dumpy one-bedroom above a filling station and a fat cat with whom I didn't particularly get along. Staring at a three-hour drive back to New Hampshire, long stretches of desolate highway, with too much time to think, I would've done it for free. Not that I was telling Tom that.

"Give me a few," I said. "I'm still in Burlington." I didn't need to mention what I was doing there. Tom knew about my life.

"Plenty of time. Auction doesn't start till seven. Dulac said he'd open the shop. Stop by my place. I'll give you the money."

Jacques Dulac rented the other half of the warehouse, a gardening supply outlet that didn't do much business this time of year. During slow months he didn't mind if we stashed our showcase on his side of the room. But that meant when the night was over, I'd have to drag everything back to our side. Total pain in the ass. Which was why I was stoked Tom had acquired a new warehouse in Pittsfield. With way more square footage, the new space was big enough to house a permanent display *and* host sales. No more rolling stones up a hill.

I flicked my burning cigarette into a snow bank and hoisted my gimpy leg inside the Chevy. "On my way."

"Thanks, Jay. I don't know what I'd do without you."

An ice storm poised to slam us that night. Winter had gotten an early start this season. Life on the mountain. I punched the truck in gear and tried not to think about temporary dinners, permanent missteps, and the possibility of different lives. This afternoon my wife and son were on loan. Seeing Aiden, now almost six years old, hearing the stuff that would come out of his mouth, the one-liners and comebacks, knowing I wouldn't be around to catch those little moments killed me. I turned up the radio so I didn't have to think. Springsteen didn't help.

By the time I crossed state lines I'd worked myself up. It's not the proms or weddings, the driver's license tests or Little League games. I'd catch the big stuff. The real remorse rooted in the mundane, the day-to-day. Silliness around the breakfast table, family movies on a snowy night, hot chocolate, decorating a tree, someone else playing Dad.

Another reason I was grateful for Tom's call. If I focused on work, I could avoid wallowing in the shallow ends of self-pity. And for the first time in a long time, I had my eye on the prize. Tom Gable was getting out of the antiques game. He wanted to sell. And he wanted me to buy.

"I'm tired of busting ass up here," he said. "Winter lasts too damned long on this mountain. And I've always liked you, Jay."

I liked him, too. But mutual admiration wasn't making me forty grand richer. I'd need at least that much to get a loan. My entire life I never enjoyed more than a thousand bucks in the bank. Jenny and her new husband may've shared a big house in the swanky suburbs of Burlington, but I was struggling to keep my head above water in Ashton. Tom and I had a handshake agreement. One year to come up with the cash. Otherwise he'd be forced to sell to Owen Eaton and the Clearing House.

By the time I got to Tom's farmhouse in the foothills, the sky had fallen hard, a slate curtain lowered. Tom met me on the porch with a fat envelope. He was drunk, the big man unsteady on his feet, another reason not to get behind the wheel on these twisty, frozen trails. Sounded like a helluva party inside. I peered around my boss' hefty frame, smelling hot brandy, apples, and cinnamon. House was packed, a middle-aged rager. Old-timey Christmas music blared. I saw his wife, Freddie, who smiled and waved me in. I held up the envelope, and she returned an understanding nod.

Tom clasped my shoulder. "Thanks, Jay," he said, slurring, leading me off the porch to my truck as silver flakes floated down from the heavens. "Really bailing me out."

"Not a problem."

"Really bailing me out," he repeated.

On my way off the mountain, I got a call from my buddy Charlie, who was at the Dubliner, the pub on the other side of town where he spent most nights, drinking beer, playing darts, wasting his life. He'd often try to drag me down with him. I usually begged off. I had to be up at the crack of dawn, and at almost thirty-five years old, I'd grown sick of the bar scene. I heard the desperation in his voice tonight. Even though I was running late, I invited him along, hoping he'd say no. He jumped at the offer. After his latest DUI, Charlie wasn't able to drive, so I had to pick him up. I tried to convince myself it's always better to have an extra set of hands, even if Charlie's bad back and lazy disposition made him a lousy helper. Divorced or never married? What difference does it make? Holidays suck when you're alone.

"How's this work?" Charlie asked as we walked in the warehouse, ice shellacking snowdrifts into frozen waves like some postmodern sculpture. Several trucks cluttered the lot. Lamentation Mountain always bore the brunt of nor'easters.

"You never did an auction for Tom?"

After I quit the business a few years back to try my hand at corporate, a brief experiment that did not end well, Charlie left the phone company to take over for me. Sort of. Charlie was a shiftless employee, and Tom stopped using him.

"I guess Tom didn't trust me with that much money."

Charlie's current gig was milking workman's comp for a back injury he sustained climbing telephone poles. His back *was* messed up. Putting on the pounds hadn't helped. He looked like Jon Favreau, improbably fatter every time I saw him.

The showroom crazed chaotic, merchandise being wheeled in, set up, staged. I pulled my notepad and started taking inventory.

"How was dinner with Jenny and Aiden?" Charlie asked.

"Fine."

In addition to cataloging, a painstaking task, I was also doing surveillance, scoping out what to bid on. I was rolling with five large in my pocket. There were certain items Tom always liked to target—dining- and living-room sets were a favorite because of the considerable markup—but I had leeway. Right now I had my eye on a Horner end table and Claremore sofa. The Flemish buffet looked good, too. I began adding dollars and cents. A 10 to 15 percent markup was my sweet spot.

"Was he there?" Charlie asked.

"Was who where?" I spotted a Serapi carpet. New, those things went for ten grand.

"Y'know . . . him?" Charlie mimed jerking off, my nickname for Stephen, Jenny's new husband.

"Are you fucking serious? No. Just us three."

"That was nice of him."

"Of *him*? Yeah, he's a real fucking sweetheart."

First time I met Stephen, I almost punched him in the head. And that was before he was fucking my wife. I still called Jenny my wife. Didn't matter that we had been divorced for three years, which was almost three times longer than we'd been married.

Jenny and I had been together since high school. Someday we'd all sit around the table—me, Stephen, Jenny, Aiden—a modern TV family. I was fine with that day not being today.

"I mean, it's his family, too."

"They were my family first."

I led Charlie across the floor. A group of buyers huddled around a dark oak Wright Mansfield sideboard and Mid-Century Modular sofa. I was about to put in a bid when I saw Owen Eaton, the other man standing in the way of my dreams.

Almost didn't recognize him at first—Owen, too, had packed on a few pounds. Everyone got fatter but me. He was talking to a slight, brown-haired man, off to the side, whispering. When he spotted me, he whisked the little man outside, beelining to gladhand.

They say the mark of a man is how he treats others who can't do anything for him. By that standard, Owen Eaton was a prick. Unless the guy personally profited, you might as well be squeegee-ing windshields at a traffic light. Cozying up to me wasn't helping his chances of buying Tom's company. That he'd come rushing over, chirpy as a junkie following a fix, a dead giveaway something was fishy.

"Who was that?" I asked, pointing out the back door where the brown-haired man had been jettisoned.

"Oh him?" Owen said, dismissing my query as if I'd just asked about the key grip in a B-movie. "Keith Mortenson." Like the guy who'd orchestrated today's major sale of high-end merchandise was but a minor detail.

They were still rolling in bigger, more elegant pieces. Milo Baugham loungers, Soren Georg rocking chairs. Not the kind of score you often found in Ashton. Why was a guy who lived in North Carolina in such a hurry to hawk gems like this up here?

There were pieces from all over the world. Each part of the globe carries unique markers. Europe, South America, Mexico. To the trained eye, even gold sparkles differently.

"Not bad," Owen said, eyes roving disinterested over the room, a con man's lowball strategy. "Might be a decent find or two."

"Who's helping you tonight?" I asked.

"Flying solo." He feigned consideration for his underlings. "Didn't want to bother my men on Thanksgiving."

"Charlie," I said, nodding at a Wepner stool on the other side of the room. "Do me a favor. See what they are asking for that?"

"Huh?"

I pointed at a stool I didn't give two shits about. Tom already had a set.

I waited till he was gone.

"What's the deal?" I said.

"Same as you. Tryin' to land a few quality—"

"Cut the shit, Owen." The Clearing House was big enough to employ top-flight appraisers, a whole division for purchasing. "Spare me the holiday crap." Owen Eaton would turn out his own mother on Christmas if he thought she'd fetch a nickel.

Owen glanced toward the back door. I pushed past him, bulling outside into the dark parking lot and biting mountain air.

The man he had been talking to, Keith Mortenson, waited across the snowy gravel, beside a small moving van, its doors closed. He squinted in our direction through the slashing sleet.

Owen came trotting after me, reaching for my arm, out of breath.

"You're trying to buy a piece off-site? In *our* parking lot?"

"No, we were about to . . . Okay, you caught me," he said, hushing his voice, which was a stupid precaution, since Keith Mortenson couldn't hear us above the swishing winds. Owen feigned a smile, but it came out more a leer. "Tried to sneak off without payin' the taxman." He pulled a fifty from his clip.

How stupid did he think I was? Confessing to a lesser crime so I'd look past the elephant hiding beneath the bedsheet. Classic misdirection.

I nodded at the moving truck. "What's he got in there? Don't bullshit me."

"Chaucer antique French-carved dresser display cabinet and sideboard."

In decent condition, the eighteenth-century piece could be flipped for twenty tomorrow. Excellent condition, twenty-five wouldn't be out of the question.

Keith Mortenson, with his limp hair and tender frame, didn't have a clue.

"What are you offering?"

Owen fumbled with his hands, chewing on the inside of his cheek. I started toward the truck.

"A grand," he said.

"You're a dirtbag."

"I'll cut you in, Porter. A thousand to keep your mouth shut. Pay Tom his percentage. Or don't. You come up big just by walking away. What do you say?"

If Owen was giving Mortenson a grand and offering me a thousand more not to say anything, he already had a buyer.

"How much are you selling it for?"

"I'm not at liberty—"

"Hey," I called out to Keith Mortenson. "Open that truck." Mortenson checked with Owen. "Don't worry about him," I said.

Owen muttered obscenities while Keith Mortenson opened the doors.

Holy shit.

I climbed in the back of the van and pulled the flashlight on my phone. Not a single ding or dent. "Do you have any idea what this is?"

"My . . . mother's . . . old dresser."

"Did she ever use it?"

"Huh?"

"Mr. Mortenson, that is an antique. One of a kind. Vintage. Top of the line. Mint."

My news didn't register.

"I've been in estate clearing most of my life," I said, hopping down. "I have never seen a piece like this."

"What are you saying?"

"I'm saying that man there—" I glanced over my shoulder, not bothering to shield my disdain "—is trying to fuck you."

Owen Eaton wedged in front of me, in full spin mode. The snow and sleet had begun accumulating at our feet. A fierce howl ripped up the ravine, making it hard to hear.

"Antiques are a tricky business," Owen said. "Not an exact science."

"Don't pull that horseshit. You know how much this is worth."

"Yeah? And where do you suggest Keith here go?" He appealed to Mortenson, before glancing up at the unforgiving sky. "You need to get home to North Carolina? Feel free to try the pawn-shop." He pretended to check his watch. "They'll be open in another twelve hours." Owen laughed like we were all old pals. "This is why you come to men like us. Yes, I plan on makin' money. That's my job. I'm giving you a fair price."

"The fuck you are, Owen."

Mortenson looked to me. "My wife's waiting for me. I have a flight to catch."

"Tell you what," Owen said. "I can go as high as two five."

"A real fucking prince."

"Do better."

I had five grand in my pocket. Cold, hard cash. I knew I could get *at least* twenty. I mean, I was pretty sure. But it wasn't my money. "Can you give me a minute, Mr. Mortenson?"

"Maybe he can," Owen said. "But I can't. This storm is getting bad. I need to get on the road. Listen, Keith, I will pay you three thousand. Right here, right now. But I need your answer."

I could go all in. I had wiggle room but I couldn't go entirely off script. I knew Tom would love to quadruple his money. If I was right.

Keith Mortenson checked with me one last time.

What could I say? Owen had called my bluff. I wasn't a gambler.

"Just make sure we get our cut," I said.

Owen handed me back that fifty and added one more. "Keep the change, Porter."

I headed inside and let Owen complete his swindle. So much for being noble. Mortenson was handing over the prized possession. Owen Eaton was about to make a killing. And for my effort? I was out a thousand bucks.

I'd almost gotten to the door when Mortenson called after me, running up and passing me a wadded ball of fabric.

"Really appreciate you doing this last-minute sale, Mr. Porter," he said.

I opened the gift, holding it by the shoulders. A winter coat. I could use a new one. Mine was threadbare and worn to shit, frayed at the cuffs. I knew I should say thanks, but I'd lost my family, was out a lot of money, and just wasted my Thanksgiving. I wasn't thanking anyone for a fucking coat.

CHAPTER TWO

THE REST OF the night wasn't a total bust. I put in solid bids, brought a decent haul. Sorlie sofa. Pendant chandelier. Travertine end tables. A sturdy, dependable night in which I played it safe, took few chances, and made someone else money. I'd get paid, as always, and when you subtracted bills, rent, child support, groceries, gas, I'd have a couple bucks left over. If I didn't blow it all on Dunkin' Donuts coffee and too many cigarettes, packed my lunches, I'd be able to squirrel away a few nuts for a rainy day. And in about a hundred years I'd have that forty grand I'd need to buy Tom's business. Assuming I didn't die as early as my folks and brother. In my family, mid-fifties constituted old age. The American Dream is terrific, as long as you don't wake up.

After I'd logged items for Tom, I collected fees and said my goodnights, doing my best to smile or at least not scowl. Some day, I hoped, this company would be mine.

Sad as it sounded, my biggest victory of the night might've come via that winter coat. I didn't often get jazzed about new clothes, but when I slipped it on, thing fit like a glove, like it had been tailor-made just for me. I checked my look in the mirror. Heavy, tan corduroy with furred camel collar. Had to admit, felt pretty cool. Also made me laugh. The coat was my first new stitch of clothing in years. Not counting tee shirts that came in a ten-pack. I owned one pair of jeans.

After I hooked up and secured the U-Haul, Charlie wanted me to drop him back at the Dubliner. He had sobered up by then, but of course planned on getting drunk again. Like making your bed in the morning, what's the point? Charlie lived in his dead mother's house on the plains, at least a couple miles away in the deep, dark wood. Staring into that starless abyss chilled me to the marrow. I couldn't fathom making that trek on foot.

"How'd you get down here?"

"Got a bike."

"Like, what, a dirt bike?" Charlie was my best friend, but I didn't see him all that often. I didn't see anybody that often; my closest friends were empty houses and long solitary drives. Still, I figured I'd know if he got a motorcycle.

"Dude, after that last DUI, I can't drive anything with an engine. I mean bicycle."

"We're in northern New Hampshire. It's fifteen degrees." And that might've been optimistic. Ashton was closer to the Canadian border than it was Massachusetts. "You're too old for a bicycle."

I understood riding one in the summer months for exercise, maybe. Although I'd rather shoot myself in the head than get bunged up in skintight latex and a pointy helmet. Charlie was as old as me. At our age, there's a big difference between hobby and necessity.

"Throw the bike in the back of the truck. Let me drive you home."

"Nah." Charlie nodded at the bar door. "Already here."

Fine by me. Truth was, I wanted to be alone. Since the divorce, I'd been hermitting hard.

That auction with Owen Eaton highlighted a bigger problem: I had a tough time pulling the trigger. I didn't think of myself as risk-averse—I'd taken plenty of chances in my life—it's just that those choices usually turned to shit. My life began spiraling out of control because I'd taken *too* many chances, starting with believing my dead junkie brother, Chris, after he said he'd uncovered a town-wide conspiracy. And it hadn't gotten any better the following year when I signed on as an investigator for NorthEastern Insurance. My last case in Plasterville cost me my marriage. That's not fair to say. My marriage was already on the skids before I met Nicki. And without her help, I wouldn't have been able to uncover the kids-for-cash scandal that rocked the state. Besides, by then I'm pretty sure Jenny was already fucking Stephen. Both Chris and Nicki had been telling the truth. And each time the root of evil traced back to the most powerful family in town, the Lombardis. And up against that competition, I was out of my league. I was done sticking my neck out and taking needless risks. I'd never walk right again. Winning battles at the cost of losing the war is still losing.

I'd reheated my Denny's leftovers, grabbed a beer, and propped up my feet in the recliner, ready to catch a few minutes of high-lights from the football games I'd missed, when someone knocked on my door. I lived atop an auto shop, same dumpy one-bedroom I'd rented out of high school. Used to be only Jenny Price or Charlie Finn rang my bell. Now my ex-wife lived a state away with the jerkoff, and Charlie hadn't had time to peddle his little bicycle across the tundra.

I took a bite of cool, rubbery turkey, hoping whoever it was would get the hint. The knocking started up again.

Walking back in the kitchen, I slid the dead bird in the trash, dropped my plate in the sink to signal being pissed, and yanked open the door.

A stocky, well-dressed man, with a head polished shinier than an apple fresh out the tumbler, stood there. I'd never been a suit guy. Didn't know the difference between an Armani and Men's Wearhouse off-the-rack. Not counting my brief, disastrous foray into corporate, I'd worn a suit exactly two times in my life: when my brother Chris died and when I got married—and even then I'd been rocking the rolled-up sleeves and no-tie look before the priest finished last rites. Part of the reason I didn't fit the corporate mold was my utter disdain for suits.

But I could tell this suit wasn't cheap. The fabric practically shimmered in the stairwell light, individual threads glinting, almost crackling with the sound of crisp hundred dollar bills.

"Can I help you?"

The man extended his hand. "My name is Vin Biscoglio." I sized up the hunk of gold around his wrist. We auctioned off enough watches for me to tell when one was the real deal. "I was hoping to speak with you. Mind if I come in?"

"Sort of. It's late, man. I'm about to go to bed. Plus, I don't know you."

Did this dude go around all hours, visiting strangers, thinking his fancy suit and expensive watch was a free invitation?

"Apologies for the late hour. I've been sitting in my car, waiting for you to come home. Must've missed you." Vin Biscoglio glanced over his shoulder, out the tiny window that framed the white tips of Lamentation, the mountain range that goldfish-bowled our quaint, rustic town. Didn't know what he hoped to find. I'd spent enough time traversing those icy peaks to know the only thing that waited up there was heartbreak. "I promise I won't take up much of your time."

I couldn't place the accent, but he wasn't from here. I left the door open and headed to the fridge for another beer. I'd been trying to cut down, no more than a six-pack a night. I was better off managing lingering panic attacks with the pills the shrink prescribed. But beer was still my primary staple.

I snapped the magnet opener off the fridge, popped the top, and lit a cigarette from the stove because, as usual, I couldn't find a lighter or matches fast enough. I'd given up trying to quit. My fat cat walked in the room, rubbing her belly against my leg. I stooped to pet her. Standing, I almost forgot what I was doing because no one was in my kitchen. Guy stood on the landing like the world's most insecure vampire.

What was he waiting for? A corsage?

I waved him in.

I swear if he had a hat, he would've folded it over his chest. For a dude resembling a linebacker able to bench press Humvees, he was oddly nonassertive.

"You want a beer?" I asked. Vin acted like the kind of guy who wouldn't drink anything not aged in an oak barrel. My discount schwill was below his pay grade. But I liked to be courteous.

"I'm okay, Mr. Porter."

"It's Jay. Now what do you want?"

"I need your help finding a missing teenage boy."

I waited for the rest. Because unless the boy had gone missing in some couch cushions, this had nothing to do with me.

But he didn't say anything else.

"I'm sorry a boy is missing," I said. "But, like, go to the cops."

"I'm afraid we can't go to the cops."

"You can't come to me either." I laughed. "I think you have the wrong Jay Porter. I work in estate clearing. Moving dressers, cleaning out the shit nobody wants from dead people's houses."

Vin Biscoglio only stared.

"I'm a scavenger."

Vin glanced around my cramped, ugly apartment, uneasy. "You worked as an investigator for NorthEastern Insurance?"

"Yeah. Worked. Past tense. It's been a while. And I didn't exactly set the insurance world on fire. Lasted less than a year. Pretty much got canned." My stomach gurgling, I made for the fridge, holding open the door. Weak yellow light bled across my floor as I confronted the startling lack of food. Beer, mustard, slab of cold cuts that had turned a funky shade of gray. I think it used to be chicken. Without Jenny, I'd fallen back into the trappings of bachelorhood. Trips to the market were reserved for beer. I picked up most of my food at the gas station downstairs. "How'd you find me anyway?" All I could think was my name remained on the NorthEastern website.

"Your friend Fisher."

That little mutherfucker.

Fisher was a friend of Charlie. I liked him fine, okay, not really. If it wasn't for Charlie, Fisher would be off my radar completely. He'd been with Charlie and me when my brother found that hard drive. Fisher worked for NorthEastern, too. But down south, at the big office, in Concord. I hadn't talked to him in years, but this made sense. Fisher was the sort of guy who would send a stranger in an expensive suit to my doorstep on Thanksgiving.

"Fisher says you may be able to help out."

"Fisher's full of shit." Couldn't the guy at least call and warn me?

Vin stepped to a rolling side table, which housed Jenny's old recipes. He plucked a cookbook, held it up. "You like to cook?"

"No."

Vin Biscoglio placed the book back between the others. He pointed at a kitchen chair. "May I?"

"Knock yourself out." I wished he'd stop with all the formal crap. He was creeping me out. "You change your mind on the beer, feel free. Need to take a leak, the can is over there. Now finish your pitch so I can say no." The pause gave me a chance to apologize. You live alone long enough, you forget manners. There was a boy missing. "I don't mean to be rude, man. It's been a long day, but I don't work investigations."

"You broke the Lombardi pedophile case, yes?"

"We found some pictures. We couldn't—"

"And your work at NorthEastern in the Longmont kids-for-cash scandal was instrumental in sending Judge Roberts to prison."

"Not exactly. Sort of. Yeah." I stopped. "How do know about any of this?"

I *had* been behind uncovering Gerry Lombardi was a pedophile. Wasn't easy. There were bikers working security—one nasty bastard in particular named Bowman tormented me endlessly, knocked me out cold, almost killed me. But allegations never reached the press, and no charges were filed before the old man died. Judge Roberts taking bribes to ship kids to private prisons? Sure. And for my efforts, I received a big fucking headache and a whole lot of nothing.

Biscoglio's demeanor changed, the pretense of politeness gone. I now saw this was a man who wore nice suits because he could afford to wear nice suits, a device employed to get what he wanted. Clothes don't make that man; he is born that way.

"I know all about Adam and Michael Lombardi's involvement, too," he said.

Vin Biscoglio was going for the hard sell. The Brothers Lombardi were my personal bane. During both scandals, they, like me, remained nameless, behind the scenes, at least as far as the law was concerned, which only intensified my hatred for both. Evoking their names now was a cheap ploy to elicit my help.

"Let me guess," I said. "This is my chance to put the Lombardi brothers away for good."

"No," Biscoglio said. "I'm afraid this one doesn't have anything to do with the Lombardis."

It was funny. My brief moment of annoyance gave way to disappointment. No matter what lies I told myself, until the brothers were behind bars—or six feet under—I knew I'd never find solace.

"I bring them up," Biscoglio said, "because it shows how deep you are willing to dig for the truth. It's what's caught the attention of my boss, and why your services are being sought."

Man, only me.

I hopped up and headed for the cupboard, rooting around. "Who's your boss?" Pack of stale graham crackers, tin of tuna, can of protein patties that had always been there.

"I work for Ethan Crowder." Vin Biscoglio waited for my acknowledgment. Name meant nothing. "Steel."

"You want me to steal something?" I spun around, gunning for the freezer. I remembered I had frozen bean and cheese burritos lurking inside. They were about a thousand years old. Those things never went bad.

"Mr. Crowder is in the steel business. Crowder Steel? Out of Boston?"

I found the burritos buried beneath a crystal ice cave, packed like a prehistoric Mastodon in the glacial shelf. I reached in the utensil drawer for a butter knife. I had no idea who this Crowder was. At this point, I didn't much care. I wanted those burritos. Solid block of ice. Would not budge. I'd never defrosted the freezer, which left me a very tiny window in which to operate. I jammed and wedged the tip, stabbing.

"Right now," Biscoglio continued, "Ethan and his wife, Joanne, are going through a nasty divorce. You may have read something about it in the tabloids?"

"Uh-huh."

"Joanne relocated to the Coal Creek Mountains a short while ago, which is where the Crowder family is originally from, taking their son with her."

The knife slipped out of my grip and sliced my hand, or as much as a butter knife can slice, more like a serious chaffing, leaving a raised, ragged pink line. "Fuck!"

Biscoglio startled. I sucked on the meat of my palm, winding with my other hand to get on with it.

"Their son, Phillip, is caught in the middle. He's a good kid, but he's fallen in with a rough crowd, experimenting with drugs. Small-time stuff. Pills. Pot. Mrs. Crowder, Joanne, has taken drastic actions. We think she has had Phillip taken, against his will, to one of those military rehabs you have up here. Are you familiar with Middlesex County?"

I shrugged, nursing my wound. Middlesex was untamed wilderness rife with doomsday preppers, halfway houses, and radical recovery types. My brother had spent a lot of time up there when we were trying to get him straight. So had his girlfriend, Kitty, the mother of my nephew, Jackson. Of course Vin Biscoglio, having done his homework, would've known this.

"Place called Rewrite Interventions. Have you heard of them?"

I shook my head.

"Rewrite Interventions employ controversial techniques for teenage addicts. They send someone in the middle of the night, throw a pillowcase over the addict's head, and toss them in the back of a van, basically a kidnapping. Except totally legal. They take away cell phones. Allow no contact with friends, loved ones.

Even the parents. As a divorced father whose ex has custody of his son, you can understand how terrifying this must be for Mr. Crowder."

Nice try. "I'm sorry. I still don't know what this has to do with me."

"Our mutual friend, Fisher, explained about your brother, your personal interest in drug-related cases. Given your impressive investigating record, we were hoping you might be willing to help. For a fee, of course."

"It's late. I have to get to bed. I don't know what Fisher told you, but I am *not* an investigator. I don't take on cases or sign clients. Pretty sure you need a license to do that sort of thing, and the only license I have is the driving kind, so I can haul junk. If you can't go to the cops, hire a private investigator."

"Mr. Crowder would like to hire you."

"Tell him, thanks. I'm flattered, but—" I put on the brakes. "I am sorry about the kid. How old is he?"

"Sixteen."

"Sixteen. Shitty age. Hope it all works out. I have to go to bed, man."

Vin Biscoglio stood with a gracious nod, returning to his airs. He plucked a business card from his inside pocket, placing it down on the table. "That's my number. If you change your mind. I wrote Mr. Crowder's offer on the back." He closed the door behind him.

Fitting end to a fucked-up Thanksgiving. In the morning I was going to tear Fisher a new one. It was too late to do anything about it now. I walked to the window, making sure the guy wasn't stuffing auto parts in his trunk. At that point, nothing would've surprised me. The snow continued to fall. I didn't see a car leave. There were no lights below. I had a strange feeling he was still down there. I bundled back up, stepping into my untied work boots, tramping down the stairs, out into the frigid night. With the wind blowing so hard, I didn't even see footprints. I slid on my cell flashlight. Still couldn't see jack. Not a single print. Not one tire track. Like no one had been there at all.

CHAPTER THREE

THREE YEARS AGO, at the tail end of the Roberts investigation, I suffered what my shrink called a psychotic break. When I protested that assessment, because it was fucking ridiculous, my doctor let me plead down to post-traumatic stress disorder. She broke it down into gentler, less bat-shit parlance.

"Basically, Jay," Dr. Shapiro-Weiss said, "you harbor guilt over your parents' and brother's deaths. I'm not saying you're crazy. Only that for you, during stressful times, reality can be tenuous. When that stress becomes too much, you sever ties with what is really happening."

Standing in Hank Miller's parking lot, my little flashlight out, clearing garage windows, peeping in the backseat of rusted cars like a tweaker in search of invisible bugs, examining evidence that wasn't there, snow piling high, freezing my ass off, I felt that creeping sensation return. Like everyone was in on the joke but me.

If not for the business card left behind, I might've lost my mind.

The first big storm of the season hit overnight, and I woke to a foot and a half of the heavy, wet stuff weighting the world. I was glad to see Hank Miller when I peeked out my window, waving good morning in the new day's light. I bundled up and helped him dig out the parking lot. Hank was getting old, and the wear of shoveling, especially this thick, goopy kind, takes a toll on a man's back.

Strange to think I'd been Hank Miller's tenant for close to twenty years. We averaged about a dozen words a year. I could go months without seeing him. Even now as I shoveled, he nodded his appreciation, but we didn't speak. I knew next to nothing about the guy. I had witnessed him age, going from forty-something to pushing seventy. The best years of his life gone, spent changing oil for housewives, patching up punctured tires, easing his way out to pasture. And what did he have to show for it? This garage, a tiny house out back. I knew he'd been married at one point. I had no idea what happened to her. Maybe he had grandkids. If anyone came to visit, I never saw them. After Charlie, Jenny, my son, perhaps Tom Gable, I was as close to Hank Miller as I was anyone on this earth.

The thought of such a lonely life might not have depressed the living shit out of me had I not just returned from Thanksgiving dinner with my ex-wife and kid at a fucking Denny's in Burlington.

About a half hour in, I heard Hank curse.

I turned and watched him shuffle toward the side of the garage. The door was ajar, striker dangling off a screw.

"Goddamn junkies," he muttered, before wincing a mea culpa. Hank knew all about my brother.

I brushed aside the comment. We did have a drug epidemic up here. Addicts frequently wandered into town from the Turnpike. Especially before they tore down the old TC Truck Stop. That place was a breeding ground for degenerates. Hard to believe anyone would be out boosting in the middle of a blizzard.

When Hank inspected the rotten wood flaking around the plate, he pretended the wind could've blown in the door. "Storm got pretty bad last night."

Which was bullshit. A hurricane didn't take a door off its hinges. I knew he felt bad about the junkie comment. I didn't mention my strange late-night visitor. Hank had already poked his head inside and determined nothing was missing. Last night's paranoia aside, I couldn't imagine Vin Biscoglio breaking and entering in his expensive suit, pilfering spark plugs.

I got out my toolbox. I had an extra rim and mortise lock set floating around. I reinforced the frame with a two-inch-wide steel strip, inlet the jamb, drilled four heavy-duty decking screws. Should hold. But, I told Hank, with the wood being so rotten, he'd need a new door hung. Took me another hour to clear the rest of the snow and ice in order to get the station operational.

By then the roads had been plowed. Still took forever to get across town to meet Tom Gable for breakfast at Julie's. I preferred the Olympic Diner, the twenty-four-hour diner on the Turnpike, but the boss liked Julie's. And he always picked up the tab.

The traffic lights along Farmington Avenue had been knocked out by the storm. Four-way stops and the whole town loses its head. A bunch of power lines were down at the Christian Lane intersection, cars backed up, bumper to bumper. I saw Sheriff Rob Turley directing traffic, bundled up in his town browns and fuzzy hat. He waved hello. A former classmate, Turley and I had a complicated relationship, stemming from all the times he'd busted my brother over the years. Turley had also bailed my ass out of a few jams. I'd returned the favor. I guess that made us friends. Or at least even.

I spotted Tom's Ford, his truck the only vehicle in Julie's parking lot. Which wasn't surprising. Being Black Friday, most of Ashton would be headed to the mall in Pittsfield.

Tom sat in a booth by the window, his usual spot, reading the *Herald*. A cold sun threatened to break through silver clouds, refracting dull shine off frosted glass. Julie's still had a newspaper dispenser out front. In this new digital age, where everyone got their information off smartphones and the Internet, I dug the old-school touch.

Bunching my Patriots hat in the pocket of my new winter coat, I stomped snow, mud, and rock salt from my cuffs, and nodded to Christine, whose family owned Julie's. Christine brought me a coffee as I slipped opposite Tom, who held up a finger to let him finish whatever he was reading. I remembered coming here with my dad and Chris. Layout remained the same from when I was a kid. Six booths. Five tables. Counter with four stools overlooking a cook's window and fry stove, coffeepot and muffin basket. I liked knowing some things would never change, even if Julie's made a lousy breakfast and burned the shit out of their eggs. There was no one actually named Julie.

Tom folded his *Herald*, placed the paper on the tabletop, pushing it away. "Don't know why I read the thing. Nothing but bad news."

I passed along the itemized list from last night's auction, including Owen Eaton's grift, the rental fees, and four hundred and change from his original five thousand.

Tom strapped on his reading glasses, tallying the inventory. Since we'd hosted the event, Tom got a straight percentage off the top, but he'd have to handle taxes, too, a pain in the ass, cutting into any significant profit. In the end, he might've cleared the three hundred he was paying me.

He tucked the note in his breast pocket, then passed back the envelope with the four bills and change. I went to pick out my three, but he said to keep it all.

"An early Christmas bonus," he said. "Thanks for overseeing that sale." Tom scratched his big, bushy beard. "Heard about your run-in with Owen Eaton last night."

"You heard about that, eh?"

"I hear everything."

"He was just being a dirtbag."

"What else is new?" He paused. "You get a look at the dresser?"

I nodded.

"The genuine article?"

I nodded again. I saw the hurt in his eyes.

"Not gonna lie," he said. "Would've loved to land a piece like that. But you did the right thing. That's not how we do business."

I stuffed the bills in my shirt.

Tom studied me, as if something burdened his mind. Like a lot of mountain men, Tom Gable, with his logger forearms and stolid girth, wasn't big on heart-to-heart conversation. Neither was I. Probably why we worked so well together. But the way his brows clipped together now—the pained expression, the stuttered starts and aborted sighs—I dreaded he was about to say something tender. Instead all he said was, "Nice coat."

"A tip from Keith Mortenson."

"Glad it was worth it."

Christine brought his breakfast, and Tom dug in to the mound. The Lumberjack Special featured a pile of eggs, hash, home fries, pancakes, grilled breads, sausage and Canadian bacon, assorted layers of carbohydrates and fats, which Tom slathered in maple syrup. If there's one thing this part of the state's known for, besides our drug epidemic, it's maple syrup, 100 percent, grade-A. You don't get a body like Tom Gable without working at it.

"How about you, Jay?" Christine asked.

"I'm good with the coffee. Thanks." For as famished as I was last night, having failed in my attempts to liberate the bean and cheese burritos from my freezer, I was strangely not hungry at all.

I felt my body knotting up, tense, anxious. I'd popped a couple lorazepam when I woke up. Hadn't helped. Vin Biscoglio's visit had unnerved me, the break-in leaving me on edge. As soon as anyone evoked drugs, like Biscoglio had done with the missing Crowder boy, the back of my brain started tickling with thoughts about my dead brother, outcomes I wished were different, shit I couldn't do jack about now.

Tom stuffed his face with greasy links and starches, slurping coffee, returning to impervious. Maybe I'd mistaken empathy with heartburn or gas. Just as well. Last thing I needed was tenderness. I can handle insults fine. Kick me in the balls when I'm down, no problem. Just don't say anything nice to me. Breaks my fucking heart.

Biscoglio's job offer had wormed into my brain, which got me examining everything else wrong in my life. Starting with Tom's even entertaining the notion of selling to a cretin like Owen Eaton. I began to pile on the misery. Like listening to sad songs when you're already depressed. I didn't know why I did this to myself.

I must've been making faces, because Tom put down his fork, giving me his full attention. "My first choice is to sell the business to you. We have time. That year deadline? It's not real. If I have to hang on another three, four years, I will." He caught my eye, earnest as homemade pie. "We'll find a way to make it work."

"Thanks."

"Owen is a backup plan; in case you can't come up with the money."

It was a nice thing to say. And I appreciated the reassurance. I believed he was sincere. But it was also lip service. Four years, five years—another ten, twenty—I'd never have the cash I'd need to buy the business. Which was why I fingered Vin Biscoglio's card in the pocket of my new winter coat. That was a lot of scratch to leave on the table. It would put me almost halfway there, but the skeptic in me was, well, skeptical. Why pay me that kind of money? Must be a dozen licensed private investigators to handle the gig.

"Something else happen last night?" Tom asked.

"This guy stopped by my place."

Tom waited for the rest. I could use the sounding board. I supplied the abridged version, omitting names and exact figures, highlighting the offer to investigate a disappearance. For a lot of money.

"Don't you need a license for that sort of thing?" Tom's face twisted up, a telling expression that told me nothing. He was responding to more than my news. Like he had a question he was afraid to ask. I wrote it off as too long with the in-laws and turkey-day hangover. But it was an odd expression from a man I knew so well. "Be careful," he said. "Strangers don't often knock on doors offering money for nothing."

"Not since Ed McMahon died."

Tom laughed. Christine brought the check. Tom peeled cash from his wad. We headed out into the blustery parking lot, where snow dusted off plowed mounds, swept away with the rest of the scrapings.

I lit a cigarette.

"Those things'll kill ya."

Tom smoked three packs a day when I first met him. Nothing like the glibness of the reformed smoker.

"What's on the agenda?"

"Got a house to clear on Worthington Ridge."

"Address?"

"I'll text you later." Tom pointed at the breast pocket where I'd stashed the four hundred. "Another reason I thought you could use that. Until I move the merch from last night's sale, money is going to be a little tight."

Tom fished out a key, placing it in my palm.

"What's this for?"

"New warehouse space in Pittsfield is available."

"Thought that wouldn't be ready for a few weeks?"

"Me, too. Got the call this morning to head down and sign the lease. You can start moving Monday."

I nodded and turned to go, but he called me back.

"I'm going with your suggestion for the new name."

"Yeah?" I'd thrown out an idea the other day. Off the cuff. Wasn't sure it worked, given our perpetual winter. "You don't think it's too cheesy?"

"No, I like it," my boss said. "Everything Under the Sun. Has a nice ring to it."

"I'll stash last night's score in the unit down the Turnpike. Safer than the back of a U-Haul." We'd been doing so much clearing of late, Tom had been forced to rent a temporary pod at You Store, no space left at the warehouse. Until the summer flea market sales, we did more storing than selling.

"Good idea. I know it's extra work. Starting next week, you won't have to keep reconfiguring layouts." He reached into his truck, retrieving a brown paper bag, passing it along.

"What's this?"

"Smart thermostat. I know how cold you keep your apartment to save on heating costs. Hooks up to your Internet, monitors usage, peak hours, turns on and off automatically. There's a Osram lightfy in there, too."

"I don't know what that is."

"Turns on your lights remotely."

"Like via computer?"

"Wi-Fi."

Who the hell needs to turn on their lights if they aren't home? I didn't say that. Tom often gifted me things like this to make up for the lack of pay or medical benefits.

"Tech stuff is out of your comfort zone, I get it." Tom laughed, pointing at the bag. "Picked that up from an estate sale last week. Brand new. Never opened. Wanted to give you something to show my appreciation."

I patted the cash in my pocket.

"I mean more than money. You mean a lot to the business." He paused, hand gripping my triceps. "To me, too."

I waited for him to say he had cancer and was dying. What other reason could there be for all the touchy feels?

"Are you all right, Tom?"

"I'm fine." He smiled and started to climb in the cab. "Just glad Mortenson is on a plane back to Boston. That last-minute sale was a pain in my ass. I know it was a pain in yours."

"Boston? I thought he lived in North Carolina."

"Owns a house down there, but he works up in Boston. Accountant for that steel firm."

"What steel firm?" I asked the question, although I already knew the answer.

"You know. The big one. Crowder. Crowder Steel."

CHAPTER FOUR

I KNEW CHARLIE was home when I pulled in his driveway because handlebars poked out of the snow. Of course he hadn't shoveled the turnabout, and I had to abandon my truck like a schooner on a sandbar in Antarctica. Odd angles of twisting metal contorted, jutting haphazard from snowy reefs, a bizarre artifact of a long-dead civilization. Walking past, I made sure Charlie hadn't blacked out and now lay under there, a giant blue popsicle, frozen dead. I was relieved to find just the bike. I wrenched the spokes free from the snow and wheeled the bicycle against the side of his house, propping it beneath an overhang. Guy just bought the thing and had already left it outside to rust. The door was unlocked. It was always unlocked. Charlie lay facedown where he'd passed out on the floral print couch. Like another ten feet to his bed presented too monumental a task to contemplate.

I parted the curtains. A low winter sun crested over the ridge. Cold sunlight cracked the pane, brightening the room by limited degrees of fractured glare. Charlie started flapping, covering his eyes, convulsing. Pure visceral response to stimuli, no higher critical thinking skills involved.

Charlie cradled a pillow around his ears, remaining faceplanted in the cushions, kicking his feet. "Come on, man," he whined. "I'm sleeping."

I kicked the couch frame until Charlie flipped over. He peeled off the afghan, revealing fat pink ham flopped over tighty whities. "What?!" Deep fabric grooves imprinted his bloated beer face.

"When was the last time you talked to Fisher?"

"Wha—huh? Fisher?"

"Yeah, Fisher. When did you talk to him last?"

"I don't know, man. Couple weeks ago. Why?"

"Get him on the line. I don't have his number anymore."

Charlie pinched between his eyes, willing clarity, or trying to stave off the start to another day. "Come back later, Jay. I'm beat."

He started to lay down. I kicked the base. He sat up.

"Why you need to talk to Fisher so bad?"

"Where is he living these days?"

"Lakeland."

"Where the hell is that?"

"Like thirty minutes outside Concord. Another town to hide."

"Hide?"

"Stay off the grid."

"What's he doing?"

"You mean for work?"

"Never mind."

Fisher got out of the insurance business around the same time I did, albeit for different reasons. Since then, he'd grown out his hair, gotten a pair of glasses that he didn't need, and turned into a typical New Hampshire radical. He'd also grown increasingly conspiratorial, like my brother Chris but without the excuse of drugs, wary of government intrusion. You encountered a lot of that up here.

"Why the sudden interest in Fisher? Thought you hated his guts."

"Just give me his number."

I didn't give a damn what Fisher was doing for work. I needed to know why he'd sicced Vin Biscoglio on me. Something wasn't right. What were the odds of Keith Mortenson working for Crowder Steel? I recalled something Fisher, of all people, once said: in the world of investigation, there's no such thing as coincidence.

With great, heaving effort, Charlie rolled himself up, snatching his cell from the dirty jeans crumpled on the floor, mumbling, pissed off to be awake and sober. He found Fisher's number and passed me the phone. I used Charlie's line to call rather than mine. Knowing Fisher, he wouldn't accept a call from a number he didn't recognize. We hadn't spoken in a while, and my number had changed more than once.

He didn't answer. No one ever answers when you need them to. I could go my whole life and never use the telephone again and it would be too soon. People bothered me all the time. When *they* wanted something. Just show up on my doorstep unannounced, no big deal. But whenever I actually needed to speak with someone, they didn't pick up.

I left a detailed albeit strongly worded message that I didn't appreciate the referral or the stranger he sent to my place at midnight.

"What was that about?" Charlie asked.

"Missing teen. Hiding in rehab. One of those military ones in Middlesex. Someone wants my help finding him."

"Middlesex? Isn't that where your brother's ex lives?"

"Lived. Kitty's in California now. With my nephew, Jackson. Remember?"

Charlie bobbed his head like he knew what I was talking about, but I knew he didn't. The more he drank, the less he retained.

"So you're, like, what? A private investigator now?"

"I didn't say I was taking the job."

"How much are they offering?"

"A lot."

"Weren't you bitching last month about not having the money to buy Tom's business?"

I ignored his question and breezed past him into the kitchen. I cracked the window and lit a cigarette, but the wind spat back, flicking ice chips into my corneas. I slammed it shut. Charlie didn't care if I smoked inside. Place stank to high heaven anyway. He'd neglected cleaning. Hungry Man boxes, tins upended, cereal tipped on its side, spilling kernels. I had no idea how he was getting groceries, unless he was strapping the sacks on the back of his bicycle with a bungee. In the corner, I saw scattered black flecks. Little pellets, the size of uncooked rice grains. Took me a minute to figure out I was staring at mouse shit. Garden trash bags that Charlie hadn't bothered to close up or tie off toppled with empty beer cans and liquor bottles by the door. How hard was it to walk the rest of the way to the garbage bins?

Tying up the trash, I hauled the bags outside and dropped them in the cans.

From his stoop, Lamentation Mountain loomed terrifying. Ragged peaks disappeared high into the sky, past the blue, past the gray, into the storm that still raged, refusing to end.

"Jay?" Charlie stood in the doorway. "What are you doing?"

I brushed past him up the stairs, back inside.

"Your place is a mess."

"Been busy."

Busy? What could I say to that? Charlie was unemployed, living off workman's comp, and getting sloshed every night, sleeping well into the afternoon.

"I don't understand why you wouldn't jump at the offer," he said. "You investigated claims and stuff at NorthEastern. Might be an easy payday for a few phone calls."

"Don't worry about it, Charlie."

Last night I'd said no to the job because it had come at the end of a long, shit day, and my default position was almost always no. When I woke up, the opportunity didn't feel any more appealing or sincere. I'd come to Charlie's for more than Fisher's number. I could use someone to talk to. But right now just being around the guy pissed me off. Charlie and I used to be partners, pals; my buddy was always up for an adventure. Back in the day, I'd be able to talk to my friend about this. Weigh the pros and cons of taking the gig, better judgment be damned. As I watched Charlie tug the thinning curls on his swollen head, staring past my eyes to the stains on the wall, canned ham gut slung over elastic, I knew I couldn't talk to Charlie about this or anything else. Charlie Finn stood in front of me. He glanced in my general direction. But my friend wasn't there anymore.

"Go back to sleep. I'm going to wait for Fisher to call back."

Charlie sloughed off toward his bedroom.

"Your Internet still work?"

He pointed at the back room that used to be his mother's sewing den, before continuing on to his room. Within seconds Charlie was sawing logs, that alcoholic's snore rattling deep within dried-out sinus chambers and a gutted soul. His place looked like shit. He looked like shit. Like he'd given up attempting the bare minimum that makes us human. Bathing, brushing teeth, pest control. Then again, who was I to judge?

I pulled out Vin Biscoglio's card, turning it over in my fingers, studying the numbers. Who turns down that many zeroes without due diligence? I called. Of course Vin Biscoglio didn't pick up. Not even a beep or robot asking me to leave a message. I felt like a dope for being so gullible. There's no such thing as free money.

I booted Charlie's computer and rooted around the web. Nothing Vin Biscoglio told me was an outright lie. But it hadn't been the truth either. First off, Ethan and Joanne weren't going through a divorce. Not yet at least. But the high-society marriage was on the rocks, and the tabloids didn't shy away from dirty laundry. Far from the victim, Ethan Crowder came across the bully. There were allusions to a history of violence, domestic abuse charges in past relationships, hints of payouts, another powerful family with the means to cover up messes, sweep dirt under the rug. Turned out Joanne wasn't even the first Mrs. Crowder. Ethan had been married once before when he was much younger, to a showgirl named Isabelle from Wyoming. The two-day Vegas marriage ended in an annulment. The guy sounded like a real prize. I was able to find Joanne Crowder's address in Coal Creek, which I scribbled down, the next logical step if I wished to pursue this further. And I did not.

Back in the kitchen, I rummaged cupboards. I found a near-empty tin of Folger's and made coffee. Waiting for the pot to brew, I craned my neck out the window to see if I could find the top of the mountain now. The fog had grown worse, cloud cover descending, visibility reduced, swallowing the dim white dot that used to be the sun.

I didn't know what Vin Biscoglio or Crowder Steel stood to gain from involving me, but I couldn't shake the feeling I was being pulled along, forced to participate.

Someone was playing me.

Playing you? What's the game?

* * *

Fisher never did call back, and neither did Vin Biscoglio. By noon I was sick of stale coffee, cigarettes, and my neurosis. I had both cells on Charlie's kitchen table, along with his landline. Sitting in that cold, dark house, waiting for one of them to buzz or ring, I felt like I did in middle school, holding out hope Tracy Barnett would agree to go with me to homecoming dance, a sap. Any trace of daylight had vanished, replaced by angrier gray clouds churning, swirling, chucking ice and snow at the glass. I could've moved, turned on a light. But I did not. Instead, I sat in the darkness and contemplated mouse turds and dust bunnies while my bloated alcoholic best friend raised the roof beams.

I didn't have time for this. I still had to deal with last night's score, which sat outside locked up in the back of the U-Haul hooked up to my Chevy. I still had to drive down to the storage locker, a good half hour south on the Desmond Turnpike, drop my load, and get ready for the next one. Felt like I worked twenty-four seven, three sixty-five, and for what? To tread water. Break even. A tie. I hoped Vin Biscoglio didn't call back. Nothing good was going to come from me poking around.

Part of me also knew it didn't matter if he called back, if I formally accepted his offer or took one red cent. I was already working this case whether I wanted to or not.

I wrote Charlie a note telling him if Fisher called to make sure he called me. I'd left my number in a voice mail, but I didn't trust that tiny mutherfucker as far as I could throw him.

Unlike Charlie, I was not a lazy, shiftless worker. I seldom cut corners. A job worth doing is a job worth doing right. I was tempted to leave last night's score in the U-Haul, go home, eat my dinner from a box, switch on the tube, because come Monday, I'd be packing up again. But with all the sketchy motels in the area, the wretchedness of the strip, crackheads, meth freaks, guys like my brother, I couldn't risk it. Junkies loved to break into private property. They'd swipe anything not nailed down, running off to trade hot electronics for a fix. Over the years, Tom and I had been hit plenty. We usually found whatever had been stolen in surrounding pawnshops. Recovered most of the items. Most of the time. Still a pain in the ass. Someone had to go down to the station, file the paperwork, make a statement. And charges never stuck because junkies just say they found it. Unless you caught them red-handed, who could prove otherwise? It was a big game to them. What did they have to lose besides the time? And time is the only commodity a junkie has. I knew by emptying the U-Haul, I was creating more work for myself, digging a hole just to fill it back up. Had it not been for the break-in at Hank Miller's garage, I might've chanced it. Better safe than sorry. U-Hauls were pretty easy to pick.

On my way to the You Store storage pod, I stopped at the grocery store and grabbed a case of beer.

Took me all afternoon to unload the U-Haul. I could've saved time, but knowing I'd be restrapping the wagon again in forty-eight, I had the foresight to restock, rearrange, and make reloading easier on the flip side. I pulled forward the biggest, bulkiest items, like the chest of drawers and headboards, sticking smaller goods—wall clocks, coatracks, knickknacks and bric-a-brac, paintings—in the rear. I also had some old hard drives belonging to Tom. He had gotten a new computer for his home office and asked me to dispose of them properly. Which, if anyone knew my history, was hilarious. My brother had gotten his hands on those pedophile pics because some moron working for Lombardi thought it a good idea to entrust a couple junkies with sensitive data. Like Chris wasn't going to root around for personal financial info. I wasn't going to make the same mistake. I had to find a proper electronic recycling center, and I hadn't had the time to do that yet. I didn't know why Tom even needed a new home computer. We didn't use one at the warehouse. Tom Gable had a mind like a steel trap. Every item ever purchased logged upstairs in the mental microfiche, more secure than an NSA database.

I dragged everything into the pod, and beat my body up good. In this weather, my leg chewed at the bone. With no one to help carry the load, I wrenched the hell out of my lower lumbar, and when I was done, my hands were raw and bloody. I'd left my gloves in the pockets of my old winter coat. Exposed to the blustery elements, I felt like I'd been jacking off a prickly pear.

Finally finished and ready to call it a day, I was deciding between takeout Chinese and Mickey D's, when I realized, like a fucking idiot, I'd missed a chair. And not a tiny one, either. A big cushy one in the back corner of the U-Haul. Which defeated the purpose of the extra hours, undermining all the hard work I'd done. So frustrating. So typical. The way I'd stacked everything, there was no room to cram it in. I could've left it, except I'm nothing if not a stubborn sonofabitch. Especially when I've had a lot to drink. I'd already made a decent dent into the case of beer.

I hopped into the U-Haul, dragging my bum leg, telling myself I was *not* pulling everything out again, knowing damn well I was pulling everything out again.

A call came in on my cell.

It was not any of the calls I was expecting.

CHAPTER FIVE

"WHAT'S UP, TURLEY? Sorta busy here."

"Jay, I don't know how to say this."

I put the call on speaker while Turley hemmed and hawed on the other end. I was in the middle of gripping a giant chair, like one of those ESPN strongmen with a log too hard to handle, arms stretched wide around the base, wrenching ligaments and soft tissue. "Spit it out, man. I got shit to do."

"Tom Gable's had . . . an accident. He's in the hospital."

I dropped the chair. Lucky for me the leg landed on my big toe, splitting the nail. Hurt like hell, but I was glad to have something to break the fall. Goddamn chair was worth more than my whole foot. I switched off speaker, putting the phone to my ear, plugging the other so I could hear above the wind tunnel racing through locker alley.

"Did you know he was down in Pittsfield earlier?"

"Yeah. To sign the lease on our new property, dual showcase and auction room we're renting. Why?"

"Oh boy." Turley groaned like my knowing that somehow made this news worse.

"What happened?"

"On his way back into town, at the bottom of the mountain— you know that secluded stretch entering into the foothills?"

"I am familiar with the area."

"Tom must've pulled over to help a stranded motorist. There were two sets of tire tracks in the snow. We're still trying to piece together—"

"Tom. What happened to Tom?"

"Someone beat the shit out of him. Looks like a car jacking gone wrong. Found the crowbar they used, covered in blood, bits of hair and bone. He was outside in the cold for a while."

"How bad is it?"

He didn't answer.

"Turley?"

"Bad. It's bad, Jay."

We didn't have a hospital in Ashton. The closest emergency room was down in Pittsfield, which was where I'd ended up when I severed the nerves in my calf. Maybe it was phantom pain, a sympathy reaction on my part, but my leg hurt worse upon hearing the news.

I jammed everything back in the pod, organization be damned. I locked up the shed, and unhitched the U-Haul, leaving it in the parking lot with the rest of the moving vans. I'd be able to drive faster without the extra weight holding me back.

When you don't have parents, you latch on to different people to fill those roles. That's what the shrink told me after Chris died. Normally I'd laugh off such psychobabble, but, man, I was a mess back then, desperate for any explanation. Dr. Shapiro-Weiss said when you don't have a father—or in my case, one who died so young—you glom onto others to do the job. My skin crawled with all the hokey terms she used—inner child, reparenting, mourning a loss of innocence—but I'd worked for Tom most of my life, and didn't need a doctor to point out the obvious. Tom Gable was about the age my dad would've been had he not driven the family car into Echo Lake. Even though ours was a business relationship, Tom had taken me under his wing. Speeding to the hospital, not knowing if he was going to live or die, chain-smoking like a mad man, popping lorazepam like breath mints, I tried not to dwell on tragedies and fallouts, the parallels of repeating patterns. In particular where that mountain was concerned. My parents died on Lamentation Mountain, Chris not far from it. I almost died up there, too. Moments like this dredge up shit you'd prefer remain buried; they force you to confront demons you'd rather stay asleep. I had enough disappointment in my life. I didn't need this. Making me feel even lousier, my first thought when Turley told me Tom was in critical condition: What would happen to the business if he died? I mean, it popped in my head for a split second. In, out, one of a myriad flashing thoughts. But admitting I'd even considered that, however fleeting, made me feel like a terrible person.

Stepping into the ICU, first thing I noticed were the machines doing God's work. Atomic hearts beating. Morphine dripping. Artificial pipelines to veins and brains. Despite the high-tech medical equipment, the scene reminded me of Hank Miller's repair shop. Janky alternators and transmissions hooked up to diagnostics, attempting to isolate the problem. The human body, no different than any other engine. Other species have the dignity to die gracefully. We don't go down without a fight. We patch up solenoid bearings with solder and duct tape, anything to milk a few more miles.

I spotted Tom's wife, Freddie, pacing, wringing hands; she looked a mess. Her real name was Fredericka but everyone called her Freddie. I wasn't as close to Freddie as I was Tom. But I still saw her often. Anytime I'd venture up to the house to get money or hand over inventory lists, like last night, we'd talk, exchange pleasantries, say hello. She knew who I was. I'd had dinner at their place plenty over the years. They didn't have any children. I wondered if Tom Gable thought of me the same way I did him. Like the son he never had. Hard not to get sentimental at times like this. I started toward Freddie to offer my condolence, let her know if there was anything I could do, please, don't hesitate to ask, but the daggers in her eyes stopped me dead in my tracks. Her husband was in the hospital. He was in bad shape. I tried to not let her chilly reception hurt my feelings. There was no reason for her to blame me.

Maybe I was mistaking disdain for grief. Before I could make a move and find out, Turley intercepted me, pulling me into an adjacent corridor, sticking me behind a defibrillator. I could feel Freddie's vitriol boring through the walls.

"What's up?" I asked, peeking around the corner, toward Tom's room. "Is he going to be okay?"

"Still critical. Bleeding in the brain. Doctors operated to relieve the pressure. He hasn't woken up. Right now, it's touch and go."

"I saw him this morning."

"I know."

"We were having breakfast . . ." I stopped. "What do you mean you know?"

"Talked to Christine Erickson."

"The waitress at Julie's?"

Turley rubbed the back of his thick neck, muckling his mouth.

"Why are you talking to Christine?"

"Listen, Jay. There's no easy way—"

"You know I hate when you do this."

"What?"

"You have something to tell me, then tap dance like a pussy. Get to it, man."

"We found Tom's truck. About a mile down the road. Someone had driven it off into the woods."

"Thought you said it was a carjacking?" Why ditch the ride so fast?

"I said it *looked* like a carjacking." He adopted his lawman's stance. "Where did you go after you met Tom for breakfast?"

"Charlie's."

"Finn verify that?"

"For the ten minutes he was awake and sober."

"What time did you leave?"

"I don't know? Noon?"

"Where did you go?"

"Work. I have a goddamn job."

"Alone?"

"Yeah." Call it stress, strain, or chalk it up to sheer obliviousness, I still didn't comprehend what he was getting at. My sole focus was on who would want to hurt Tom.

"Why were you snooping around Hank Miller's garage late last night?"

"I wasn't snooping. Who told you I was snooping?"

"Hank Miller. The crowbar used to beat Tom came from Miller's garage."

And like that it all came rushing back, twenty-five years of pain, hurt, and remorse. The crash. The rumors my brother Chris had been responsible. You could trace the exact moment my life veered off course to the night my folks went off that bridge. At the time of their accident, my brother had been working at Hank Miller's garage. A burnt-out head case at seventeen, with a nasty temper and penchant for violent outburst, Chris had begun experimenting with drugs. Known for his erratic behavior, he and our father had gotten into legendary brawls. Tawdry grist can't escape a small town's gossip mill. After the crash, the cops determined someone had tampered with the brake line, and because of the drugs and attitude problems, the fights and easy access to the garage, Chris got accused. My brother was a whiz with mechanics, which didn't help. The preposterous allegations dogged my brother the rest of his no-good life.

Now here we were again. Another Porter brother in trouble with the law. Only this time, it was me.

"No one is accusing you of anything, Jay."

"You're shitting me, right?"

"Hank Miller said around eleven o'clock last night, he saw you, outside the garage, poking around windows with a flashlight. He tells me there was a break-in?"

I pulled out the blank business card from my mysterious visitor, holding it out. Turley stared at the handwritten number and dollar amount scrawled on the back. Might as well have been written by me.

"What's that?" Turley asked.

"Nothing." I stuffed the card back in my pocket. If I started rambling about a frame-job now, I'd sound like my dead junkie brother. My anxiety kicked in, making me act jumpy and skittish, which comes across as guilty to the untrained eye. If I tried to pin this rap on a boogeyman, Turley would have me committed on the spot. I was a Porter, first and foremost, and my brother had left a legacy. In his absence, I'd stepped right into those shoes; and you can't outrun your name. I turned back to the hospital room where my friend and boss clung to life, trying to muster indignance. My outrage came across manufactured and phony. "Tom Gable is laid up in there—maybe dying—and you're investigating me?" I wanted to laugh but couldn't. "You got a pair of balls."

"I'm doing my job. This isn't twenty-plus years of innuendo, okay? And this has *nothing* to do with your brother. You were the last one to see Tom. The weapon came from the garage below *your* apartment."

"So fucking what?"

"And then there's the matter of—"

"I don't care if you are a cop, Turley. You're lucky I don't slug you."

Turley brought up his right hand a bit, still loose but at the ready. "I wouldn't try that if I were you. Didn't work out so well the last time, remember?"

I wrapped my head around the corner. Freddie glowered. No wonder she was giving me the stink eye, Turley filling her head with this garbage.

"What were you and Tom fighting about last night?"

"What are you talking about? I saw Tom for like six seconds on the porch before the storm. To get cash for the sale."

"Freddie said she heard Tom fighting with someone on the telephone. Late. Like two a.m. She thinks it was you."

I bent over, inflating my lungs, holding back the air, trying not to scream. It was happening again. Blood surged between my ears making it tough to think, heart thumping, temples throbbing, circulation rushing behind my eyeballs, a siren wailing in the distance, growing louder, chasing me down.

Turley crouched to meet my eye. He reached out to touch my arm. I flung him off.

"Whoa." He held up his hands. "Let's take a minute to calm down, okay?"

I could see his deputy up the corridor take a step in our direction.

Turley held him back. "I started this conversation by saying no one was accusing you of anything, didn't I?"

"Goddamn right. Why would you? The suggestion is a fucking joke."

"I want you take a deep breath. Then pay attention to what I am about to say. Don't leap to conclusions. Take what I am saying at face value. Can you do that?" Turley pointed at a nearby bench. "Maybe we should sit down?"

"I'll fucking stand, thank you."

Turley kept his hands high.

"I thought I was past this bullshit." I shook my head, like if I could shake hard enough I'd be freed of these thoughts forever. "Why on earth would I want to hurt Tom? He's my friend. He's my boss. He's selling me the company, for Christ's sake. I mean, if I can come up with the money."

"About that . . ." Turley trailed off.

"Maybe you should be talking to that dirtbag Owen Eaton. He wants to buy the company, too. He's a real piece of shit. Should've seen the stunt he pulled last night—"

"Oh boy," Turley said. I didn't appreciate the condescending tone. It was the same attitude he'd adopted when I admitted knowing Tom had gone to Pittsfield. Like he knew something I didn't. I hated when people did that.

"What?"

Turley pulled an envelope from his back pocket, slapping it in my waiting palm like a fiver owed on a football bet. My name was on the front, Tom's handwriting clear as day.

I held the envelope at arm's length, not wanting to look, because I knew whatever waited inside was not good news.

"Go ahead," Turley said. He peered past, as if to make sure the coast was clear. "Freddie found that in Tom's office this morning. Right after he left the house to meet you. Propped on the keyboard." Turley nodded at the letter in my hand. "Read it."

I opened the envelope.

I read the note. Didn't take long. It was a short letter.

What the fuck?

CHAPTER SIX

WALKING BACK THROUGH the snow-covered lot toward the garage, I wasn't pissed that Turley had told me "not to leave town"; I didn't have anywhere to go. The only place I wanted to be was with my wife and son, and they weren't mine anymore. My next scheduled visitation was two weeks away. If I wanted to see my son before that, I had to get clearance, ask Jenny if it was okay. Then she had to run it by Stephen, see if it fit into *his* schedule. I hadn't gotten a divorce lawyer, couldn't afford one, and I wasn't fighting Jenny on custody anyway. My wife was more qualified to raise our son. And the truth was she'd never tell me I couldn't see Aiden. She was a wonderful mother, who was more than fair with visitation rights. She only asked that I call first, not drop by unannounced, a reasonable request born of the fact that I was liable to punch her new husband in the head. Maybe I was touched. Had I crossed that line? Everyone's the hero in his own story. Even the bad guy.

I reached in my inner pocket and dug out my prescription bottle. A couple more should calm me down. But I was all out. A month's supply gone in less than two weeks. Why would Tom write that letter? And that morning of all mornings? Of all the times to make a grand gesture, why did it have to be then? Made no sense. The note wasn't even typed. It was handwritten. Tom's writing. Right there in black and white. Or rather blue ballpoint. Signed and left where someone was meant to find it.

If anything happens to me, I, Tom Gable, leave Gable Liquidators LLC to Jason Porter of . . .

Then a few hours later, the accident.

How's that even possible? Who would want to hurt Tom? He was a junkman, like me. We didn't make enemies in our line of work. Besides Tom, the business was valuable to exactly two people. Me. And Owen Eaton. And for as little as I thought of Owen Eaton—as big a dirtbag as I knew him to be—I couldn't picture him throttling Tom Gable to within inches of his life. Owen Eaton was a snake oil huckster. Tom Gable, a barrel-chested mountain man. No way Owen was getting the jump. Which left me. Obviously I was innocent, but that letter sure made me look guilty.

There was no rumor this time, no whispered innuendo inside the Farm Shop or outside Central Pizza. That directive fingered one person. Yours truly. Like I'd forced him to write it at knifepoint before beating the shit out of him and leaving him for dead on the side of Lamentation. Hank Miller saw me last night, flashlight in hand, poking around the garage where the potential murder weapon was stolen. Christine had ID'd me from the restaurant, where I'd been with Tom right before the attack. Freddie said she overheard me on the phone, threatening Tom. Which was total bullshit. But all of that put together? Along with the note saying the company was mine if he died? I would've suspected me, too.

Tom wasn't dead, I kept telling myself. They'd drilled into his skull to relieve the swelling. Critical but still alive. Looked bad. But not over yet. Tom would wake up and set the record straight. He was a tough SOB. Something must've spooked him to write that letter. That was the only explanation. He was looking out for me. Unfortunately in trying to help, Tom had painted a bull's-eye on my forehead. No wonder Freddie seethed with murderous intent.

In the three years since my brother died, I'd blown the only decent-paying job I ever had, and lost my wife and custody of my son. I'd survived a near-fatal attack on the ice of Echo Lake, shredding my calf muscle like fresh mozzarella, leaving me with permanent nerve damage and a considerable limp. Worst of all I'd started to lose the parts of me that made me *me*. It had been a rough stretch. But I was beginning to bounce back. I was starting to heal. I was still lonely, miserable, and pissed off most of the time. But I was me again. I'd take a lifetime of broken bones over that kind of self-doubt. I didn't need this now.

Stalking to my Chevy, I'd fired up a smoke, inhaling like a rat bastard, when my cell rang.

"How's the King of Shit County?"

"Took you long enough, Fisher."

"Sorry, Porter. I don't sit around all day waiting to see if you'll grace me with your presence. What do you want? I got shit to do."

This was how Fisher always talked.

"This guy stopped by last night—"

"I know," Fisher replied, bored and agitated. "I got your message. It's why I'm calling you back? I also talked to Charlie."

"And?"

"And I don't know what to tell you."

"A man named Vin Biscoglio, who works for Ethan Crowder—"

"Don't you listen? I told you: I got your message. I don't know anyone named . . . Vin Biscotti—"

"Biscoglio."

"Whatever. Don't know him. Don't know Ethan Crowder, either. I know *of* him. Everyone does. Heir to a steel fortune. But

I haven't spoken with either one, ever, and I sure as shit didn't recommend *you* for any investigating job. Get over yourself, man. You fucked up the last gig I got you in record time. Made me look like an asshole."

"You'd already quit NorthEastern."

"Whatever. You worked investigations for, what? Eight months?"

"Whoever this Biscoglio is, he's offering me a lot of money to find Crowder's missing kid."

"And I have a Nigerian prince who wants to entrust me with his family's fortune. So fucking what?"

I got to my truck, climbed in the cab, and blasted the heat. "Think, Fisher. Are you sure—"

"How many ways can I say it? Yes, I am sure. Think about what you're asking. Someone has that kind of money, they hire a professional, dude. Why go to a guy who clears crap out of dead people's houses?"

"It's called estate clearing—"

"Yeah, yeah. Save it for the college girls. Are we done here?"

I ran my fingers down my face, clawing at my own eyes, jaw and throat tightening. Then I let out a bellow, a demented screech that sounded like a cross between a possum stuck in a bear trap and that scene in *American History X*. Scared the hell out of Fisher, though.

"Jesus Christ!"

I didn't respond.

"Porter? You still there, man?"

"Yeah, I'm here."

"Hey, man. Sorry. Okay? Didn't mean to bust your balls so hard."

"It's fine."

"I don't know anything. I swear. I never suggested you for a job. If you knew what I did now . . ."

I'd barely spoken to the guy in three years. I had no idea what he did now. And I couldn't care less.

Fisher laughed without prompt. "I don't get out of the house much, let's put it that way." He waited. I could feel his remorse bleeding over the line for coming on so strong. Good. Let someone else feel like shit for a change. "You going to be all right, man?"

"Fucking peachy. Remember my boss, Tom Gable?"

"What about him?"

"Someone tried to kill him. Brained him on Lamentation Mountain with a crowbar. Cracked his skull open. He's in ICU in Pittsfield."

"Someone tried to kill Tom? Whoa. Why? Who . . . what . . . do they have any suspects?"

"Yeah, Fisher," I said. "They do. Me."

* * *

I got back to my place late, agitated skies eddying over Lamentation. Hank Miller's house was dark. At the steps to my apartment, I pulled my cell, flipping on the flashlight, sweeping the grounds. What was I looking for? Sinister tracks in the snow? Cracking a wrecking bar over Tom Gable's skull didn't require breaking into Hank's garage. Any hardware store would do. Stealing it from here served one purpose: to set me up. The question was why.

Across the field I saw the porch light switch on. Hank Miller waved from the stoop, before heading over. I knew he was coming to apologize, but I didn't blame Hank for telling Turley he'd seen me out here last night. The law asked the questions. An old man, he had a lot of ground to cover, his little house a good fifty yards from the filling station, across the ironweeds of an automotive graveyard. My brother didn't kill my parents. I knew that. But the rumor had legs because of this garage. The same garage where I now rented a room upstairs. Truth was, I think the only reason Hank Miller rented to me was because he felt bad about my brother. Wasn't his fault his auto shop linked to the tragedy, but providing me a place to live—at a very reasonable rent—represented a form of reparations for Hank.

"Hey'ya, Jay." Even in the dark, I saw the remorse wash over his face. "Cops come by earlier."

"I know. Ran into Turley at the hospital."

"If I'd have known . . ." Hank panned to the gas pumps populating tiny islands. "They asked if anything was missing. Before they told me what happened. I says, 'Yeah, now that you mention it, I'm missing a pry bar. I only know 'cause I had it on the hood of a car I was working on.' Strange thing to notice missing. But they asked. I thought they'd come because of the break-in."

I put a reassuring hand on his shoulder.

He bobbed his old man head. "I told them cops they had it all wrong. About you. About your brother."

"Why don't you go in, Hank? It's cold out here." The guy didn't even have on a coat. "I'm going to have a look around if that's okay."

"Sure, Jay." He waited, manufacturing a smile. "I went to bed half an hour ago anyway."

I waited until he was indoors and the lights switched off. Holding the cell to the windows, I searched for anything out of the ordinary, boot prints, discarded candy wrappers, matchbook, which was pointless since the garage had been open all day, business as usual. A couple dozen people had come and gone.

Something felt off, a presence I couldn't place, the same one I'd gotten last night after Vin Biscoglio's visit. Last night, the sensation wasn't overpowering. More unsettling, like a color you can't quite describe, trapped between shades, flames flickering beyond peripheral. Now the lunatics danced in the clear moonlight and their voices screamed in my ear. The offer for that much money coming when I needed it most? If I were to compete with Owen Eaton, I needed a miracle. Was that miracle my friend and boss having his head stomped in? Once upon a time, I believed God was looking out for me, like there was rhyme, reason, some serendipitous Universe seeking to even scores, settle wrongs, balance the scale. I'd view good fortune as providence. But for the grace of God there go I. Which is all well and fine until you think about the poor bastard over there.

CHAPTER SEVEN

I WOKE THE next morning to the simultaneous sounds of fists pounding on my door and my landline ringing. Total sensory overload. I kept telling myself I was going to cancel my home phone because the only people who called it were bill collectors and solicitors, neither of whom I wanted to talk to. And I sure as hell wasn't up for company.

Crawling out of bed, I zipped my sweatshirt, shivering. I left the heat off to avoid hefty bills. Nighttime wasn't so bad because I could pile on the blankets. When I woke, though, it was like stepping into a meat locker. Tom had given me that fancy automatic heating system. I could handle the electronics, no problem. Hooking up to the Internet? Not with step-by-step directions and an extra set of hands.

I checked out my bedroom window, scanning for police cars, as fists continued to rain down. The usual cars dotted the block. Fat flakes floated through slate skies. Icicles jagged from telephone lines, threatening preemptive strike. More snow had accumulated overnight, winds gusting hard. The glass bowed with each blast, perforating plastic insulation.

For a brief, glorious moment, the thumping stopped, calls abated, my temples didn't pulsate, and I wasn't cursing things I couldn't see for just being born. Then the ringing started back up, the thudding returned, and without thinking, I yanked the landline from the socket, ripped the cord, and smashed the thing against the wall, cheap Radio Shack piece-of-shit shattering into a million little pieces.

"Jay? It's me. Come on, man! Open up."

I hadn't seen a bicycle below and couldn't picture Charlie peddling his pork chops across town in this weather anyway, which meant one thing.

A while back I saw a terrible movie with Nick Nolte and Jessica Lange. Tim Hutton was in it, too. I can't remember the name. It was about a football player. The film spans many years, and to show this passage of time, the filmmakers made the unfortunate, ham-handed decision to alter Hutton's facial hair every scene he's in. Early on he's clean cut, and then as we pass through the sixties, he's sporting longer hippy locks, and then the seventies, all disco 'stache, et cetera. At one point, I think he even rocks a goatee, never a good look on a man. I was thinking about that movie when I opened the door.

Fisher's appearance had grown increasingly radical, and the years had not been kind. His stringy, greasy hair was tied atop his head in a sloppy knot. And he had a fucking goatee. Beneath his beaver coat, he was still a runt, compensating by wearing thick-soled boots, painting the false impression of height.

"What was that noise?" Charlie said, nodding past my shoulder, scouring my party-of-one remnants. I hadn't collected empty beer bottles in ages. Place was such a mess, you couldn't pick out the landline bones among the rest of the carnage.

"Bumped into the table."

"You were passed the fuck out. Been standing out there for fifteen minutes. Could hear you snoring down the block."

That was rich. Charlie Finn had no business commenting on anyone's snoring.

Fisher grunted, "Yo," before blowing past. He never waited for invitations. He had his leather satchel with him. Anytime I saw him, he carted the man purse along. His big bag of secrets.

"Why are you guys here?" I asked, even though I knew the answer.

Fisher began extracting papers from his handbag, ignoring the question like it was so beyond obvious he wasn't condescending an answer. "You have any coffee?" Then before I could respond: "Charlie, find some coffee. We got work to do."

"Fisher came up this morning," Charlie said. "He told me about Tom Gable's accident. I know how much he means to you. I'm sorry, man."

"Yeah, me, too." I pointed at the cupboard. "Coffee's in there. I'm out of milk."

"That's okay," Fisher replied, perusing his papers. "I like my coffee like I like my facts. Fast, black, cold."

"That doesn't make any sense."

He looked over. "It does if you think about it."

"No one drinks iced coffee in this weather. It's twenty degrees outside."

"Tell me about it. It's freezing balls up in this place. Don't you have a heater?"

"Yeah, Fisher, I do. But heat is expensive."

"Maybe you should take the money this Biscoglio is offering." Fisher snickered. "You're on the job regardless. And that offer is the key to this whole thing."

"What whole thing?"

"Try to keep up, Porter. Why you're being set up."

"Who says I'm being set up?" Sure, I'd suspected the same thing but that didn't mean I had to lend credence to Fisher's goofy theories.

"I do," Fisher said, talking over my head. "How we coming with that coffee?"

"On it, Captain." Charlie mocked a salute.

"Good. Now let's get down to brass tacks. Have a seat."

I hated taking orders from the pipsqueak, but I sat down.

"After we got off the phone last night, I got to work, and—"

"What is it you do for work these days?" I knew Fisher had quit the insurance racket, and judging by his out-there, raggedy appearance, no one was hiring his mangy ass for a traditional nine-to-five.

Fisher reached into his bag of tricks, plucking a thin pamphlet, one step up from those stapled jobs bedraggled poets try to sell you outside the coffee shop, clearly homemade.

"Most of what I do is online," he said, proudly presenting his product. "I print out a few issues. Pass them to folks at Price Chopper, libraries, take the fight to the streets."

I unfurled the paper. *Occam's Razor*. Typical wackadoodle conspiracy theories: "10 Truths About GMOs, Monsanto, And What Big Pharma Doesn't Want You To Know"; "We Are On The Cusp of Interstellar Travel—And Why The Government Won't Tell You"; "Proof Jet Fuel Doesn't Burn Steel." Strap on the tin foil helmet and buckle in for a bumpy ride. All the bylines by one author: Fisher. I glanced back at Charlie, who shrugged.

"Don't look at him, Porter, like I'm inconveniencing you with some truth."

Just what I needed, help from a conspiracy nut and a thirty-five-year-old alcoholic who used a bicycle as his sole mode of transportation.

Fisher dragged his laptop from his shoulder bag, flipped the lid, and spun it around.

"What do you want me to do with that?"

"Just look. Page is bookmarked."

The website had the same name, with amateur flashing graph-
ics and visual aesthetic culled straight from ColecoVision, circa
1985.

"What's *Occam's Razor* even mean?"

Charlie brought two mugs of coffee and set them on the table.
"Mind if I grab a beer, Jay?"

"Occam's Razor means the most obvious answer is usually the
right one."

"Great."

Fisher tapped the screen of his laptop, encouraging me to read
his ridiculous ramblings.

"I have no interest in this lunatic fringe horseshit, okay? I dealt
with that crap when Chris was alive." My dead junkie brother
did a lot of meth, and that drug in particular turns your brain inside out, unleashes a hall of never-ending mirrors, multiplication
charts reflected back on itself, all numbers irrational.

But Fisher wasn't pointing at an article. He was pointing at an
ad. A commercial for stomach ailments accompanied by a picture
of a vivisected rock, innards red, as if it were bleeding. The banner
underneath: "The Secret Cure For All Your Stomach Woes." His
entire website was covered with similar ads.

"Know how much companies pay to advertise on my website?"

"I don't know how computers work."

"I do. So shut the fuck up. Remember last time I saw you I said
I was taking journalism classes?"

"Sort of."

"I got an Associate's."

"Good for you."

"Laugh it up. But my blog gets five thousand hits a day. On
average. Which means businesses want to advertise with me. I
charge five bills for a tiny ad like that one." He pointed at a small

picture of an engorged tick. "I make more money selling ads and writing these conspiracy pieces than I ever did at NorthEastern Insurance." He stared me dead on. "And I guarantee I make more money than you."

He jabbed a hand over the table and snared the brown paper bag Tom gave me the other day outside Julie's.

"Do you mind?"

He unwrapped the thermostat and auto-lighting kit. "Why haven't you installed this? Your apartment wouldn't feel like the goddamn Arctic."

"It hooks up via the Internet. I'm not good with that shit."

"You have Wi-Fi?"

"Jenny made me get it."

"What's your network name and password?"

"Some long-ass number. It's on the fridge."

He hopped up, snatching the password from under a magnet, fishing a screwdriver and clippers from my junk drawer.

I pointed at his newspaper articles. Bright, scintillating titles, which were all variations of "What *they* don't want you to know . . ."

"You don't really believe these things?"

"Some of it I do. Some I . . . embellish." Fisher was at my thermostat, prying panels. "Point is, beats a day job. I'm my own boss, I'm making bank, and I've learned a thing or two about digital investigation, which is ninety-nine percent of the game these days. Charlie, hand me that Nest and Osram unit."

Charlie followed orders. Fisher threaded a ribbon cable, snapping the plate in place. An LCD glowed. He plunked down at the computer, pecking away. Charlie drank his beer, leaning against the stove. When my friend first walked in, he'd seemed twitchy, on edge, like his skin were a too-tight suit. A couple sips of beer and he was right as rain.

"Have you searched Ethan Crowder online?" Fisher asked me.

"A little."

"You might want to start taking this a little more seriously. Give me your cell."

"Why do you need my cell?"

"Lights and heater hook up to it. It's called an app. What century do you live in?"

I keyed in my passcode, Aiden's birthday, and handed him the phone.

"So, Crowder," Fisher prompted. "Talk to me. What'd you find?"

"I told you. Not much. Silver-spoon trust-fund kid. Inherited the company from his father. Used to be a bit of a player. Had a habit of knocking women around. Mended his violent tendencies, or at least found a way to keep them out of the spotlight. Learned about an ex-wife in Wyoming. Got Joanne's address in Coal Creek. Didn't get much further than that."

"What did your unexpected guest have to say?"

"Oh you mean Vin Biscoglio? The guy you've never met? Know nothing about? And definitely did not refer to me?"

"Don't be a smart-ass, Porter."

"Works for Ethan Crowder. Says Crowder's estranged wife, Joanne, had their sixteen-year-old son, Phillip, shipped off to a radical rehab in Middlesex. Overreaction to pot and pills. Gave me the name of a place. Rewrite Interventions."

"You call the rehab? Talk to Joanne Crowder? Have you done *any* legwork?"

"I told you. I haven't had a lot of time."

Fisher flipped me my phone. "Real simple. The heater and lights will monitor your usage, get accustomed to your schedule, automatically dim, adjust, turn the heat down when you aren't here. Tap that app."

"Why do I need to automatically dim lights if I'm not here? I barely use the heat, period."

"This shit saves money. Think about your friends. No one wants to freeze their nuts off when they visit. Now I suggest you get your ass up to Joanne Crowder's."

"If it were that easy, why wouldn't Biscoglio have already done that? This whole thing stinks. Why come to me at all?"

Fisher placed one finger on his nose, the other pointing at me as if we were playing a game of charades.

"I'm not taking the money."

"I didn't say to take the money. But you have to take the job."

"I already have a job."

"And now your boss is laid up in a hospital."

"And the cops suspect you put him there," Charlie said.

I glared over my shoulder at Charlie.

"Don't shoot the messenger," Fisher said. "Our best defense is a good offense."

"Turley knows me better than to think I'd hurt Tom." I didn't mention the letter, which would further murk already muddy views.

"Unless Tom doesn't make it, and they can't find anyone else to pin the rap on."

The way Charlie said that scared me. Of course, I knew I had nothing to do with Tom's attack. The truth would come out. Eventually. Unless it didn't because Tom died with it. Facts were facts, true or not, and that letter leaving me his business could convince a jury. The way things stood, they had enough evidence to arrest me now, which invited its own mess. Exonerated didn't mean squat; any legal action would drain my limited resources. I bypassed the coffee for a beer, too. I needed to refill my prescription.

"Ask yourself this," Fisher said. "Why wasn't Ethan, rich and powerful as he is, able to get custody?"

"One, they aren't divorced."

"All the more reason the boy should be with him."

"Maybe he doesn't want custody?" I hadn't contested with Jenny. "If they're headed for a divorce, judges tend to side with the mother."

"For a mere mortal. Ethan Crowder is royalty."

"How many times has the dude been married?" Charlie asked.

"Two," replied Fisher. "Don't know about number one, but he was smart enough to get a pre-nup this go-round."

"Live and learn."

"Except he's still paying out the nose to Joanne," Fisher said. "A lot of money to a woman he supposedly hates. And before you say he's providing like a good father should, Crowder treats people like possessions. He has a long history of violence against women. He'd be fucking Joanne six ways to Sunday. If he could."

"Then why isn't he? Maybe the charges against him are bullshit. Pissed-off exes lie. Wouldn't be the first time."

"Oh, Ethan smacked these women around. Black eyes, broken bones. There are hospital records, if you dig deep enough. The guy has real rage issues."

"And you know all this how?"

Fisher shook his head, slow and full of pity. He pointed at the laptop, like every answer was contained within that tiny machine. Who knew? Maybe it was.

He began scrolling webpages. "Let's get started."

"Doing what?"

"Coming up with a strategy." Fisher closed his computer and took off the glasses he didn't need, staring me down with those beady eyes of his. "We need to find the boy."

"I'm not interested in doing Ethan Crowder's bidding." I grabbed my new winter coat from the back of the chair and snagged another beer for the road.

At the door, I turned around. "I appreciate you both stopping by. I know you're looking out for me. But I am not taking on any 'case,' especially one I can't get paid for. Regardless of whoever turned Biscoglio on to me—" I made sure to look at Fisher when I said that last part "—I don't see how beating Tom Gable senseless connects to a missing teen. And *that* is what I care about. Finding who attacked my boss."

CHAPTER EIGHT

THE CLEARING HOUSE was a couple hours south of Ashton, all the way to Moultonborough and Lake Winnipesaukee. The lake saw a lot of tourist action, making it a better location for an auction house than Ashton. Getting there was a headache. Around the mountain, down the 93, over the 113, tracing the shoreline halfway to Wolfeboro. Too much time alone. Too much time to stew in my own juices.

If Turley were doing his job instead of harassing me, he'd have taken a harder look at Owen Eaton, who had as much of a motive as I did, maybe more. Tom goes down, his main competition is gone. Freddie sells the business, she's not waiting around until I scrounge up the capital. Owen had better credit, the bigger name. Banks would line up around the block to loan the guy money. If he didn't already have the cash on hand. My chances were a long shot to begin with. And that was before Freddie blamed me for her husband's death.

I knew I could be a stubborn sonofabitch and that I wasn't the easiest guy to be around, especially when the heat was on. If I were the sentimental type, I'd say it was cool having friends like Charlie and Fisher who had my back. But while I loved Charlie like a brother, Fisher bugged the hell out of me. Just being around him irritated me, like slow-flying flies hovering above a dirty sink. Which made me a lousy person, I knew, because Fisher tried to be my friend. At thirty-four, I didn't want any more of them. Friends, I mean. People who demanded my time. When I was younger, I was always up for a party, going down to the reservoir, drinking life to the lees, like this poem I read in high school. I don't remember who wrote it but that line always stuck with me, this idea that life was meant to be lived. Go big or go home. It's the kind of crap you believe in high school because you aren't going to settle. No compromise, you are going to have it all. Then you hit a certain age, and you don't want to be awake after ten o'clock.

Before Aiden was born, Jenny bought a bunch of baby books, strategically placing them around the apartment for me to read. My wife really wanted to bring up our boy right. Titles like *How to Raise a Strong Sensitive Boy*. How's that even possible? You can't be strong *and* sensitive. They tell you that you can. But you can't. It's a lie. And that's the thing with all these platitudes they shove down your throat—they're all lies.

Most of the information in these baby books was common sense—set firm but caring limits, let the child know actions have consequences, love, logic, that kind of thing. There was one passage, though, that really resonated, like that drinking-life-to-the-lees poem. It was this bit about teen angst. Even though I was thirty-four, a huge part of me was still stuck at sixteen. This one baby book—I can't even remember the name—maintained teen angst stemmed from the realization you'd been lied to growing up. Like a few weeks ago with Aiden. He'd gotten into trouble at school, and Jenny wanted me to talk to him. So I took him out for pizza and ice cream, my dad money move. He was slow to warm up, which is another part that sucks about being a part-time dad. Every time I'd see my son, I'd have to prime the parental pump again, re-win his trust. Anyway, he'd gotten into trouble at school because he didn't share. Kindergarten is big on sharing. Aiden didn't want to share, and so he got a time-out, which is how they punish kids these days.

At the restaurant, I said, "Aiden, why didn't you want to share? Sharing is fun." I was trying to teach him a valuable life lesson, be a role model.

My son stared across his pepperoni pizza and said, "No, it's not."

And I thought about that. Fuck, he was right. Sharing isn't fun. It's a pain in the ass, a compromise none of us wants to make except for the fact that we are all stuck on this spinning blue orb together. It might be necessary, but it sure as fuck isn't fun. Why was I telling him it was?

That was the point of this book, how as parents we tell our children the way the world is *supposed* to be. Shit like sharing is fun, and if you work hard enough you can be anything you want to be, and it's what's on the inside that counts, money doesn't buy happiness. Then we hit sixteen and realize we've been lied to. Poor people get scraps. Fat people get made fun of. The richest and the prettiest get all the spoils. Our entire lives we've been lied to by the people we trusted most. And it pisses us off. Most move on. I never got over that. Which I recognized at my age was counterproductive. How much do you cling to your vision of the way the world should be in the face of mounting evidence that it's anything but? Going down with a sinking ship ceases being heroic when land is in sight, a stone's throw away. I'd begun to suspect my moral compass was seriously broken.

Pulling into the sprawling Clearing House parking lot, I felt like I was hitting the mall at Christmastime. On non-auction days, we were lucky to draw half a dozen window-shoppers. People on their way to somewhere else who'd stop by on a whim because they'd seen our sign from the Turnpike and thought it might be fun to look at a couch.

Midday, the Clearing House was packed with families, shopping carts rolling in and out revolving doors, a sea of big-screen televisions, chandeliers, gigantic artwork. I had to circle the lot twice to find a space.

Out front, big red banners boasted sales in between the inflatable wacky wavers, long arms berserking wild in the wind.

My son, Aiden, had a fear of dolls and dummies. Jenny was terrified of squirrels. I didn't have any phobias, other than ending up the same man I was now. But, Christ, those wacky wavers freaked me out.

This current sale was for Cyber Monday, which made no sense. I thought the whole point of that one was online deals. Didn't matter. It was a ruse. A new sale would highlight whatever bullshit holiday landed next on the calendar. Every day is a holiday in America. Presidents' Day. Arbor Day. Fucking Feast of the Immaculate Conception. Next week Owen Eaton would be knocking off 40 percent to commemorate Pan American Aviation Day.

I hadn't been to Owen's place since moving home from Plasterville three years ago. He'd expanded operations. Bigger showroom. Larger auction house. Double down on the glitz, ramp up the glamour, rake in the profit. I knew he was on-site. His truck occupied the same primo spot closest the door. The vanity license plate gave it away: LKQUID8.

Owen was either on his way out, or he had been warned. Before I could grab the handle, he was at the door, holding it wide, carnival barking for me to step right up.

"Come on in, Jay," he said, ushering me into his sanctum, which splayed out as if it had been decorated by a Louisiana Purchase trapper. Pelts furred the walls in between huge skulls of dead beasts, longhorns and mounted muskets, the rest of his office littered with the assorted knickknacks that hallmark the profession. Glass figurines. Whittled walking sticks. Tea sets. Made me wonder why I didn't at least have a new Keurig coffeemaker. Tom often gave me picks of the litter. Didn't have much interest in acquiring more stuff, I guess. Looking over Owen's riches, I promised myself: next time I saw a decent coffeemaker, I was snagging it. That swill Charlie made last night tasted like it had been brewed through a sweaty jockstrap.

"Good to see you," Owen said, pointing at the tiny chair in front of his long cherrywood desk. "Have a seat." Cowboy boots kicked up, fat ass plushing the captain's chair, he reminded me of a Texas oilman, not that I'd ever seen a Texas oilman other than on campy late-night soaps. Probably the boots, these obnoxious snakeskin things no one in northern New Hampshire had any business wearing.

"Can I get you something to drink? Tea? Coffee? Scored one of them Keurigs at auction recently. Kind that uses those little pods? Tasty." He pressed a button on his phone, bringing up the speaker. "Marlene, mind brewing a couple fresh cups?" Then to me: "Cream, sugar?" Before I had a chance to answer, he was back on the phone. "The works. And hurry up."

"I'm sorry to hear about Tom," he said clicking off. "Got a call from your sheriff up there. Nice fella. What's his name?"

"Turley."

"That's right. Told me what happened. Awful. Just awful." I thought I detected a slight grin. Then again, the smarmy bastard always seemed to be smirking. I wondered how much Turley had told him. I doubted he'd go so far as to mention the note. But that smirk didn't make me feel too confident.

"Did he tell you it was a botched carjacking?"

"He implied as much, yes."

"Don't you think that's a little weird?"

"A carjacking in your hick town? Very."

"Turley said it was meant to *look* like a carjacking. Someone pretended to be stranded, setting a trap for Tom. So they could crack his skull open." I waited, watched his reaction. "Someone who wanted him out of the way."

Took him a moment. Owen Eaton cocked his head, sizing me up with a squint. "Don't tell me that's why you're here?"

The door opened and a dowdy woman with field mouse brown hair and a body shaped like a bowling pin waddled in, presenting a tray, a house maiden in some old film noir. Except instead of sterling silver and ornate spouts, she carried paper cups with mini creamers, the kind you get for free at 7-Eleven or the Gas 'n' Go. No matter how much money Owen made, he'd always be a chintzy SOB. I wasn't complaining. Gave me time to think how I wanted to play my next move.

Marlene set the coffee on his desk.

"Make sure you get me in five minutes," Owen said, wrinkling his forehead, wriggling his bushy eyebrows, stopping just short of winking. "For that . . . thing."

"Of course," Marlene said, only slightly less confused.

Soon as the door closed, Owen put down his boots and leaned across his desk. "I know you've never liked me, Jay."

"That's not true." Of course that was true, but declaring your intense hatred for someone is seldom the best way to get answers.

"That's okay," Owen said, grabbing his coffee. "You don't like anyone. You think you're better than everyone else. Don't bother me none. I don't trust people who like everyone. I think we're all too friendly up here. A little distrust is a good thing."

"Glad to see we are on the same page." What an asshole.

"But walkin' into my office and accusing me of attempted murder? I can appreciate a set of stones as much as the next guy. But those balls of yours ain't quite that big and brassy."

"I'm not accusing you of anything—"

"You know the problem with smart fellers like you?" He said it like that, too, "fellers," even though he knew it wasn't really a word, the way some people will drop the "g" to sound more street, use "ain't" even if they've gone to college. This guy probably had a million plus in the bank. But Owen Eaton, one of the biggest liquidators in the Northeast, still needed me to believe he was down because he retained a twang and said stupid shit like "fellers." Dollars to donuts he wasn't even from the South. "Smart fellers like you—and I think you *are* a smart feller, Jay. Whether you like me or not—I have respect for you—but you are just smart enough to think everyone else is a moron. A little intelligence is a dangerous thing."

"I don't know what that means."

Owen slapped the table, spitting out a laugh. "Maybe you ain't so smart after all."

"Don't you think it's a little weird? Tom's talking about getting out of the business, hosts this last-minute secret sale, which also happens to be one of the biggest to date. Then someone lays him out?"

"I could ask the same of you. This ain't *Silkwood*, son." Son? Guy was ten years older than me. I wasn't his fucking son. "Can I be honest with you?"

"No, lie to me."

Owen pointed a finger, busting himself up. "No disrespect to Amos and Andy at that rinky-dinky police department you got up there, but your sheriff, Turkleton—"

"Turley."

"Right. Turley. Seems like a nice guy. But I find it hard to believe that within ten minutes of finding a man bleedin' on the side of the road, they can start lobbing theories that include manslaughter, don't you? Seems a little . . . melodramatic? I mean, who's to say Tom's truck didn't slide off the icy road—you know those mountain passes, how treacherous they get in storms. His truck's slippin' and slidin', Tom gets tossed, he's stumbling around, all shaky, falls and cracks his skull on a rock."

"And the crowbar covered with blood and bone?"

"Hell, I don't know. Throwin' out hypotheticals. Just sayin' your boy, Turley, might be fishing. Can't imagine there's much crime to fight up there in Ashton. The devil will find work for idle hands and all that. Now listen, as long as I got you here, I want you to know, your feelings for me aside, I've always thought you were a damn fine estate man. Have a real eye for antiques. I'm not blowin' smoke up your ass. When I go to an auction and see you there, I get worried, because I know I'll have to bring my A-game."

"You mean like slipping out back for a little wheeling and dealing?"

Owen slapped the table, pointing that finger at me again, beaming.

Marlene cracked the door. "Mr. Eaton, you have that meeting—"

"Dammit, Marlene!" He threw up his hands, shocked to find gambling in this establishment. "Can't you see I'm talking to my good friend Jay Porter here? I'll be there in a minute. Sheesh."

Owen caught my eye, waving me closer, like we were on the same team. "I want you to know, you'll always have a job at the Clearing House if you want one." Before I could say a word—like I already had a fucking job and that Tom was going to pull through like a champ, call Owen Eaton a dick for suggesting otherwise—the smooth-talking snake-oil salesman cut me off. "God forbid, I mean. Tom Gable is one tough sonofabitch. I am sure he's going to overcome this bump in the road with flying colors."

Owen stood up and walked around his desk, wrapping an arm around my shoulder, guiding me to my feet, offering reassurance as he escorted me the hell out of there.

"Think about it," he said.

Then he shoved me out the door and slammed it shut.

CHAPTER NINE

TOM HAD SAID to start moving Monday, but I had the key. He'd already signed the lease. The property was ours. I began schlepping the biggest, most expensive items down to the new space in Pittsfield. The security system was up and running. Tom didn't skimp on security. Couldn't risk it. I started with our main warehouse off Lamplight Lane. I'd clear the temporary pod at You Store, which housed the Mortenson haul, last. Despite some good scores from that auction, the value paled to our permanent collection. Over the years, Tom Gable had acquired more than three hundred thousand dollars' worth of merchandise. The relocation required several trips, and this was the most efficient route.

With Tom laid up, the business wasn't going to stay on course without someone's taking the reins. Freddie's feelings for me aside, my loyalty was to Tom, not her.

After dropping off the first load at Everything Under the Sun—I had to admit, the new name was growing on me—I stopped by the hospital to check on Tom's progress. I was hoping Freddie would be taking a break. But she was there, along with her two sisters, all huddled together, a clamor of harpies. Tom still lay unresponsive, hooked up to the machines that were helping him breathe. I wanted to remain optimistic, but for the first time, I feared he wasn't going to make it. My big, burly friend was shriveling up, cheeks withering gaunt, pale, like the life force was being sucked out of him. Everyone in the room pretended to acknowledge me. Freddie answered my questions. Clipped, unenthusiastic responses but she answered them. I knew they'd been talking about me before I walked in, and they'd be doing so again the moment I left. She was polite enough, I guess. Very few have the guts to call you an asshole to your face.

I'd known Tom Gable for almost twenty years, which meant I'd known Freddie that long, too; they'd been married forever. And now because of the rotten timing of good intentions, I was the bad guy.

Turley should've fucking known better. As much as I detested Owen Eaton, he had a point. How the hell can you find a man, unconscious and bleeding out his head, in the middle of a snowstorm, and say with any certainty what happened? Turley had honed in on me because of my family's history. If my brother didn't have his reputation, I don't have mine. Chris' involvement in our parents' death had become part of small-town lore, like the crane stuck on the bottom of Duncan Pond, main boom and fly jib breaking the surface, backstory buoyed by rural folks' need to fable the fabulous. My brother had the misfortune of working at an auto garage and not getting along with his dad. What hardheaded teenager gets along with his father? If Chris works at the Dairy Queen, no one is accusing him of tampering with anything other than the Mr. Misty nozzle. But he worked in a garage, had intimate knowledge of mechanics, and access to the hardware. In other words, luck of the draw, which can still be a shitty hand. If I'm back in Plasterville, working in that stupid monkey suit, denying claims to soccer moms and prematurely balding dads, and Tom has an accident? No one is pointing a finger at me, regardless of any letter. Then again, I'd always be Chris Porter's brother.

Which rendered me a fuck-up by proxy. Maybe I was selling my-self short. After all the mistakes I'd made, I'd earned that reputa-tion all by my lonesome.

With daylight savings stealing time, darkness slinked in ear-lier. Late-afternoon jet streams picked up as more flurries fell. Turnpike traffic jammed, sludged like chilled maple syrup, bumper to bumper, lights stuck on red, horns bleating. I scanned radio stations. Nothing I wanted to listen to. Tried sports talk, but everyone was screaming. Callers, hosts, even the commercials sounded deranged.

When I was growing up, the Turnpike, with its slew of off-track betting sites, fast-food chains, and single-room occupancy hotels, represented squalor, providing mean-spirited kids with endless material for the bus ride home. When Chris started living as a junkie in these flophouses along the strip, my discomfort around this part of town intensified, became more personal. This was where my brother began killing himself, one shot at a time, and long before the police fired any bullet. Now after everything I'd been through, my disdain for the diseased thoroughfare had bur-rowed deeper, eating away at me like the scabies and bedbugs that infested half these rooms.

I drove past the Kenilworth Motel, where I'd suffered the worst morning of my life. In the midst of that psychotic break, I'd holed up there to elude the tactical units on my tail, the shooters on the roof, the helicopters circling the sky, the world that waited to come crashing down. Of course none of this was true. My brain chemistry out of whack, I was imprisoned within the walls of paranoia, unable to separate fact from fantasy.

But a few hours trapped inside the Kenilworth Motel was all the fuel my nightmares needed. These days when I closed my eyes to sleep, I still saw the streaks of blood across the walls and ceiling. Long, sweeping arcs of black and red. The walking dead clearing the line, spraying unholy constellations across fractured chapels.

Instead of veering off onto Orchard Road, the straightest shot back into the center of town, I continued north on the Turnpike, past the new Coos County Center recently erected on the grounds of the old TC Truck Stop, through the unchartered territory of Coal Creek, climbing the mountain into an affluent section called Crimson Peak.

There weren't many houses on this part of Lamentation, but the disparity between the blessed and the rest was never more pronounced. Crimson Peak was the mountain's Park Avenue. In the low-lying flats my brother and a junkie pal had run their crooked electronic recycling con, easy to hide among the blight of used car lots and Chinese restaurants shut down for serving cat. On the hill, a different narrative unfolded. Grand houses, modern architectural wonders. Rich red cedar frames, gleaming steel beams, walls made entirely of glass. Postcard snapshots of brilliant blue lakes and towering green trees, the chosen ones lording over lesser peoples.

I pulled out the address I'd scribbled down for Joanne Crowder, wishing I'd come better prepared. I didn't even know what I planned to ask her if she answered the door, my decision to drive up here spurred by frustration, anger, outrage. In retrospect, coming up to Crimson Peak should've been my first move. Maybe I wouldn't feel so pissed off if I knew what the hell was going on.

From my days in insurance, I'd learned house calls were the most effective method for getting people to talk. Catch them off guard, pants down, unprepared. Folks have an easier time slamming down the phone than they do shutting a door. Though I'd been on the receiving end of both plenty.

All the lights were off, no car in the driveway. I parked my truck in the deep, unplowed snow, and rang the bell anyway. Nothing stirred inside. No light switched on. The mailbox was overstuffed with shopping mailers, letters, and bills, correspondence crammed into the tiny slit, spilling to the steps. Financial newspapers, wrapped in blue plastic bags, stuck out of the frozen ground. I thought about leaving a business card. Stick it in the door, hope for a callback. But I knew then that Joanne Crowder wasn't coming back.

The drive to my dumpy one-room pad above the garage was a cold, hollow road. I'd been hoping for a quick fix. There's no such thing. Ask any junkie. I tried not to dwell on the Crowders' domestic troubles, I had enough of my own, and I didn't want to obsess over Freddie and her family's opinion of me. I mean, if I were in Freddie's shoes, I'd be thinking the same thing. Tom pens that note, gets attacked the next day; I have no alibi, what else is there to ask? My question had to be different: Why then? Of all the times to put those wishes in writing, Tom Gable had picked *that* night. Something must've spooked him. Freddie told Turley she'd heard Tom and me fighting on the phone at two a.m. That wasn't me on the line. Even if I'd been hammered after Biscoglio's visit, lost track of time, blacked out, no way I call my boss after midnight and pick a fight. Over what? I had no gripes with Tom. Except simmering resentment over his possibly selling the company to Owen Eaton.

During our breakfast at Julie's, Tom didn't mention any argument. But he *had* been acting odd. Not his usual Zen-bear self, more hesitant, like he had something on his mind. He'd start, stop, stammer, words on the tip of his tongue before he'd clamp up, swallow them back down. I'd noted it then. Now that I thought about it, he'd addressed the issue of selling to Owen before I even brought it up, promising me we'd work it out. He and I were close, but not mind-reading close. Had I been so drunk that I phoned my boss at two in the morning? I did possess a tendency to let shit fester. In efforts to avoid conflict, I'd push grievances down deep, letting resentment build and build and build, until I blew up at the worst possible moment. Did it all the time with Jenny.

No, that wasn't me on the phone. I had no record of any such call on my cell. Although I would've used the landline. Better reception. Could check the call list when I got back. *If you hadn't Russell Crowed the thing against the wall.* Why hadn't Turley checked phone records? *Maybe he has.* Unless the threat came via e-mail? If someone stopped by unannounced, Freddie would've told the cops. *Who says she would?*

I needed to get my hands on Tom's phone log and access his computer. Lucky for me, I had two friends skilled in each. Even if I didn't like one of them much, and the other was a shiftless, chronic alcoholic.

*   *   *

I saw this movie last year about a lawyer who operated out of his car to save money on office rental expenses. Only caught the tail end of it. One of the cops from *True Detective*, Matthew McConaughey, was in it. Meeting up with Charlie and Fisher at the Olympic Diner felt like that. The twenty-four-hour dinette was like our office. And it beat all hell out of a car. For one, there was more room, better food, and the view was spectacular. The Olympic Diner on the Desmond Turnpike laid claim to some of the best-looking women in the state. Young, Greek, gorgeous. I swear I wasn't like this in high school. When all my buddies overheated from sex on the brain, I barely noticed girls. I had better things to do. But the older I got, the worse it got. I also hadn't been laid in a while, which didn't help. The longer you go without getting any, the more desperate you come across. Nobody wants to be the answer to all your problems. I wasn't improving my chances hanging out with the Wonder Twins. Charlie had let himself go, sprouting gin blossoms and bitch tits. Fisher, decked out like a Dungeons & Dragons reject, was a couple sides short of a twelve-sided die, even on his best day. No man's hair should be so long he has to wrap it on top of his head and secure it in a bun. Maybe it was for the best. Last thing I needed right now was a romantic entanglement. I'd deal with blue balls on my own. That's why God invented porn.

Charlie cradled his swollen head in his hands, receding hairline stretching temples taut, skin flush as a fat pink baby plucked fresh from the hot tub.

We were meeting Sunday morning, which meant Charlie had been partying hard last night, and I could see he was hurting. Not that the day mattered much to Charlie at this stage. Every night was Saturday night. He could use a little hair of the dog.

"Glad you came to your senses," Fisher said. "This is no joke."

I craned to watch the twenty-year-old waitress bend over to restock the muffins. "Like you said yesterday, I don't have a choice."

"Anything new on Tom?"

I shook my head and turned around.

"So what's the plan?" Charlie said, less interested in a course of action than he was in speeding up the process. Fisher was crashing at his place, and I knew he'd dragged Charlie along. No other way my best friend was making the morning meeting. Charlie wanted back under the covers until the skies grew dark again and he'd be able to drink himself back into oblivion.

"First thing we need to do," Fisher said, "is pay Joanne Crowder a visit."

"Already did. Last night."

"And?"

"No one's home. Doesn't look as if anyone's been home for a while. Newspapers haven't been picked up, mail stuffed in the box."

"Then I'm thinking we need to take this show on the road." Fisher looked deathly serious. "We go down to Boston and confront the man himself. See what Ethan Crowder has to say."

"Let's hold off on that for now." I had no interest in a road trip with Fisher, especially to Boston. Just hearing the name caused me pain. I flashed back on the last thing Erik Bowman said to me three years ago when he quit the construction game, giving up leg-breaking to go on the run from the Lombardi Brothers: anywhere but Boston. One of the few things we agreed on. I'd been down there to see the Sox play a couple times. Loved the team. Hated the city.

The pretty waitress came to take our order. I needed to start dating again. I felt like a fat guy ogling a cheesesteak stand.

Bypassing his usual chicken wings, Charlie asked for a beer. He didn't care what this pretty girl thought of him. The minute you stop caring what pretty girls think about you, might as well pack it in, get some black socks and sandals, move to Florida.

Fisher and I said we were good with coffee for now, and then Fisher called the girl back, said, on second thought, he'd order half the fucking menu. So I got a mushroom omelet and some hash. Even if I'd lost my appetite, I knew I needed to eat.

"Charlie," I said, "you still have friends at the phone company?"

"I know a few guys over there, yeah. Why?"

When my brother got his hands on that hard drive, Charlie was working for the phone company. He had offered to tap Lombardi's line. At the time, I'd talked him out of it, told him he was crazy to jeopardize the steady paycheck, never mind the legal repercussions. Obtaining phone records without a warrant was a serious criminal offense. Now here I was, outright encouraging him to break whatever law he could, implicate former coworkers, friends, whoever, throw the whole town under the bus, personal welfare be damned. Funny what a potential murder charge does to belief systems.

"How hard will it be to pull Tom Gable's phone records?"

"A lot easier once I get something to drink. My fucking head is killing me." Charlie whiplashed down the aisle, willing his beer to arrive faster. "I didn't eat enough yesterday." His bulging belly pinched over the countertop.

I didn't point out he hadn't ordered any food to remedy that.

"I need all incoming and outgoing calls for Thanksgiving night. The morning after, too."

"I don't think I drank enough water yesterday," Charlie said to no one.

"Can you access Tom's e-mail?" I asked Fisher.

"Tom have computers at the warehouse? I'd rather not go up to the house and break and enter."

"You need his actual computer?"

"Makes life easier. A lot of times passwords are saved, stored via autofill. Beats hacking."

"You can do that? Hack?"

Fisher slid along a slip of paper. "How do you think I got that?"

The address for Rewrite Interventions. I hadn't been able to find a physical address anywhere. Rewrite's actions were clandestine, under lock and key—the only way to reach them was filling out a form and waiting for them to contact you.

"I'm a man of many skills." Fisher hoisted his coffee mug with a smarmy grin. "Wasn't that hard. Buried in a chat room. Couple pissed-off junkies. Everyone's a tough guy on a message board. Your problem, Porter, is you give up too easy."

"We're in the middle of transplanting everything. Tom scored a new space for us in Pittsfield." I nodded out the Olympic Diner windows, down the Turnpike, through the low-lying fog sweeping in with tractor-trailer drift and obscuring faster-moving headlights. "Got one of those temporary U-Storage places down the road. You Store. We don't have any computers at the warehouse but I have some of his personal hard drives stashed there that I'm supposed to recycle."

"That'll work. If Tom asked you to wipe the hard drive, means he hasn't done it himself. All the passwords should still be accessible."

"I'll give you the key to You Store."

"What are you going to do?"

I waited till the waitress set down Charlie's beer with a mild scowl of disapproval. She wasn't being overly judgmental. Only people drinking at this hour are hobos. Not that Charlie paid any heed. He chugged half the glass in one long swallow.

"Guess I'm taking a ride over to Rewrite Interventions."

"You really think they got the Crowder boy?"

"That was Biscoglio's story."

"Ulterior motives?"

"Possible."

"Biscoglio hasn't returned your call yet?"

I shook my head. "I think it was a bogus number."

"You know anything about this Rewrite Interventions?"

"I looked into *a lot* of rehabs for my brother. I may've come across the name. Or maybe I read about it when I was inquiring into that Judge Roberts business." I took a sip of coffee. "Last thing I feel like doing, believe me. Middlesex creeps me out. Place is crawling with Mad Max types, *Hills Have Eyes* extras. Nothing but halfway houses, AA Nazis, and strapped libertarians."

"Be careful," Charlie said, already flagging down the waitress for a refill. "Remember our visit to the North River Institute a few years ago on the Roberts case? They chased us off with handguns."

"Thought you said those were flashlights."

"And you said they were handguns."

I turned to Fisher. "Do private investigators have badges?"

"How the fuck should I know? Look it up on the Internet. You must have something shiny and silver from all the junk you haul. Anyone starts acting suspicious, whip it out."

"I'm sure that'll work."

"Put on a suit first," Charlie said. "It's all about how you present yourself." He belched before tilling ear potatoes with his little finger.

"I could be the goddamn FBI. Rehabs are confidential. And if Vin Biscoglio's right and it *is* Rewrite Interventions who nabbed the Crowder boy, we have the added wrinkle of kidnapping. Rewrite will be used to getting shit from authorities. I'm not expecting any pretty blondes to offer me tea while I wait."

"Maybe one of us should come with you?"

I looked at Fisher, all one hundred twenty pounds of him, at bloated Charlie, still trying to flag down another brew. I'd take my chances solo. "Thanks. But I need you guys here. Too many angles to work. I'll be fine."

"What's your plan?"

I faked a smile. "Be charming."

It was true. If I concentrated all my efforts, stopped scowling and tried to look pleasant, I could pull off charming in short bursts. Usually took me at least ten minutes before I wore out my welcome. Just ask my wife.

CHAPTER TEN

EVEN BY RURAL northern New Hampshire standards, Middlesex was the sticks. One road in, one road out, gas station in the middle, the township the preferred residence of the recovery community. In the middle of nowhere, drugs are harder to come by. Or so goes the theory. Most permanent citizens in the region leaned hard right. Impenetrable tree cover and natural rock formations made it tougher for the government to come for their guns. I had nothing against guns. When all that shit was going down a few years ago, I considered getting one but decided against it. I had a kid. I didn't want to be that moron who has to bury his boy because he forgot to lock a box or pick a better hiding place. I'd eaten my share of venison but wasn't big on hunting. The deer I ate tended to be the dumb ones that ran in front of my truck. I never saw the need for assault weapons or stockpiled automatics, even at my most paranoid. I never debated gun control, though, a simple matter of self-preservation. The other side had the firepower.

I didn't know what to expect. The little bit of research I'd compiled on Rewrite Interventions came via a modest website. A picture of some trees in a meadow, barn in the background, small, cursive font offering bumper sticker sound bites and fortune cookie wisdom. Wait for the Miracle. Work it, You're Worth it. Let Go, Let God. No phone number, no hard copy address. The sole contact option via e-form. I had no intention of leaving my address for three masked men to cart me away in the middle of the night to who-knew-where. Guns outnumbered people twelve to one in this county. I anticipated hostility.

Even armed with an address, I ended up driving in circles, although it was hard to say if I was backtracking or forging new ground, because there were no street names out here. Every so often, I'd spot a felled tree branch that looked familiar, a snow bank iced a particular shade of blue.

The rehabs I'd brought Chris to resembled traditional hospitals, institutions with walls designed to keep the public out and the patients in. Some had gates, others fences. Most displayed open spaces to create illusions of tranquility and freedom. But they weren't houses; they were facilities.

I'd driven by the big green farmhouse a couple times. A picturesque home with snow on the roof and chimney puffing perfect white clouds. In the middle of the boxed lawn, a weathervane pointed due north. The sort of place where a nice old lady sat inside drinking hot cocoa, shawl draped over withered shoulders, darning ugly sweaters for her grandkids. Should've known better. Those kinds of people don't live in Middlesex, and nothing in the northern wilds is ever what it seems. On my third pass, I spotted the dangling wood sign.

With all the gun nuts up here, you didn't go trespassing on private property, so I pulled to the shoulder, focusing on the triangular sign through the tree line. The letters were shaky, childish, like a grade school art assignment. But I'd seen those words before—Unity, Service, Recovery—and I knew what they meant.

Turning around, I pulled into the driveway. I got out and stood beside my door. Waiting in the boot-deep snow, I glanced up at the surrounding mountains, which formed a perfect half circle. Would make a pretty painting. Or great hiding spot for a marksman's rifle.

The door opened and a woman came down the steps. I had parked a considerable distance from the house, in case reason presented itself to hop and run. I could only make out the long dirty blonde hair, but even from that distance I knew she was beautiful. That's the thing with beautiful women. You can tell from the back of their heads, twenty feet away, by the sound of their voice; you don't even need to see their face. Just the way the beautiful carry themselves. Even though it was freezing and snowing, she didn't wear a coat, and as she drew nearer, instead of the aggression I'd been expecting, she greeted me with a warm, empathetic expression. And since it was cold and she was wearing only a shirt, no jacket, I couldn't stop staring. She rolled a towel over in her hands, like I'd interrupted drying dishes. I pretended to monitor treetops, captivated by canopies. Amazing how even at my age a pretty woman could reduce me to high school awkwardness in seconds.

"Can I help you?"

"Is this Rewrite Interventions?"

"It is." She wrinkled her nose. But not in a nasty way, more a playful, curious fashion. "People usually call first." She started walking back toward the house. I wasn't sure if that meant to follow her or if she was going to get someone bigger to escort me off grounds because I didn't follow the rules.

She stopped to turn over her shoulder. "Are you coming? Or would you rather freeze to death out here?"

* * *

"Can I get you anything, Mr. . . . ?"

"It's just Jay."

"Nice to meet you, Just Jay." She leaned across an island in the airy kitchen, taking my hand. "Alison Rodgers."

She had a genuine, kind smile. And the home was gorgeous. The rustic exterior augmented by modern interior upgrades. I spent so much time clearing out old homes, I'd developed an eye for different time periods and styles, schools of design. Colonials and Saltboxes were my favorites. New England, with its rich, storied history, had the most magnificent homes in America. Of course, I hadn't been west of the Hudson my entire life. Best I could tell, the old farmhouse, a Georgian, had been built in the late 1700s, and had maintained many of the original features, like bookcases carved in the walls and ornate wainscoting. Such touches increased resale value. I had a tough time reconciling the presentation with rumors of kidnapped teenagers, a theory further complicated by the fact that Alison wasn't exactly built like a linebacker, more like a cheerleader, or that waitress back at the Olympic. The perky all-American girl routine was throwing me off my game. No doubt Alison employed serious muscle to make this operation work.

"Are you okay?" she asked.

"Sorry. I didn't expect . . . this."

Alison cocked her head to the side. "And what were you expecting?"

"A rehab? Place where alcoholics and junkies come to get clean?"

Alison pulled a pendant out of her shirt, presenting the gold medallion. "Twenty years last March."

I did the math. When did she stop drinking? Fifteen?

"I was a wild child." She winked. "You never answered my question."

"Huh?"

"Can I get you anything? Coffee? Tea?" Alison walked to the giant, stainless steel refrigerator, which sparkled sans smudge. The whole kitchen was like that: untarnished and sexy. Such overhaul did not come cheap. "We have some mineral water."

"Sure. Okay. Sounds good."

She bent over to grab one from the lower shelf.

I turned away and checked out the latticework on the cupboards. "Quality carpentry."

"Ice?"

"Huh?"

"Would you like ice in your mineral water?"

"That's great, sure, whatever."

Alison filled the tall glass with ice and bubbly water, then slid a stool next to me, sitting near enough I could see the blue of her eyes, which were so light they almost appeared gray. When she slipped closer, I flinched.

"It's all right," she said. "No reason to be nervous."

She made me uncomfortable by invading my personal space. Like we were in a bar and she really, really wanted to get to know me. Somehow, at the same time, I had a hard time being offended.

Then Alison grabbed my hand, right there in her kitchen, clasped one over the other, stroking it. Forcing me to look her in the eye, which wasn't something I liked to do with anyone, not even my wife.

Over the past few years, I'd stared down my share of guns and taken plenty of hits, kicks, punches, and blows. I'd gone toe-to-toe with an ex-biker named Bowman who killed people for a living. A pair of dirty cops beat the ever-living shit out of me on a dark country road, fucked me up so bad I couldn't piss right for a week. A hit man pretending to be a big-city detective lured my brother up to Lamentation Mountain, aiming to blow his brains out, dump his body in the ice. I got there first and ran him off the road. He died. Life had been very eventful of late. But sitting this close to Alison Rodgers, faint hints of warm vanilla sugar radiating off her body, was the most uncomfortable I'd felt in a long time.

"Tell me, Jay. Aren't you sick and tired of being sick and tired?"

"Huh?"

As Alison continued patting my hand, so soothing, so kind, nurturing, maternal, I realized what I'd mistaken for a come-on was nothing but an old-fashioned sale's pitch.

I jerked my hand away, hopping up when I got the joke. "Whoa, whoa, hey. That's not why I'm here."

"It's not?" Alison's reaction was sincere. Which was the worst part. She thought I was another bum, junkie, drunk, a pill-popping loser. Me. The humiliation overwhelmed. Like when you think the pretty girl has been staring at you all night, but it turns out there was a clock over your head the entire time.

I stared down at my clothes. I wasn't wearing the suit Charlie suggested, but I wasn't dressed like a hobo, either. I had on my usual dirty jeans, but I'd put on a fancy tee shirt, and by that I mean one with a logo. Even wore my new camel-fur coat. Looked pretty sharp, if you asked me. Hadn't showered in a couple days, but nobody sweats in this cold, and even when I did sweat, I didn't smell too bad. And, goddamn, at thirty-four I was still a good-looking guy. Alison was what? A couple years older than me, tops? But the way she looked down on me now, I might as well have been a student in her sweet pickles class.

I affected an exaggerated laugh, but it only made me appear more hapless. "Why would you think I was here for me?"

"You do know what this place is?"

"Sure. It's a fucking rehab. But couldn't I be here for, like, a friend? A family member?"

"Are you?"

"Well I sure as shit ain't here for me." I pushed in my stool, erecting my back, taking the high road. "What makes you think I have a problem? You see my truck? That Chevy is new." I'd upgraded. Same make, model, size. Tom had gotten a helluva deal on a repo, and his welcome-back gift to me came with a very reasonable low-interest loan.

Alison's eyes widened and she clamped her teeth, biting her lower lip, gaze cast askance, the way people do when they are embarrassed for you.

"What?"

"Honestly?"

"I can take it."

"This is my job. I help run a drug and alcohol center. You do this long enough, you start to see patterns, recognize reoccurring looks. An expression in the eye."

"I have a . . . reoccurring look?" I scoffed, inviting commentary with a two-finger curl. "Okay, let's have it. What's my 'look'?"

She didn't miss a beat. "You look like a guy who drinks every day. Mostly beer. So you don't think it's a problem. You look like a guy who set limits for himself. No more than a six-pack a night. Most nights he keeps that promise. Except sometimes he gets stressed, and then, fuck it. But that's okay, because it's just beer, right? You look like a guy who knows people who drink way more than he does, people with *real* drug and alcohol problems." Alison glanced at my callused hands. "You work outdoors. Heavy lifting. In the trenches, man's work. None of that cubicle bullshit for you, and out in the fields, men like you can handle their alcohol. Most of all, men like you don't ask for help even when it's beginning to affect their personal life."

"My personal life?"

"I'll go out on a limb and say you are divorced?"

"Anything else?"

"Since you asked." There was that smile again. "Judging by the dark circles under your eyes, I'm guessing you don't sleep too well, high strung, anxiety issues. You need something to relax, help you rest, sleeping pills, benzos, the occasional painkiller. But you don't touch anything illegal. Anything you take, a doctor prescribes." Alison smirked. "Am I close?"

"Not even. I don't touch painkillers."

"I noticed the limp, so I figured—"

"You figured wrong." I shook my head, incredulous. "It's been a bad few years. But I *don't* have a problem."

"Okay."

I turned to go, stopped, spun around. "How did you know about the divorce?" That one was downright creepy.

"I cheated." She wrinkled her nose and nodded at my left hand.

I looked down at the faded band where a ring should be.

"I don't have a drinking problem," I repeated. "But, yeah, I *am* prescribed medication for panic attacks. After I watched my brother shot dead in front of me."

"I'm sorry. I had no idea—"

"What gives you the right to make judgments like that?" I tried to manufacture self-righteousness, summon spite and rage. It was hard to find. Because, one, she was right. I didn't have a drinking problem, but she'd nailed the rest of it. The second reason was, well, she was really attractive, and I hadn't misread the situation entirely. There *was* a little flirting, at least playfulness, going on. I wasn't picking out the matching dining sets just yet, but it felt nice to be around a pretty woman, doing whatever we were doing.

Then the door opened, and he walked in. One of those confident bastards who isn't the least bit fazed to come home and find a strange man talking to his wife in his kitchen. I already knew they were married before he walked over and kissed her on the cheek.

"Richard Rodgers," he said, squeezing my hand with a self-assured grip.

I gave my name, explaining I wasn't joining their stupid program.

Alison Rodgers got her husband a mineral water.

"Okay, Mr. Porter, why are you here?"

"I'm looking for someone."

"Someone? As in someone who might be receiving services from Rewrite Interventions?"

"I've been hired by the father of one of your clients. He is separated from his wife, and would like to know his son is okay." I made a show of looking around an empty house devoid of guests. It was just Mr. and Mrs. Rodgers here. "Wherever his son is. Wherever you stash your patients."

I wished I'd had business cards other than the ones I carried, an old batch with a goofy, thumbs-up cartoon character in a hard hat. Tom's idea. I should've searched out a shiny make-believe badge. Making it worse, my number had changed so often, I'd had to pull the rookie move of scratching out the old number and handwriting the new one each time.

Passing off a handyman logo didn't project professional investigator. But it beat sticking my hands in my jeans and playing pocket pool.

I put my card on the table. Alison placed the mineral water in front of her husband. He remained smiling, smug and disingenuous. I didn't care about him. It was Alison's expression that caught my attention. The change in her demeanor reminded me of how Jenny looked after she started dating the jerkoff. Except the roles had been reversed. Alison's levity and ease with me, her smiling eyes and effortless sparring erased, replaced by cold indifference in her husband's presence.

"I think it's time you go, Mr. Porter," Richard Rodgers said, clinging to his agreeable demeanor.

"Perhaps I could leave a message?"

"You are free to leave anything you wish. But I can't verify who has or has not retained our services. Nor can I promise any message will make it past that wastebasket."

"People can sign confidentiality waivers, a release."

"Yes, they can," Richard said, not taking his eyes off me. "That's my wife's department. Honey, has anyone signed a release for us to talk to Mr. Porter here?"

Alison tried to smile but only shook her head.

Richard stood up. "I'm going to get changed." He checked with his wife. "We have the DeWildt Gala tonight. Would you mind showing Mr. Porter out?" Richard Rodgers did not offer to shake my hand goodbye.

Alison walked me to the front door.

"Confidentiality waiver?" she asked. "So you have been through this process before. Then if not for you . . ."

"My brother."

"The one who died?"

I nodded.

"I'm sorry, Jay."

"Me, too."

CHAPTER ELEVEN

EXITING THE DRIVEWAY, I pulled across the street, same way I'd come in, engine idling, watching the Rodgers' house through the rearview. My cell buzzed. Fisher. The call dropped before I could answer. In the house behind me, a curtain peeled open, then fell softly shut. I didn't know who'd been watching me. But the thought that it might've been her delivered a rush. Also could've been him. I punched it in gear before Mr. Rodgers had a chance to call the cops. Although I doubted Rewrite Interventions' avant-garde practices were winning many fans with the local PD.

Couple miles down the road, Fisher called again. I answered to garbled static and another drop. He had *one* job. How hard was it to complete without me holding his hand?

Driving back to Ashton, I ran through possibilities of where Rewrite Interventions housed their clientele. Nobody was staying in the house, unless inmates were chained up to boilers in the basement. Breaking you down to build you back up has its limitations. Alison had preached the AA party line, but I'd expected that; most rehabs lean hard on the Twelve-Step Model. I hated Richard on principal. He had a beautiful wife, elegant home, and thriving business. I was divorced, living above a gas station, and ate my dinner most nights from a can. Why hadn't I taken Vin Biscoglio's money on the spot? The same reason I'd turned down Owen's at the Mortenson sale. Because nothing in this life is free.

Fine, Richard Rodgers was a jerk. But I didn't see a kidnapper. Middlesex was a sprawling county, one of the most expansive in the state, making for some very good hiding spots. Phillip Crowder could be anywhere.

Once I was out of the deepest cuts, Fisher's call came through.

"Dude! Why don't you answer? I keep calling and you don't say anything—"

"I did answer! No one was on the other end. You know cell service out here sucks. What's up? You make it down to the storage unit? Any luck with the computer and e-mail?"

"Yeah. I made it down here. And so did someone else. Looks like they took a sledgehammer to the roll-up. Tried to break in."

"You're shitting me. What's it look like inside?"

"Can't open the door. They beat the hell out of the lock. Key won't fit the tumbler. Gonna have to cut it."

"Any of the other units tampered with?"

"Nope. Just yours."

"Let me call you back."

I rang the Ashton police and got Turley on the line.

"No change," he said, anticipating the reason for my call. "Critical but stable—"

"I know. I stopped by the hospital before going to Middlesex."

"What were you doing in Middlesex?"

"Don't worry about it, Turley. I'm up to date on Tom's health status. Had to deal with Freddie and her sisters giving me the stink eye, thanks to you."

"I didn't do any—"

"Yeah, yeah. I don't want to hear any of that right now. Can you send someone to our warehouse on Lamplight, make sure everything looks all right?"

"Thought you guys had that new space down in Pittsfield?"

"I'm in the process of moving. Takes time. Can you have one of your men check it out?"

"Why?"

"Got a call from Fisher. He's over at You Store, our temporary storage pod south of the Turnpike."

"Why do you need two places up here if you're moving down there?"

"Because we have too much shit to house everything in one warehouse. Which is why we're getting the new space. What do you care?"

"Fisher's up here?"

"I told you he was. He's at our temporary storage locker. Says it looks like someone took a hatchet to the lock. No one else's but ours was targeted. If someone's trying to break and enter there, I want to be sure the warehouse is safe."

"I wouldn't worry about it, Jay. Probably one of the junkies on the strip attempting a smash and grab."

"It's your job, man. Got a lot of money tied up there, and I can't be two places at once. I don't want Tom to wake up and find his life's savings gone. Have a car drive by, make sure everything is cool?"

Turley huffed and groaned.

"Please?"

"Sure, Jay. I can do that."

I hung up. Maybe Turley was right and I was being paranoid. Maybe the attempted B&E was totally random. My gut told me otherwise. The entire Mortenson sale was stashed in that pod. But five grand worth of furniture, however nice, paled in comparison to what the warehouse held. Why the pod? What was someone hoping to do? Lug a dresser onto a flatbed? My mind went to the hard drives. For obvious reasons. This wasn't like when my brother was running around with Lombardi's computer, and I wasn't willing to entertain notions that Tom's old desktop harbored dark secrets. History wasn't repeating itself. *Keep telling yourself that, little brother.*

Taking the one road out of Middlesex, I searched my phone's Internet for You Store's contact info. Tom had set all that up, and last I looked, he wasn't talking. Took me twenty minutes to patch together enough cellular service to find the name and number for Yu Chen, owner of You Store. Called. No answer. Left a message.

The snow was really coming down by the time I pulled inside the You Store lot, whipping winds and blizzard conditions. Didn't see Fisher's car. Didn't see any vehicles but the moving vans. Who'd be out in this weather anyway except lunatics like me? I curled my shoulders, braving the alley, fighting off gusting ice shards with the wall of my coat. I found Fisher sitting on the hood of his car, which he'd driven right up to the pod's door, despite a dozen posted warnings saying to leave cars in the lot and use the dollies. What is so hard about playing by the rules? Rules are meant to be followed. That's why they are called rules and not suggestions.

I was smoking, seething, stalking with the driving snow. Fisher hopped off the hood when he saw me. I bypassed the fist-bump or whatever the fuck he was doing with his hand. I bent to inspect the damage done to the lock. At least whoever it was hadn't been able to get inside. For a two-bit, small storage unit off the Turnpike, the doors were seriously fortified.

"What the hell?" I said, turning around.

"Beats me. Found it like this."

"I mean your fucking car. Can't you read? You're supposed to use the dollies. You're blocking the whole walkway."

"Who's coming out in this weather?"

I scanned the area, searching for signs to back me up. That's when I noticed the cameras. At least two of them had a partial view of our door. I hadn't noticed them before. Whenever Mr. Yu Chen rang back, we'd have a decent snapshot of our would-be intruder. Better still: there might be footage from the day Tom was attacked, and I'd be able to prove I was working here all day long and couldn't possibly have bludgeoned my boss.

Who'd want in our pod this bad? Had to be some stupid junkie. Unless another buyer realized he'd missed out on a score? The Mortenson sale had been chock-full of rare finds. The inventory played like a greatest hits package. Maybe in his zeal to scam that French Chaucer dresser and sideboard, Owen had overlooked a painting or something, and sent one of his underlings to snatch it from under our noses. Or maybe someone really was trying to steal sensitive data from those hard drives.

I pulled my padlock key.

"Already tried that," Fisher said. "Tumbler is damaged. Key won't fit."

He was right. Thing beaten to shit. Like trying to get laid in high school, couldn't even slip in the tip.

"We need bolt cutters. Don't suppose you have a pair?"

"Sorry, Porter. I don't go around with bolt cutters in my trunk."

"I don't have any either." Ironically, I was pretty sure there was a pair of bolt cutters inside the unit. "Guess I'll head down to Eagle Hardware. If they haven't closed because of the storm. Wait here." I'd begun walking back through the mounting drifts when I saw the strobing cruiser lights. I heard a door slam in the distance.

And here came Turley, hitching his giddy, strutting our way, wide-brimmed lawman hat donned proud. I didn't care if he was Ashton's head honcho. Turley would always be a dork to me. It's hard to shake high school reputations.

"Hey'ya, Fisher," he said. Then touching the brim of his cap like I were a southern belle and not someone he'd recently accused of attempted murder. "Jay."

He squatted at the door, inspecting the lock. "Yup, looks like someone went to town on this bad boy."

"No shit, Turley. I already told you that on the phone. Did you have someone check out the warehouse?"

Turley creaked to his feet. With that expanding waistline, the strain on his knees had to be considerable. Hurt my back just watching him. He nodded. "Locked up tighter 'n a drum."

"This doesn't make any sense."

"You have bolt cutters?" Fisher asked.

Turley's roly-poly bat face pinched up in thought. "Think so. Why?"

"Um, to make sure everything's cool?" How did this guy get to be sheriff?

"No one got in there."

"I know," I said. "But I have to get in there. Something I need."

"What?"

"What do you care?"

"Can you drop the attitude, Jay?"

"Can you drop the implication I had anything to do with Tom's accident?"

"You think Porter had something to do with Tom's accident?"

"No, I don't." Turley paused, panning between the two of us. We'd all been the same age in high school. I was living in Concord at the time, but I'd see Turley and Fisher when I came home, which was almost every weekend, at the house parties and bonfires by the lake. Here we all were, seventeen years later, waiting for the calendar to flip over into December, a bunch of boys playing grown-up. "You tell him about the letter?" Turley asked me.

"Why would I? And why would you bring it up?"

"What letter?"

"Tom Gable wrote a note," I said. "A last-minute will, leaving me the company should anything happen to him."

"When?"

"When what?"

"When did he write the letter?"

"Morning of the accident, I guess."

"Looks bad, is all," Turley said.

"Ya think? Can you get the fucking bolt cutters? Please?"

Turley sloughed back to his squad car, its swirling, silent lights splashing bright colors against white walls.

"Give the guy a break," Fisher said. "He's just doing his job. If I remember right, he saved your ass up on Echo Lake a few years back."

"I don't know why he gives me such a terrific pain in the ass." It was true. Turley had always been nice enough to me. Nicer to me than I was to him. He bugged me. Same as Fisher bugged me. Same as everyone bugged me.

When have you ever been happy, Jay?

"Why didn't you tell me about the letter?" Fisher asked.

"Why would I? It has nothing to do with this."

"Yeah. It sorta does."

"Not you, too—"

"Despite what you think about me, Porter, I don't hate you. I think you act like a conceited jerk, like your shit don't stink, but I don't hate you. You haven't had it easy. With your mom, dad. Chris. Jenny, Aiden. I also happen to think you are a talented guy."

"Talented? At what? Moving shit in a truck?"

"I remember those stories you used to write in high school. Charlie would get your letters from Concord, pass them around English class. We'd bust a gut."

"High school was a long time ago."

"Tell me about it." Fisher tightened the hair bun atop his head. "And I didn't ask when Tom *left* the letter. I asked when he *wrote* it."

"Wrote, left. What difference does it make? They found it the morning he went to meet me."

"It makes a difference because he could've written that letter years ago, for all you know. He's always liked you, right? Would it be that weird if one night, after a few drinks, Tom writes an addendum, says if the unexpected happens, he wants you to have first shot at the business?"

"Yes, it would be pretty fucking weird."

"You know a sealed letter is basically a will?"

"Bullshit."

"Dude, you worked in insurance, too."

"For about a week."

"Trust me. I worked that shell game for years. And, yeah, a sealed, dated letter serves as a makeshift will, and saves you about six hundred bucks in probate costs. People do it all the time."

"Still doesn't explain the timing or attack. Tom writes a do-it-yourself will, *then* someone breaks into his house? Leaves the note where Freddie can find it, before trying to kill the guy? To frame me?" I made an okay sign with raw digits. "That makes sense."

"None of this makes sense, man. But you need to start asking the right questions. Was the letter dated? One page? Part of a page? Who *did* know about it? You said Tom was in the process of rearranging his home office, right? That letter could've fallen out of a box. You're sure the envelope was properly sealed? And not steamed open?"

"How the hell should I know?" I shook him off, waiting for fat-ass Turley to lumber back with the cutters. "I know you're trying to help, but you're not." I also knew Fisher was right. I did act like a self-centered prick sometimes. I felt like I gave enough to this world, had a firm grasp on how everyone should act, and if they acted that way, this world would be a better place. Which is pretty much the definition of a self-centered prick.

Turley came huffing back, hoisting the cutters above his head like he'd just won the Most Improved Swimmer Award at Weight Watchers Camp.

"Give me that," I said, swiping the cutters. I dropped to a knee. With one good chomp, I bit through the steel.

I rolled up the garage door.

We all stood there, seeing the same thing.

CHAPTER TWELVE

WHICH WAS NOTHING. As in we'd been robbed, cleaned out, hit. The entire space, top to bottom, bare. Might as well have dusted and vacuumed the place for us, too.

"There was a lot of stuff in there?" Turley asked.

"Packed to the hilt. Mostly merchandise from the auction Thanksgiving night. Sofas, chandeliers, carpets. A lot of furniture. But some other shit, too. Couple empty filing cabinets. Box of tools." I paused. "Old hard drives."

"Was the furniture that expensive?"

"There were good pieces, sure, but nothing so out-of-this-world awesome someone would go through all this hassle to get it."

Turley looked up and saw the cameras.

"I'm hoping the footage shows something, too," I said. "Already called the guy who owns the property, Yu Chen. Waiting for him to call back."

"Wouldn't count on it," Turley said.

"You know him?"

"No. I mean, no wires running from the cameras. They're not working. Purely for show."

"What about wireless?" I asked, then realized how unlikely given the spotty reception up here, my fleeting hope of exoneration gone as fast.

"Doubt it. Tom get a cut-rate on this place?"

"Tom doesn't skimp on security."

"Even the doors," Turley said, inspecting the frame, slipping his fingers along the edge. "They look heavy, but you can jimmy the latch, slip it off the rollers with a claw hammer or crowbar. That's how they got in." He pointed at dented metal rims.

Turley walked up and down the alley, checking other pods for the same telltale signs, shaking his head. "You already called the owner?"

"I told you I did."

"You can ask about wireless security when he phones back. But I'd be surprised." Turley gestured toward the cameras. "Plastic crap, novelty. Used to be able to get them in the back of magazines. Now you got hundreds of websites hawking this garbage. Pop in a battery, light turns red. Better than nothing I guess. Might scare away some stupid junkie. Seeing more and more of 'em these days." He readjusted his hat. "Want to follow me down to the station, fill out a report?"

"Will it do any good?"

"Doubt it," he admitted. "Not with a heist this big. If you want to give me a list of the items, I'll put a call out. Have my boys check the pawnshops and secondhand furniture outlets along the Turnpike. Might get lucky."

"Sure, I can do that." I already knew what it would yield: a whole lot of nothing. This wasn't drug addicts or garden-variety theft. Whoever had targeted our pod had done so for a reason. Someone had been looking for something specific. Out-of-this-world awesomeness aside, I could only think of one thing: those computers. I'd read this book before. Except when Chris had gotten his hands on that hard drive, we're talking about the most influential family in town. The Lombardis were state senators, helmed one of the largest construction outfits in the Northeast.

These were men of power and ambition, with skeletons hiding in very large closets. Tom Gable? He collected the garbage no one else wanted. What possible secret could he be harboring? What did he know worth stealing and killing for?

"You got a pen and paper?" I asked Turley. "I'll write down what's missing."

Turley patted his pockets, coming up empty. Fisher went to his car, returning with a pen.

"What about some paper?"

He shook his head.

"You don't have a fucking scrap of paper in your entire car? What about your satchel?"

"My briefcase is at Charlie's, and I keep my shit clean, Porter."

"Old insurance card? Back of the owner's manual?"

"I'm not defacing material I need because you don't have the foresight to carry a notebook."

"I'll head back to the squad car," Turley said. "I'm sure I got something back there."

Turley started walking. I patted down my new winter coat. "Hold up," I called after him, surprised to find a sheet of folded scrap inside the breast pocket. "Can you get me something to write *on*? Or is that too much to ask?"

I cleared the snow from the trunk. Fisher let me write on his owner's manual. Big of him. Ten minutes later I'd done the best I could to recollect the stolen merchandise. I didn't possess Tom Gable's iron-trap memory for this kind of thing but I'd gotten most of the big-ticket items. I passed the folded paper to Turley.

"Might've missed one or two things," I said. "Tom has the complete inventory. I gave it to him when we met at Julie's for breakfast."

"Who's Maria Morales?" Turley asked.

"How the fuck should I know?"

He held up the paper with the list of stolen items, flipping it around. "This is her death certificate."

"Beats me. I picked up this coat at the auction. Must've been left by the previous owner." Was supposed to be my tip. Was supposed to be new. Why are the rich always the cheapest fuckers?

"Mexican." Turley tried reading the death certificate, stumbling over the foreign-sounding words. "*Accidente . . . de . . . coche.*" He looked to Fisher, pointing down at the paper. "What's that mean? *Hemor-ra-go por . . .*"

"*Traumatismo.* Means she hit her head in a car accident and died."

Turley spun it back, straining. "Zi-hu-at—" He tried giving it to me.

"What do you want me to do with it?"

"What's that word?"

"Zihuatanejo."

"Isn't that where Andy Dufresne escapes to in *Shawshank Redemption*?"

"Yeah. So what?"

"Why do you have this woman's death certificate?" Turley asked, unable to hide his natural police suspicion.

"Because I'm running a credit card scam like my dead junkie brother, Turley. You caught me." I bound my wrists together. "Tom found out and I bashed his skull in to keep him quiet." I nodded back at the pilfered pod. "Then I broke in and stole the hard drives to cover my tracks. But the jig is up. You got me."

"There's nothing funny about this, Jay. Tom is in bad shape."

"No shit. And he's *my* friend. Why don't you stop busting my balls because I found some dead woman's crap in a jacket I got at auction? We get shit from all over the world. Stop wasting my time, and go find Tom's missing merchandise, or when he wakes up—and he will, because Tom Gable is one tough sonofabitch—I'm going to tell him you didn't do jack to find out who robbed him."

"Are you threatening me?"

"Yeah, Turley. I am."

He stepped to me, and me him. Fisher intervened, wedging between, pushing us back.

"Hey," he said, appealing to Turley. "Jay is upset, all right? That's his boss, his friend. He's been working for Tom Gable longer than you've been a cop."

Turley took a deep breath, like he had to think about it. He tucked the piece of paper away, backing up but keeping an eye on me. Like I was hiding a bazooka behind my back. This was why I couldn't get along with this guy. Or any cop.

"I'll run those items through the system," he said.

"Glad to see my tax dollars at work."

He hadn't gotten ten yards away when he shouted above the mounting storm winds. "And when I said don't leave town, I meant it."

I didn't bother responding to that.

Fisher waited till Turley trudged off. "I'll have to hack into Tom's e-mail accounts the old-fashioned way." Fisher made for his car. "Send me a text with Tom's birthday, name of any pets, favorite band, that kind of shit. Might not even matter. Half the time it's Password1234."

As soon as Fisher backed up and drove away, I called in my refill for the lorazepam. The pharmacy was closed. I'd have to pick it up tomorrow. I'd held it together okay, but my heart was racing through my forehead. I was pissed off and in dire need of some relief.

I was not my brother. He'd been dead for years. Why did everyone want to compare me to Chris?

Because a brother is as close as you get to another you.

I had to get off the road. The latest weather report had the blizzard continuing through the night, so I made a quick stop at the grocery store for more beer and a carton of Marlboro Lights. I'd made the switch from full-flavored Reds. It's the little things you can do for your health. I also grabbed a few items to make the next twenty-four livable. Like food. Soup, milk, cheese, hamburger meat, bread, eggs. Which covered the extent of my cooking skills. This was a hunkering-down, waiting-it-out kind of storm. The Price Chopper was always the last to close, capitalizing on fear and hysteria. Nothing moves product like impending doom.

Maneuvering back to my apartment, I enjoyed limited visibility, threading fifteen miles an hour. What a clusterfuck this had turned into. I had an auction's worth of merchandise missing, my boss laid up in the hospital, and a manslaughter charge hanging over my head—with the not-so-subtle implication I was as batshit crazy as my brother. And this had all started because I agreed to host that last-minute sale. Reminded me of something my dad used to say: no good deed goes unpunished.

Except where did it really go wrong? Slimy Owen Eaton swindling Keith Mortenson in the parking lot? That was par for the course in our crooked game. Vin Biscoglio, the stranger who showed up out of nowhere with the job offer too good to be true? Or did it start much, much earlier than that?

After a nervous breakdown, nothing is ever the same. Even after life returned to normal, stable, I still made the trek back to Plasterville once a week to see Dr. Shapiro-Weiss. I trusted her. And it helped. Not the talking part so much. Maybe I got something out of that. But the meds worked wonders. More than the pills, it was the idea that I had a safety net, a stopgap to prevent me from free falling. Knowing sanity was a tab away provided the real benefit. I hated relying on pharmaceuticals. Made me feel like a hypocrite. I busted Chris' balls—society busted Chris' balls—for relying on drugs to regulate his moods. How was I any different? Alison Rodgers was right. My medicine was legal. His wasn't.

I couldn't keep going to the doctor because of the cost. No such thing as health insurance in my line of work, and Dr. Shapiro-Weiss had offered a sliding scale as long as she could. Now I had to check in every few months, and she did me the solid of writing my prescription. I never planned on being one of these fruitcakes who needs to go to the shrink every week anyway, a fragile bunny who has to talk about how his dad didn't love him. That wasn't my problem. My problem—then much like now—concerned my brother. A ghost. No, a dead junkie ghost, whose voice I still heard. I didn't admit that to anyone, not even the doc. But it was something Dr. Shapiro-Weiss said during our last visit that was haunting me now.

"The thing with PTSD, Jay, is symptoms can manifest themselves any moment. Blindside you. Flair up when you least expect them, when you are least equipped to deal with them."

When that Roberts situation was coming to a head, things got so bad I began seeing people who weren't there. Hearing people who weren't there. You know how fucked that is? Seeing and hearing people who aren't real? Freaked me the fuck out.

Driving in that whirling wind and snow, Chevy sliding all over the dark road, not a soul out because everyone else was smart enough to have already walled their asses indoors, I started wondering if it was happening again. I mean, what if I was hallucinating all this? No one else had seen Vin Biscoglio. None of the research I'd done online yielded the name. Not a single picture. Ethan and Joanne Crowder, sure, but not this Biscoglio character. Nothing in the company directory either. He was a phantom. That entire conversation we'd had, witnessed by an audience of one. What if in some fugue state *I'd* written that number on a blank card? That I had to even *ask* the question terrified me. I couldn't trust my own version of events. Was my grip on reality so tenuous I'd invent an imaginary friend at my age? Maybe I was a nutty bunny. Of course Vin Biscoglio was real. I felt like I was reading Jim Thompson's *After Dark My Sweet*, how Collie, the punch-drunk prizefighter, randomly meets that psychiatrist in the diner, and then every conversation they have thereafter takes place in a vacuum. I'd read that book a half dozen times, and always suspected the shrink was a figment of Collie's too many concussions. I forget who convinced me otherwise. Probably some chick in a bar.

But that's what I was thinking about, that book, and *Fight Club*, and the old *Twilight Zone* episodes my mother loved so much, memories lost, buried deep. I wasn't sure if I was relieved or scared shitless when I saw Vin Biscoglio, standing in the middle of Hank Miller's parking lot, unwavering in the nor'easter howl, stone-like at midnight. An absurd amount of snow crossed my headlights, an opaque sheet of white chopping shadows, as if an impatient stagehand had dumped all the confetti at once, because that's how hard and heavy it was coming down. His animal yellow eyes breached the assault. I saw him. Sure as I was sitting behind the wheel. He was there. Except I had nothing to hold onto, no one to blame, bearings too slippery to grasp, reconfiguring orientation a zero-sum game. My reflexes lagged behind my brain, synapses slow to catch up, picture distorted, surreal, unreal. Is this what hard drugs felt like? A week of sleep deprivation? Had I gone mad? The way he stood there, smirking in the fast-approaching headlights, unimpressed, immovable, even when I slammed on my brakes and fishtailed, missing him by inches, he did not move, until all that was left behind was the smug satisfaction burned on an overtaxed brain, everyone in on the joke but me.

I smacked my head on the wheel, snapping my neck back. I cleared the cobwebs and blinked away the exhaustion. Hitting the high beams, I saw the front of a plow freed from the grill. Two yellow reflectors stared back through the snowfall like eyes.

I needed to sleep and everything would be right in the morning. That's what I told myself. But I needed my medication more.

It was happening again.

CHAPTER THIRTEEN

Two feet of fresh powder had accumulated overnight, and I saw I had several missed calls. I slogged out of bed and staggered to the window. My bones ached, which happened with drastic changes in barometric pressure. Always thought that was an old wives' tale. My bum leg dragged behind me like an underachieving childhood friend. I gazed out the window. The new day blustered, covered in white. The worst of the fast-moving storm had moved out to sea but the fury of wind remained. I saw Hank Miller in the filling station lot, trying to shovel, and threw on my new winter coat. I dug gloves out of my old one and headed outside to lend a hand. Caught the clock on the microwave, a little before eight, sleeping in for me.

By the time Hank and I were done cleaning up, I didn't get back upstairs until ten thirty. I had more messages. I started at the beginning.

Turley checking in to give me an update. No, they didn't find our stuff. No, Tom hadn't woken up. Stay in town.

A bunch of calls were from Charlie, the first ones starting out fun-loving and optimistic at the bar the previous afternoon, inviting me out, everything wonderful like it always is when the party first starts, oblivious to the approaching blizzard, no mention of his friend at the phone company, no indication he recalled our conversation from yesterday morning period. Just Good Time

Charlie tying one on. I was tired of Good Time Charlie. Working with my friend these days required increasing handholding, something I'd lost patience for. The final call saw the return of rambling, drunk, incoherent, lonely Charlie. Like the one on Thanksgiving, his voice dipped in sorrow. I wanted to console the hurt. I hated seeing him like this. Maybe when this latest tragedy was over, I'd meet him for a beer. We'd laugh again. Someday. Right now, much as it pained me to admit, I had to avoid the guy. I couldn't let his habit become my problem.

My only ally in any of this was Fisher. He had also phoned in with the latest developments. Unable to access Tom's e-mails via conventional methods, he was going "in the back way," whatever the fuck that meant.

The final voice mail was from my ex-wife, Jenny. She hadn't heard from me "in a few days and wanted to be sure everything was okay." I didn't know if that meant I called her too often, because most divorced couples, even ones with a kid together, probably didn't talk as often as we did. Maybe she missed the sound of my voice. I knew I missed the sound of hers.

I threw yesterday's coffee in the microwave, got distracted, heating it too long. The black liquid boiled over, spilling everywhere. While I was sopping up the mess with a wad of paper towels, another call came in that I couldn't get to in time. I checked the message I'd missed, dreading whatever bad news was headed my way, because all I got these days was bad news.

But this was the first message to make me happy.

* * *

Middlesex comprised one restaurant, Fanny's, in the middle of town, next to the one gas station. Never ate there so I couldn't vouch for the quality of food. Open for breakfast and lunch, Fanny's closed in the early afternoon. We still had time to make it, I said, and I was more than happy to meet her halfway. But Alison Rodgers rejected any offers, insisting on driving all the way to Ashton. Which told me one thing: she didn't want to risk being seen with me.

I arrived at the diner first. Trace flurries lingered, but by then roads had been plowed and weekday lunch crowds packed the Olympic Diner. This time of day, you got a lot of White Mountain Tech students soaking up hangovers with skillet grease and fried foods before rushing off to make afternoon classes.

Old folks dined on liver and onion specials, a staple of the septuagenarian sect. Factory boys and utility workers perched on stools, scarfing burgers in the allotted forty-five, before scrambling back to the mills and assembly lines, gassed up on caffeine and processed meats in order to survive the second-half drudgery.

With plenty of places to sit—there was never a waiting list at the Olympic, no matter how busy—I found our booth in the back, the same one we—Fisher, Charlie, and I—always sat in. Felt like it was reserved just for us. I liked believing there was at least one place where they knew my name.

No one knew my name. In fact, I was never closer to disappearing. One of the beautiful Greek waitresses brought me coffee. She'd waited on me at least two dozen times. Didn't even toss off a courtesy smile. I sniffed my shirt to make sure it didn't stink too bad, checked my reflection in the glass. I needed to shave. I kept staring out the window, waiting for Alison.

Up and down the Desmond Turnpike, riff-raff—lowlifes, addicts, alcoholics, welfare cases, assorted sad-sack losers who called these dumpy motels home—crept out of their holes, prepared to meet a cold and uncaring world. Some cracked the door, easing into the harsh new day's light, like stepping into an icy pool, one painful toe at a time. Others jerked the door open, ripping off the Band-Aid in a single violent motion. Tear some skin, spill a little blood, but get the shock over with.

Plows barreled along, scraping up pieces of permafrost asphalt. Cars veered off the boulevard, into the Shell station next door, taking advantage of the free coffees that came with fill-ups, before peeling back onto the ice-slicked road, racing to be somewhere else. Where did all these people go? Thousands of lives I knew nothing about, men and women I'd never come into contact with, existing in bubbles that had nothing to do with me.

"Is this seat taken?"

It was a cute but clumsy line. I hadn't seen Alison pull up or walk in, too stuck in my head.

They brought her coffee. She looked older in the brighter natural light. At first I'd pegged her for thirty-five, tops. Now I saw the faint crow's feet around her eyes, betraying a harder life than I'd first assigned, adding another five or six years. It didn't matter. Alison Rodgers was still a beautiful woman.

"I was surprised to get your call." I wasn't sure of the reason behind the call. She'd only left a message to call her back, and when I did she asked if I was free to grab a bite. I hoped she was ready to tell me something about Phillip Crowder and Rewrite Interventions, opinions and facts she hadn't been able to share in mixed company. In other words, I hoped she was willing to trust me. There weren't many of those people left. *Brother, it sucks when there's no one left to let down because no one believes in you anymore.* The truth was, I didn't give a damn why she wanted to meet. I liked being near her.

"This is what I do for a living, Jay. I try and help people when I can."

"Good," I said, ready to catch a break. "I could use some help."

I knew violating confidentiality was a big deal in the recovery community. It was called Alcoholics *Anonymous* for a reason. I appreciated she recognized how dire my situation was.

"Can you tell me about your brother?"

"Huh?"

"We're going to talk about what you want to talk about, okay? But first I'd like to talk about you, if you don't mind."

"Me?"

"I want to hear about your brother. The one who died. The one you mentioned yesterday." Alison glanced around the room, unsure what to do with her hands, the way people do when they are stalling for time. When she turned back to me, her eyes were red, rimmed with tears. "I haven't been able to get your face out of my mind."

Normally when a beautiful woman says she can't stop thinking about you, it is a good thing. This was not a good thing. I already saw where this conversation was headed—down Pity Street, by way of Woe Is Me Lane. This was the second time in as many days I'd misread Alison's intentions.

"You seem like you are in such pain," she said.

I dragged my bum leg out of the booth, running a finger down the length of my inner thigh to the calf. I nodded out the window, toward the mountain above us. "You know Echo Lake?"

"I've heard of it, yes. Up on Lamentation Mountain."

"Few years back, I was working an insurance investigation, and I ran up against a couple dirty cops." I didn't detail the whole Judge Roberts drama, didn't mention the young clerk, Nicole Parker, who'd fucked me over, selling me out to Michael Lombardi, who, it turned out, had been funding Roberts the whole time in order to build his private prison pet project, the new Coos County

Center. None of that was germane to this story. "These cops brought me up to Echo Lake and made me walk the thin ice. The thaw of spring. Gun pointed at my skull, I didn't have a lot of say. The ice cracked and I fell in. You know where the saphenous vein and nerves are?"

"I'm not a doctor."

"The saphenous runs up your leg. It's pretty much responsible for keeping the blood pumping in your body since the leg is so goddamn big. Turns out the nerve's important, too. And I sliced the fuck out of mine." I stomped my boot on the floor, prompting several customers to turn around. "Can't feel that." I rubbed my thigh. "Parts of my leg, I could stick a fork in. Wouldn't feel a thing." I took a sip of coffee. "But, no, I don't take painkillers."

"I'm trying to help."

"Yeah? Then tell me where I can find Phillip Crowder."

"I didn't mean like that. I can't talk about Rewrite Interventions." She stopped. "Except how it might help you."

"Rehab?" I entertained brief fantasies that this might be a means to an end. Play on sympathies, parrot back what she wanted to hear. Let her take me in, find Phillip that way. Some old-school undercover. Except I wasn't a cop, and I wasn't an investigator, and I'd be damned if was giving her or anyone else the satisfaction of admitting to a problem that didn't exist.

"Are you happy, Jay?"

"Thrilled. You said we were going to talk about what I wanted. I'd like to talk about Phillip Crowder."

The waitress came for our order. I waved her away. It was just us now.

"I can't confirm a patient—"

"What was all that 'I promise we'll talk about what you want' then?"

"Let's just say some kids are better off where they can't be found."

"What's that mean?"

"You said you are working for someone? As impetuous and angry as you come across, I would hope you'd check out any client's true motives."

"Let's make a deal, Alison. I won't tell you how to do your job. You don't tell me how to do mine."

She laughed. "All you've done is tell me how to do my job. You want me to break a confidence."

"And you called to meet me for lunch. You *want* to tell me something, and you don't want your husband—or anyone else in your town—to know you're meeting me. So why are we doing this dance? Do I need to coax it out of you? Why not save us both the time? Someone's life might depend on it."

"Maybe that's the point."

"I'll make it easier for you. You say you want to help me, right?"

"Very much."

"Will you believe me if I tell you the only thing keeping me out of jail right now is finding this kid?"

"What kind of trouble are you in?"

I hadn't wanted to play my ace, which in this case was the sympathy card. But she wasn't leaving me a lot of choice. I told her about Tom. The attack. The false accusation. And about the mystery man who stopped by the night before it all went down.

"So you see, I have to find Phillip Crowder. He might be the only one who can clear this up."

"I am sorry about your boss and friend." She leaned over, looking me in the eye. "And I don't believe for one second you could harm anyone."

"Oh, I could harm someone. Just not this someone. I don't care about money. If I did, I'd still be climbing corporate ladders. I don't have patience for bullshit."

"This is why, besides legally binding confidentiality agreements, I can't talk to you about this. You're so volatile."

"I opened up to you. Told you everything, the whole truth, held nothing back—something you haven't done with me—you're content to let me twist in the wind?"

"Have you been charged with any crime?"

"No. Not yet."

"And you said you think your boss will pull through."

"Sure. I mean, I hope so."

She smiled, genuine and warm. "I do, too." She stood up and collected her coat and purse.

"What? Wait. That's it?"

"Hypothetically speaking—?"

"Fine. Talk in code. Talk in tongues. Use smoke signals. Give me something I can use."

"This . . . boy. Has anyone seen his mother?"

"She's missing."

Alison's face opened up, like she wanted to say more. Then she shut it down, on a dime. Like that. "It was nice seeing you again. When you are ready to get help, I hope you can swallow some of that pride. I'd rather have you hate me for calling you out on your bullshit than let you think you have to suffer in silence."

"Thanks. That's a real big fucking help, Alison."

"Until then: be careful. You are playing with fire."

"I got more problems than a matchbook."

Alison put two dollars on the table. I told her the coffee was on me. She didn't pick her money back up.

"You are screwing with a very powerful family," she said. "And you are being used."

* * *

After my infuriating, unproductive coffee with Alison Rodgers, I pulled onto the Turnpike, heading north back to Joanne Crowder's. Messing around with a very powerful family? Where had I heard that one before? The mistake I'd made in the past was not pressing harder, taking my foot off throats. I wasn't making that mistake this time, and I wasn't getting scared off by bad reputations. I had a pretty bad one of my own.

Since my first visit to Joanne's place, I'd gotten a phone number, but that hadn't yielded anything either. I'd left several messages; no one had called back. I hadn't expected anyone to. Pulling into the gated community of Crimson Peak, I found more of the same. More mail. More newspapers. Still no Joanne Crowder. She was gone, and she wasn't coming back.

I'd done enough estate clearing to tell the difference between snowbirds on vacation and someone who has left this mortal coil. I didn't go for hippy bullshit of auras and energy fields, none of that New Age-y crap. But I could feel Joanne Crowder's absence the moment I stepped out of the truck. The yard smelled of abandon and loss.

I cupped my hands and peered in house windows, the garage, too. Didn't have the best view, but the car was still there. A woman with her financial resources could've caught a limo to the airport, or maybe she had more than one car, a driver, so that told me nothing. I tried a couple doors, relieved to find them locked, because knowing dumbass me I'd walk in, trip an alarm, and have to explain to the cops what I was doing there, a question to which I'd have no plausible answer.

Leaving the mountain, heading south, I was planning to take another load down to Everything Under the Sun before zipping over to the hospital to check on Tom. Let Freddie throw all the shade she wanted.

I didn't need Alison to plant the idea. I'd already considered the possibility I was being manipulated, and I had a good idea who was jerking that chain. The question was why they had chosen me.

Sliding over to the left lane, I saw Owen Eaton's truck fly by, heading north. I had no reason to follow him. But with no sales or clearances on the docket today, Owen didn't have any reason to be in Ashton either.

I cut through an emergency-only turn lane and blended into Turnpike traffic, lagging behind several lengths for a few miles, exiting Orchard Road. As we wound through the foothills, heading up the mountain into the subdivisions, I recognized the familiar route. Without benefit of other vehicles, I had to grant wide berth. Didn't matter. By now I had a good idea where Owen Eaton was headed.

I pulled up well short of Tom Gable's house, one whole street over in fact, watching though the evergreens as Owen exited his truck, bouquet of flowers in hand.

Freddie greeted him at the door. He handed her the flowers. They embraced. She panned the woods, straining through the thicket to make sure secrets stayed safe, before ushering him inside and softly shutting the door.

CHAPTER FOURTEEN

AND LIKE THAT my picture got a whole lot clearer. Why Freddie "found" the letter that morning. After inheriting the company, Freddie could sell to Owen outright, the logical play. But there would still be that minor detail of murder. Tom writes a note leaving the company to me, then is beaten to death? Same end accomplished with none of the messy suspicion. And you have your patsy. Clearer didn't translate to crystal, though. Like Tom's having written the letter and signing it himself. What about the garage break-in? Owen didn't know Vin Biscoglio. Or maybe that was how Owen knew about that dresser to begin with. Both Biscoglio and Mortenson worked for Crowder. Trying to tie together all these intersecting plot points was giving me a headache.

An accusatory wind rustled loose canopies of snow, clods crashing down on the roof of my ride. This connected to that, but that didn't necessarily connect to this. Was Owen so worried about Tom selling the company to me that he'd resort to murder? Owen Eaton, that aw-shucks hillbilly huckster? The Clearing House did plenty of business on its own. Crime of passion? Owen Eaton banging Freddie Gable while Tom lay in the hospital fighting for his life made the guy an asshole. But it didn't make him a killer. Freddie wants a divorce, she files. She'd be leaving a good man, but if it was Owen she wanted, she'd be moving up, financially speaking. No one had to die.

I thought about going to Turley with this latest discovery. Couple things prevented me. One, Turley was a moron. This was the same cop who'd let a hit man pretend to be a Concord detective, pick up my brother from the county jail, and haul him to the mountain to put a bullet in his brain. Four years was a long time ago, and Turley had done a lot right by me since then. But such incompetence and gullibility was tough to overlook. The bigger reason, though, I didn't have proof of anything besides a man showing up with flowers. If I went to Turley now, Owen Eaton would spin it as an act of compassion and support, with Freddie backing that version. I decided to play hangman instead. Leave enough rope . . .

Digging around my glove compartment, I found something to write on and scribbled instructions. Then I crept through the forest and tucked the note under Owen's windshield wipers.

I drove out to Charlie's but didn't see a car, which meant Fisher wasn't around. I'd tried calling from the road, but it's tough getting through up here after the storm, half the town's grid—telephone lines, cell towers, power plants—out of commission. I hated leaning on Charlie, given his current state, but I wasn't flying solo. I had no idea how Owen would react to being called out.

Took a few minutes to get Charlie on his feet, but I was able to pry him upright with coffee. He was still drunk, the caffeine rendering him only slightly more functional. At least he was out of his house. I needed stronger brew. The entire ride to Dunkin' Donuts, Charlie slumped against the passenger-side door, mumbling, half asleep. Any semblance of my friend didn't appear until Charlie had drunk a jumbo hot large, bummed three smokes, and had me pull over to piss twice and puke once.

"Where we going?" he finally asked.

"Charlie, you look like shit."

"We can't all age as well as you." He pulled back his receding hairline to reveal an Eddie Munster widow's peak. He'd also begun to sport serious baloney patch. "You have more hair than you did in high school." Before I could mention the drinking, that maybe he should ease up, he cut me off. "And spare me the 'I drink too much' crap."

"You do."

"In soda you."

"Huh?" I had a hard time understanding him through the slurring.

"And. So. Do. You."

"I don't drink as much as you do."

"Keep telling yourself that." He gazed out my truck window, at our hometown passing us by, the days we were losing. "You just have better—"

"What? Luck?"

"I was going to say genes. But, sure, luck, too.

"What are you so pissy for?"

"Beside you waking me up at the ass crack of day, dragging me out in the cold, and telling me how terrible I look?"

"It's the middle of the afternoon, man."

"What do I care? I was sleeping. Fisher's practically living with me now, to help you out with . . . whatever the hell this is. Don't ask me why. You hate his guts."

"I don't hate his guts."

"Yeah, you do, Jay. You look down on everyone. Always have."

"Jesus. What crawled up your ass?"

"Sorry. I'm hungover. I feel like shit. I think I'm depressed."

I wanted to ask what he was so depressed about, except I knew depression didn't work like that, and even if it did, he had plenty of fucking reasons. He was single, undateable, an alcoholic living off workman's comp, a once handsome man turned anything but, with a future bleaker than a northern New Hampshire winter. When I thought about it like that, I wondered how he hadn't shot himself by now.

I reached over and patted his shoulder.

"Maybe it's seasonal depression. Read about that the other day in some magazine. When I was at the dentist." Charlie dug a tender thumb and forefinger around his craw, searching out the offending molar. "Damn things are rotting in my skull. Some people get depressed in the gray and cold."

I thought about pointing out that Lamentation Mountain was nothing but gray and cold. I decided to let him have his small victory.

"We've driving out to the warehouse," I said.

"What for?"

"Meeting Owen Eaton." I didn't need to go into it more than that. I'd brought Charlie along to avoid getting blindsided. If Owen had been behind Tom's accident, it meant he'd been willing to kill, which meant he'd have no qualms adding one more body to the pile.

Charlie kept fishing around his mouth, staring out the window. If I were a better friend, I'd check in more, urge him to keep it down to a six-pack a night. Like I did. Which reminded me of what my brother Chris used to say when I'd tell him to stick to beer.

Oh, so it's okay if I do the drugs you *do.*

Maybe I was a hypocrite. I also understood Charlie better than anyone. Even if he gave up the bottle, what was he going to do? He'd had a long-time job at the phone company that got him out of bed every morning, but he was miserable. If Charlie Finn quit drinking, what else did he have? The Dubliner was his social scene, where all his friends were. He had no outside passions. He was lazy as fuck. If his mom hadn't died, Charlie would still be living in that house. He'd just be living there with his mother.

We turned past the Beckly Beer Garden, an old Ashton establishment where shitty bands used to play live, way out on the southwestern front. I'd snuck in there when I was a kid. Now the once white, sturdy structure had crumbled, turned brown, wet wood decayed beyond salvation. With all the snowfall, the roof had collapsed. The Beer Garden resembled an abstract sculpture, serving as postmodern commentary on a lost, simpler time when people didn't ask so damn much out of life. But this wasn't art. This was the town where we lived. There were a lot of buildings like that.

Tom's old warehouse, the one we were abandoning for the new space in Pittsfield, Everything Under the Sun, pushed town limits. Past Christian Lane, the complex was the closest thing we had to an industrial section in Ashton. I'd picked it as a meeting spot because I wanted to be on home turf. Also gave me time to grab backup, whip Charlie into fighting shape, but that plan had taken longer than expected, and now I had to wonder if I'd missed Owen altogether.

Abandoned brick buildings populated the district, shattered glass, For Lease signs hanging in broken windows above tangles of weeds and broken pallets. Most of the mills had gone under, jobs and tradesmen moving west to Newington or one of those other faster-growing little big towns. This stretch represented an older Ashton, a more prosperous time in the flats, when businesses flourished and families wanted to be part of the community, not flee it, like when my dad was still alive. Now Ashton was an exit sign you passed on the Turnpike, maybe stopped for gas, grabbed a bite to eat, and then got the hell back on the road.

I hadn't been by the warehouse since Turley sent someone to check security in the wake of yesterday's pod theft. A few cars and trucks were spread throughout the complex. There was a coil and furnace store still open, a take-out Chinese joint. I drove around back. We had a chain-link fence secured with a Magnum Master padlock for an added layer of protection. I hopped out of my Chevy, unshackled the lock, lifted the hitch and kicked up the latch.

"What are we doing here?" Charlie asked when I climbed back in the cab.

"I told you, man. Meeting Owen Eaton."

No response.

"Runs the Clearing House?"

Charlie stared clueless.

"Guy from the auction Thanksgiving night?"

Took him a moment. "The dirtbag who lowballed that other dude?"

"That's the one."

I didn't mention the affair. At this point, given Charlie's limited comprehensive abilities, he was on a need-to-know basis. "You hang here, okay?"

I got out of the truck and made for the back of the warehouse.

"Hey," he called from the window. "Leave me a couple smokes."

I tossed him the pack, tugged on the heavy door, and went to key in the code on the pad, but the alarm wasn't sounding. The door had been locked, and I'd seen the steel grate rolled down up front when I drove in. I hit the lights. Nothing. Storm must've knocked out the power. Didn't impact security, which connected to a backup unit. Otherwise anyone could walk out with a king's ransom whenever storms hobbled a grid. Which was all the time.

Given the darkness, I wasn't able to see much, not even my breath clouding in front of me. We didn't waste money heating the place when no one was here, the warehouse emitting hockey-rink frosty. I reached for my cell to use the flashlight, realizing I'd left my phone in the truck's console. Glancing around the showroom, eyes adjusting, everything appeared in order. The alarm not being active bugged me. I knew I had turned it on after the auction. If the sensors hadn't been tripped, Dulac must've dropped in and forgotten to set it, which wasn't like him. He seldom showed up in the winter anyway. Maybe Tom had made a pit stop on the way to sign the lease? Nothing rang true.

I weaved through marble statues and grandfather clocks to hoist the roll-up gate. Without light, the warehouse so crammed, I banged my shin on a Formica countertop perched on its side. The sharp edge ripped a divot of flesh, like a drunken, wayward tee shot on 18. I was hopping like a spaz, twisted around, knocking into more shit.

Headlights swept by the front window, a bright yellow flash. That's when I caught sight of the arm slicing out of darkness. It wielded something long, heavy, and squared between my eyes. That fraction of a heads-up spelled the difference between a glancing blow and a trip to the ICU. Still clipped me good, but instead of splitting my skull, my collarbone caught the brunt. I braced for more. The next strike thwacked the meaty part of my thigh, then the back of my knee. The glint of metal. Tire iron? Crowbar? What did it matter? The hits were coming too fast. Weapon raised, coiled, unleashed, driving down ferocious. Whoever was slinging lead was in front of me. I felt a fist drive into my kidney from behind. Normally a punch that precise, lodged below the rib cage, up in the gut, knocks the wind out and I'm down, but fight-or-flight adrenaline had kicked in, and instead of hitting the mat, I spun around and launched a blind haymaker, guessing where a face might be. I got lucky. I felt nose cartilage crack beneath the force of my knuckles. A guttural cry followed an animalistic howl, and I smelled the sweet, metallic tang of blood. Best punch I'd ever thrown. The prolonged wail mapped a clear path to a pair of balls, and I lined up the shot like an extra point attempt, splitting the uprights. Whoever it was, I'd broken their fucking nose, and with any luck, I'd ruptured their gonads, too. One-on-one, I stood a chance of surviving. I turned around in time to be pile-driven over an antique porcelain sink, spine impaled on a spigot. We tumbled to the cold ground, trading blows. I gave as good as I got, getting three or four clean shots to the face. But the man on top was too strong, and I was forced to cover up. Better to protect my face and get my forearms bruised than have my teeth knocked out. I didn't have dental insurance either. He kept smashing my arms, fist after fist. Mutherfucker was tough, and young. Only a young man fights this hard. Even with defensive strategies and the thick padding of my new winter coat, I was taking a serious pummeling.

By now, Charlie had heard the ruckus and come running in from around back, shouting my name.

"Charlie! Over here!"

The screaming stopped the assault, at least long enough for me to feel around for a weapon. Soon as I fingered density, I closed ranks and swung for the head. I connected with his neck. He fell off. I glanced down at the brass candlestick in my fist. I scrambled to my feet and ran toward Charlie's voice. Dizzied and disoriented, everything moving so fast yet strangely slowed down, I crashed into a dinette set, getting all knotted up, tripping over a chair leg and eating concrete. I couldn't see who was who, what was where, or what direction was up. Ten feet or so behind me, Charlie groaned. Pulling myself to my feet, I hobbled best I could through the maze. I found my friend rolling on the floor, clutching his knee. He'd be okay. I took off after the intruders. With both legs now compromised, unable to bend joints, I couldn't run, toddling after the bad men like Frankenstein's Monster.

By the time I got to the back door, whoever they were had disappeared into the woods.

* * *

EMTs tended to my injuries while Turley and his men canvassed the warehouse. The power, which had been cut, was now back on. I'd pulled a similar stunt three years ago, slicing the phone line with a steak knife before fleeing police.

The medics bandaged me up. Nothing too serious. Nothing broken at least. Welts, scrapes, cuts, bruises, which had been listed on the official report as "deep contusions."

I'd gingerly slipped back into my winter coat when I saw Turley amble toward me.

He had his little policeman pad out, pencil poised, questions at the ready.

"Any idea who could've done this?"

"Yeah. Owen Eaton."

Charlie, who had wandered off to the woods' edge, glanced back, the way people do when they want to eavesdrop. Except I knew Charlie didn't have any opinions on the subject. He was counting the minutes to happy hour.

"What makes you think Owen Eaton had anything to do with this?"

"Because I caught him at Tom Gable's house."

Turley waited for me to add two and two for him.

"To see Freddie," I said. "He had flowers." I waited. "They were alone. They went in the house. Together. Closed the door. It was dark. You following yet?"

"Are you telling me—"

"I'm telling you what I saw."

"How did Owen know you'd be at the warehouse?"

"Because I left him a note."

"When?"

"Before I picked up Charlie. I said I knew what he was up to and to meet me here."

"Jesus, Jay."

"What?"

"Sorta egged him on, no?"

"How the fuck is this *my* fault? He's the one sticking it in Freddie Gable while her husband's laid up in the hospital. Owen's probably the one who put him there."

"You think Owen Eaton is capable of besting a man Tom Gable's size?"

"Then he hired someone else to do it. How much more proof you need, Turley? Owen wants the company, he's fucking Tom's wife—Christ, do I need to spell it out for you in crayon? Put it in a box, wrap it up with a little pink bow?"

"I'll admit it looks suspicious, but it's also circumstantial."

"So is blaming me for Tom's attack. Because of a stupid rumor my dead brother caused our parents' car crash twenty years ago. You had no problem with that, though, did you? Ran with that just fine."

"Nobody ran with anything, Jay. Were you arrested?"

"You told me not to leave town."

"And did you listen?" Turley turned around and called out to Charlie. "Hey, Finn, you get a look at any faces?"

Charlie shook his head. "It was dark. Not a lot of room to move. I heard Jay hollering. I ran in and someone whacked me on the knee on their way out." He tried to rub where the EMT had treated the joint but Charlie wasn't able to bend that low.

"Hey, Chief?" one of the patrolmen shouted. "Got someone here wants to talk to you. Says he was supposed to meet one of the vics."

I burst through feeble attempts to restrain me, hobbling fast as I could to the gate, Turley calling, trotting after me. Charlie lumbering after him. With the beating and blows, the lingering nerve damage in my leg, I wasn't sprinting to the finish line. Then again, Turley and Charlie were both out of shape. The three of us trying to race mimicked those giant sausages in-between innings at minor league baseball games.

The patrolman had already let Owen Eaton through.

I wedged past the cop and shoved Owen into the fence. "Fucking cocksucker."

Owen remained in place, shocked by the reception. What did he expect? A wet willie and noogie? Asshole had tried to lay me out.

Turley wrapped me in a bear hug from behind, hoisting me off. I relaxed long enough for him to let me go. I lunged for Owen's throat but came up short. The cops caught me by the collar, holding me back. I swung around them, rabid, a mad dog lashing on the leash.

"What's his problem?" Owen was talking to Turley, as though I were beyond reason.

"Like you don't know." I'd already stopped fighting, throwing up my hands, letting Turley and his boy know I was done with the red-ass routine.

"Someone broke into the warehouse," Turley said. "Jumped Jay and Finn here."

Now Owen addressed me. "And you think *I* had something to do with that?"

"You knew I was going to be here."

Owen whipped the note from his back pocket. "Because you left this on my windshield." The letter was wet and falling apart. "Took me ten minutes to figure out what the damn thing even said."

Turley plucked the paper from his hand, squinted to read the message. The ink had run like a Rorschach test. "What'd it say?"

"'I know what you're doing. Meet me at Tom's warehouse. Or I go to the police.'" Owen stared at me, an expression blending annoyance and pity with a touch of fear. I'd already told Turley what I'd written but hearing it played back sounded worse.

The stress was getting to me. I could feel anger surging, overpowering capillaries, bursting tiny vessels. My temples pounded out a discordant beat on my eardrums.

"Where were you when you found that note?" Turley asked.

"At Tom Gable's house. I brought Freddie a bouquet of flowers."

"What kind of flowers?"

"Carnations and daisies. To offer my sympathies."

"I'm sure that's why you went inside."

"She asked if I wanted some coffee, Jay. Is that a crime? What are you doing? Following me?"

"I saw you on the road, on your way to Tom's."

"What do you think I was doin'? Stealing the company from under you? Sweet-talkin' Freddie Gable while Tom is in the hospital to get a better deal? How big a jerk do you think I am?"

Either this guy was the world's best salesman or I'd seriously jumped the gun. He wasn't even addressing accusations of an affair. His mind went straight to business. Still, the timing was too convenient.

"You were the only one who knew I'd be at the warehouse," I said.

"I'm not a cop," Owen said, "but ever cross your mind that if someone wanted to rob you and Tom, they'd be counting on you *not* being here?"

CHAPTER FIFTEEN

AFTER DROPPING CHARLIE at the Dubliner, I swung by the pharmacy to pick up my prescription, before returning to my apartment to chew on this. If I was wrong about Owen having an affair with Freddie—and my suspicions suddenly weren't looking good—my quick-fix solution had gotten a lot more complicated. I was back to Vin Biscoglio and a phantom offer made on a snowy night.

The problem was Vin Biscoglio didn't exist. At least in no verifiable form. I'd abandoned calling the bogus number he'd left me. I didn't possess the greatest electronic acumen, but I had a few tools at my disposal. Meaning I could type a name into a search engine and hit enter like anyone else. I dragged my case of beer to my computer and hunkered down.

There was no listing of Biscoglio on the Crowder Steel website, no social media or e-mail address, none that I could find anyway. I shied away from digital platforms. I was just a good ol' shit-kicking country boy. Biscoglio hailed from the big city, employed by a hotshot CEO, high profile all the way. Yet, not a trace in cyberspace. The man existed in the ether, a cypher. I did an image search, hoping to find a picture of him at a fundraiser or charity banquet. Even a blurry pic of a stocky bald guy would've constituted victory at this point. If Lombardi or Tomassi handled most of the construction projects around here, Crowder

Steel supplied the building blocks. Their products were used in everything. Hospitals, bridges, airports. Countless webpages featured Crowder Steel events. Just none with the bald man who knocked on my door at midnight and started all this shit.

Finding no evidence of Vin Biscoglio, I turned my attention to his boss, Ethan Crowder. Cobbling together archival pieces and featured articles, I came up with a disturbing portrait.

Ethan Crowder began his charmed life behaving like a typical spoiled rich kid, an only child cracking up expensive cars, making an ass out of himself, squandering opportunity, and embarrassing the family with ill-timed photo ops. Kicked out of some prestigious university, the billionaire playboy traipsed around the globe, making social page headlines. Clubs in Morocco, Mykonos, Corfu.

When he inherited the company from his father, Ethan didn't behave much better. This was the part of his story that caught my eye: the womanizing and history of violence, especially after my earlier conversation with Alison Rodgers. There were charges that he beat women, including his first wife, domestic abuse a personal pastime. When you're that wealthy, charges have a way of disappearing. There were allusions to hush money, payoffs, backroom settlements to keep scandals quiet. But these allegations were old news. His first marriage, he'd barely been thirty. Ethan was in his fifties now. Not a word of any trouble since he married Joanne almost twenty years ago. I had a tough time believing the love of a good woman had set him straight. Maybe he had mended the error of his ways? Stranger things had happened. Didn't matter. Ethan Crowder was the last guy I'd ever work for.

There were pictures of Ethan in his younger days. I wanted to see what he looked like now. Such photographs proved nearly as elusive as those of Biscoglio. Apparently, Ethan didn't have a lot to do with the day-to-day operations of Crowder Steel, eschewing the spotlight, surfacing only at the big-money events. The few pics I uncovered were all the same. Slender, silver haired, clean shaven, well dressed, Ethan Crowder could've been any man you passed on Wall Street. In the most recent pictures, a young, petite blonde accompanied him. This was obviously not the mother of his son. Basic math would've put her around three years old when Phillip was born.

Wasn't until I scrolled through half the Internet that I found Joanne, although the name didn't match the face. Some awards dinner from a few years back. Due to my own prejudice, I'd expected upscale and uptight, highbrow, a WASP-y type. This woman was darker skinned, almost exotic looking. She, too, was a blonde—Ethan seemed to have an affinity for the flaxen-haired. Here, the peroxide yellow jarred against the natural bronzed complexion.

Pictures of their son Phillip were easier to come by if only because of Facebook and social media. Maybe I was predisposed, but Phillip didn't seem like a happy boy. Sullen, blond, ineffectual, he oozed sadness in every shot, wounded and listless. My eyes locked on a photograph of Aiden, Jenny, and me on my desk. It had been taken right after we were married, a summer day in the park. I couldn't remember who snapped the picture. I found myself studying my eyes and Aiden's, panning back and forth between Joanne's and Phillip's, uncertain what I was looking for, even when instincts told me I'd found it.

I was adamant that Jenny not post pictures of Aiden online. I didn't have a fucking Facebook or Twitter account. I knew she, like most people in the 21st century, did. Sometimes when I had a few too many beers, like this afternoon, I'd check her profile. All that stuff is public. I'd convince myself I was checking in, but

I was totally lurking like a creeper. She had a few photographs of Aiden, but I wasn't going to be a dick and give her aggravation; I knew a lot of my aversion was projection. After Gerry Lombardi, I was touchy as hell about kids' images online and what dirty old perverts did with them. I also knew Jenny lived in a different world, and that's what people did these days. Most of the pictures featured her new husband, Stephen, the jerkoff. There was even one where she was feeding him a bite of food in a swanky restaurant and him laughing. Totally staged. Every time I saw that picture I'd clench my fists, grind my jaw, and want to hit something. I didn't know what the hell she was feeding him, but it sure wasn't fucking steak because the pussy was a vegetarian. He was also an investment banker making ten times the money I'd ever see. Whenever I wanted to make myself angry, I'd look at that picture, feel the fury flame in my gut, feel the outrage, feel alive. I didn't know why I did that to myself. I'd had my chance. I'd blown it. And I wanted her and my son to have a better life. The only way that could happen was without me. So I tortured myself with these reminders to stay gone.

I returned to the best photo I had of Joanne. Something about the look in her eyes . . . Was it kindness? Character? The opposite of her son, hers was an expression of strength, resiliency.

In this scenario, the Crowders' custody battle, I knew I should be siding with the husband. Vin Biscoglio had pitched that story line, playing on sympathies. Help the poor man whose bitch ex-wife had stolen his kid. There was nothing poor about Ethan Crowder, and maybe you can't judge a book by its cover, or in this case some cobbled electronic portraits. But if you could, Joanne came across as the one you'd rather have lunch with. Ethan Crowder looked like the douche in a sports car taking up two spaces and leaving a shitty tip. Then again, I'd turned into a class warrior. Stephen, the jerkoff, was rich. The Lombardis, who I blamed for my brother's death, also loaded. All around me, money, money, money. So much money that men like the Lombardis and Owen Eaton and Vin Biscoglio could throw thousands at me to do their bidding. I pretended I was above taking their payoffs and bribes, and maybe that was true, but I was also none the richer for it.

I had two browser tabs open. One with the Crowders. The other, Jenny's Facebook page and that jerkoff vegetarian giggling about eating twigs and weeds. I had drunk all the beer.

This was getting me nowhere, other than pissed off. I reached for my prescription bottle, because any minute I was going to lose my shit and hurl that computer off the back porch into the snow, like I'd chucked my telephone, and then I'd be out another four hundred bucks. And, yeah, I was buzzed, which invites its own brand of introspection and ire. Everything I wanted, like gold in my hand, and now this grass-grazing asshole was raising *my* kid? Men like Crowder and Biscoglio, Owen Eaton and the Lombardis were scumbags. So fucking what? They were flourishing. Why shouldn't I get my piece? Last I checked, Master Card didn't let me pay my credit card bill with lofty ideals. I should've taken Biscoglio's money, Owen's as well. Going back four years, I should've accepted Lombardi's bribe, too. Maybe then I'd still have my family.

My head was swimming when I jumped up and shoved in the chair. Out of beer. Out of smokes. Pissed off. The usual. I went to power down the computer when a tiny thumbnail, like on page fifty-three of the Google image search, caught my eye. From a recent Crowder building dedication. Down in Boston. This past summer. No Ethan. No Joanne or Phillip. No Vin Biscoglio. But there was another face I recognized.

I rang Fisher. He was at Charlie's. Alone.

"Heard from Finn?" he asked.

"Assume he's still at the Dubliner. That's where I dropped him off."

Fisher was online, too. I could hear him clacking away, multitasking. No doubt designing the new issue of his wackadoodle e-zine.

"I'm worried about him," Fisher said. "He's drinking more than before."

"I know. But what can we do about it? Can't make anyone stop if they don't want to."

Neither of us said anything for a while, both thinking the same thing. Our friend had gone from a fun-loving goofball who loved beer and chicken wings, to a sad, pathetic loser who was wrecking his life with alcohol. It was like watching a man drown in slow motion.

"What do you want?" Fisher said, interrupting the melancholy. "I'm busy."

I was grateful we were getting back to busting balls. All that tenderness was making my heart hurt.

"Do me a favor. Look something up online." I gave him the URL, and waited while he cued it up.

"Yeah, and?"

"Go to page fifty-three."

"Fifty-three? How long you been sitting there? You need to get laid, Porter."

"Just pull up the image. Lower right hand corner."

"Hang on. Gonna take me a minute . . . The one of a McDonald's?"

"No," I said. "Second from the bottom. The one with two steel pylons. Looks like a football stadium breaking ground. Big Crowder Steel banner in the background."

"Do you even know how computers work? Different algo-rithms, man. Tailor-made to each user. Based on individual search history. You and I won't get the same result."

"Find the picture I'm talking about."

"Hold on . . . Is there a lady with a yellow hat?"

"Yeah, that's the one."

"For your information, that image is on a totally different page when I search. Forty-nine."

"I give a shit. Pull it up. Enlarge it. In the background, by the—I think it's field goal posts? See the guy?"

"I don't see any—" I heard the surprise in his hard stop. "Shit. Is that really him?"

"Who else has a giant Star of David tattooed on his neck?"

"Holy fuck."

Bowman.

Bowman's real name was Erik Fingaard. I called him Bowman because first time I met him in a cold, tweaker pad, he wore a wife-beater tee shirt with the word Bowman stretched across his broad chest. I had been searching for my brother Chris after he stole that hard drive, which deposited me in that hellhole. A name needs to fit the face, and this mutherfucker, with his prison muscles and neck tattoo, was a Bowman all the way. A former biker turned thug-of-all-trades, Bowman worked con-struction security until a beef with the Brothers Lombardi had him on the run.

"Thought you said he was fleeing the country?"

"That's what he told me last time we met for donuts on the Merrick Parkway."

"He works for Crowder Steel now?" Fisher said.

"Looks that way. I haven't heard a thing about him in three years."

"Photo is from last June. Guess he's down in Boston now, doing what he does."

What Bowman did was off-the-books intimidation and beat-downs, a real charming guy, the sort of cretin you hire to make problems go away.

"I wouldn't read too much into it," Fisher said. "People tend to stick in the same field. Construction's a rough game. You can always use an enforcer. Guys like Bowman will never hurt for work. Not surprised he'd land at a company the size of Crowder."

"Maybe."

"Leave the conspiracies to me, Porter."

"Any luck hacking into Tom's e-mails?"

"Not yet. These things take time. But I *do* have something that might be of interest. It's about Rewrite Interventions."

"I'm listening."

"Rewrite Interventions farms out recovering addicts."

"What do you mean 'farms out'?"

"As in literally. They have partnerships. With farms. It's part of their credo. Recovery. Unity. Service."

"That's AA's slogan."

"Same difference. Stay busy, stay out of trouble."

"What kind of farms?"

"Mostly sugarbushes. Y'know, distilleries to make maple syrup?"

"I live in New Hampshire. I know what a sugarbush is."

"That house I sent you to? That's the address for the couple that runs RI, Richard and Alison Rodgers. Couple of ex-addicts, husband and wife team. They started the rehab."

I didn't bother mentioning how much time I'd already spent in Alison's company.

"Got any names?"

"Some. Information is tough to find. They want to keep associations on the down low."

"Ashamed to hire addicts? Or profit from slave labor?" My mind instantly went to dark places.

"I knew you'd say that. Program looks legit. Junkies don't increase property value or curb appeal."

"Know which one Phillip is at?"

"Nope. These sugarbushes are all over the map, here, Vermont, even upstate New York. You could go knocking on doors. I'm guessing no one's gonna be itching to talk to you. November isn't peak season. Not sure how many will be open to the public."

I tried to figure logistics. "These addicts . . . live on the farm?"

"They work the land to earn their keep. I'd guess that includes room and board."

"How many?"

"Sugarbushes? Fourteen so far. Like I said, particulars are not easy to pin down. I've been surfing recovery chartrooms, piece-mealing shit. Graduates of the programs are *very* protective." Fisher paused. "I know you're skeptical of these places because of Chris—"

"I'm also not a big fan of kidnapping."

"Understood. But from the looks of it, Rewrite is a last resort, a desperation move. And it seems to work. They boast a high success rate."

"I'm sure. E-mail me the list."

"*You* have an e-mail?"

"Everyone has an e-mail." Jenny made me get an account a while ago. I logged in about once a month. Mostly ads to see if I wanted a bigger dick or some other scam to steal my banking information.

"Do me a favor?" I said. "Can you get contact info for Bowman?"

"How the fuck would I do that?"

"Computer?"

Fisher laughed. "They're not a magic portal, man. We don't even know for sure that's him in the picture—"

"He has a Star of David tattoo on his neck—"

"*Why* would I do that? You remember the last time we had anything to do with the guy? I still can't take a leak with the lights off."

"Never mind. Send me the list."

After I hung up with Fisher, I watched my inbox, sniffing my own rancid breath, which stank with sour beer and stale nicotine. I'd lost my buzz. No matter how much I drank these days, I never kept a good buzz. I kept thinking about Bowman. Being in the same line of work made sense. The rest? Not so much. If Fisher hadn't turned Biscoglio on to me, maybe Bowman, now working for Crowder Steel, had? But why?

Fisher's e-mail came in. All tolled, I counted sixteen farms. One dairy, two slaughterhouses, the rest sugarbushes.

I tried printing out the list but couldn't get the fucking printer to work. I did what I could to try and fix it, which entailed turning the machine on and off, and when that didn't work smacking the shit out of it. With that, I'd exhausted my diagnostic capabilities.

I ended up copying down the names and addresses by hand, a pain in the ass. Fisher wasn't kidding. Places were all over the map.

When I was a kid, I'd taken a field trip to a sugarbush in middle school. Salt-of-the-earth, ox-and-mule, Pilgrim reenactment horseshit. Like it was still 1684. We'd gone in December, right before Christmas. That was the year I'd made my aunt put me on a Greyhound to spend the holiday with my brother. Meaning Charlie's mom let me stay at their house, since Chris was already homeless. Mrs. Finn made cinnamon rolls. I could still taste the warm dough and icing if I thought hard enough. Despite being winter, I remembered sugarbush employees running around dipping cheddar cheese in wax, packing holiday baskets, hanging buckets, leading private tours. The state pumped out about one hundred thousand gallons of maple syrup each year. Production never stopped. The region flooded with amber gold, and there's always work to do around the farm.

I picked the closest, biggest sugarbush, which was just over the border into Vermont. Had to start somewhere. I'd fan out as needed. At least I'd get a sense for how this operation worked, and, maybe, if I got lucky, someone would know Phillip Crowder.

CHAPTER SIXTEEN

THE PRASCH SUGARBUSH in North Brighton was open for business and housed an impressive operation, grand in scope, shameless in its self-promotion. I'd seen the name before, the Dutch Boy britches synonymous with the Prasch name. Several restaurants carried their brand, and I'd slathered Aiden's flapjacks more than once with their sauce. But I had no clue where they actually produced the stuff. How often does one study the back of a maple syrup label?

Exiting Billington Lane, I followed the signs offering daily tours and encouraging me to "Ask About Slokey's Special." Tall trees lined the perimeter of the plantation, boxing in rolling acreage, towering evergreens cradling snowy crowns in extended arms. Big barns, where they stashed the large-tank evaporators, the type used for mass production, came into view, looming large behind the maple orchards.

I pulled my truck into the big lot, watching the performance.

Workers decked out in period costumes carried vats of fresh brew across snowy fields, long sticks affixed behind their necks, hands draped over ends, like they were toting crucifixes, buckets tied to twine, swinging low. It's all about the presentation, the illusion that times are simpler, mankind not yet corrupted. Quaint shops on Main Street that add a superfluous "e" to everything—Ye Olde Shoppe, Ye Olde Towne Pub, Ye Olde Waffle House. I knew for a fact trees were tapped in the spring. We lived in the twenty-first-fucking century, yet a huge contingency got off pretending they'd just landed on Plymouth Rock. Another rip-off. Saw that on a class trip once, too. Expected a boulder. Thing's about a foot wide. Passing off corporate as cottage industry's a goddamn pastime in these parts.

A few tourists, mostly hunched-over old people with plastic bags tied around shoes, shuffled behind tour guides dressed like Little Lord Fauntleroy and Hester Prynne. The Prasch Sugarbush was the closest maple maker on the map, but it was still a solid forty minutes away, and by the time I got there, I'd missed the day's last tour. What would I learn playing that card anyway? I wasn't a very good actor, and pretending to care about the difference between wood- and oil-burning stoves would've blown my cover. This was a recon mission, get a handle on the arrangement with Rewrite Interventions, a sense for how the partnership worked, maybe sniff out when the boys went into town for the AA meeting because all these programs force-fed the Twelve Steps.

I headed inside the gift shop, little bell dingling enthusiastic. A dowdy blue-hair waited behind the counter decked out in antiquated New England garb—poofy bowed hat, frilly apron, rosy cheeks—eager as that bell. I tried to embrace my inner 1860s shopkeeper.

"How can I help ye?" She said it like that, too. "Ye."

I asked about the tour even though I knew they were done for the day.

She seemed crestfallen, pointing at the grandfather clock's swinging pendulum. "Last group just left." She nudged forward a bowl of maple-flavored ribbon candy. "Sucker?"

Out the window above her head, the outline of a two-story building lay beyond the orchard.

"Shoot," I said. "When did they leave?"

"About half hour ago."

The two-story building was a few hundred yards over a hill and blockier than distillery barns. More like modern apartments, dormitories, off-campus housing. The newer construction felt out of place against the old-timey aesthetic. A winding path cut through the forest. I glanced over my shoulder. A bunch of cars clogged the parking lot. Still had time to investigate.

Miss Marple pointed at a side display, golden syrups glistening in glass bottles stacked inside a waxed cheddar cheese frame. "Souvenir to take home to the family?"

At $19.95 a pop? No thank you. A handle of corn whiskey costs less than that.

I buttoned my winter coat. "Maybe some other time."

In the parking lot, I slipped past my truck, slinking between cars, and ducked into the woods. Two grooves trampled snow to dirt, the kind of imprints motorized carts make. I followed the tracks. Curling through the forest, I spied a pair of Amish hats over the thatch, going in the opposite direction. Surprised they didn't make them strap on a phony Abe Lincoln beard, too. Definitely teenagers. Had to be humiliating enough getting sober on a maple syrup farm without playing *Little House on the Prairie*. Junkies are used to the humiliation. Except these weren't regular junkies. Not the street kind anyway, not like my brother. These were suburban boys kicked off the rowing team. I noted the lack of pigment, the winter tans. I decided to follow, hoping they were headed to the dorms. Maybe I'd be able to cut them off, talk to them.

But the boys angled down the valley, back into the orchard, and were soon swallowed by the dense forest. There was a lot of white between us. I didn't want to risk calling or running after them. I kept to my side of the woods, tracing the footpath until I came upon a shack, a storage shed. Peering through dirty windows, I recognized the tools of the trade, rakes and drills, trowels, shovels, hammers, buckets, ties to tap. A tractor sat inside. I peeked around the edge of the building. The dorms weren't far now, maybe half a football field away. Dusk was creeping in. There was no easy way to get there. I'd have to cross the clearing, in plain view.

I was deciding whether to play it safe or go for it, when I turned back and took a hard hook to the body. Fast, compact, the kind of punch boxers are trained to throw. Dropped me like that, sucked the wind out of me. On a knee, unable to breathe, I gazed up from the ground, surprised. We don't get a lot of black people up here. Not saying Ashton and its surrounding counties are racist. But we sure don't make it easy to look different up here.

"I got separated from the tour," I tried explaining after I caught my breath.

"The fuck you did."

I knew not every black teenager was a gangbanger; but stamped with tattoos and sporting grills, these boys weren't like Phillip Crowder either.

"Anyone tell you punching paying customers is lousy customer service?"

"Yeah. Because thirty-year-old white boys come up here all the time to inquire about maple syrup production. I ain't never seen nobody older than eight or younger than eighty on the tour. Let's go."

The other one, the less talky of the two, hoisted me to my feet. I couldn't even stand straight, a stitch in my side leaving me bent over with a wicked case of scoliosis.

"Where we going?"

No one answered as they dragged me away from the shed, beyond the dorms, deeper into the dark woods. More snow shook loose in sheaves, dumping on my head. I wondered how far they were willing to take this historical reenactment and if I'd end up shamed in a stockade. Something told me playtime was over.

They guided me through a gully of granite until we arrived at a trailer. Long and skinny, like the mobile unit to an off-site chain gang. They pushed me up the wood stairs and shoved me inside.

The plantation manager was waiting. Better dressed but with the same hard look around the eyes, older and, y'know, white. He was a graduate of the program, too. Wearing long sleeves, he sported plenty of ink, up the backs of his hands, on knuckles and between fingers. I checked the clock over his head. What was my crime? After-hour loitering? Didn't matter. This was private property, and no one itched to do me a solid. Behind us, no more lugged buckets, no more cutesy charade of early American history. Just night falling hard with me caught in the wrong place, at the wrong time, one more time. I hadn't seen any fences, no locks on the gates. These boys were here because they believed in the cause. Nothing is more terrifying than the true believer.

"Why don't you head back?" the man in charge said. "Get ready for the meeting. I'll take it from here."

The two thugs made sure to each bump my shoulder on their way out.

"How can I help you?" he said after they'd left, but he didn't mean it.

"Mind if I ask you a few questions about Rewrite Interventions?" No reason to beat around the sugarbush. I was here now, and this might be my only chance.

"Let's stop wasting each other's time, okay?" The man pointed past my shoulder, out the front door, into the gnarled wilderness now blanketed country black. "This is your one free pass. I'm going to walk you to your truck. You're going to get inside your truck and drive home. You're going to forget about this place. Understood?"

"What if I want to visit a friend of mine enrolled in the rehab?"

"You don't. Jay." He made sure to stop before saying my name, the one I was sure I hadn't given him.

When I didn't stir, he nodded through the wall, toward the bunks. "I got more boys like the ones you just met. Only not as friendly. Unless you want to find out what we do to trespassers, I suggest you get your white ass moving."

"What's your problem, man? I'm just asking about your partnership with Rewrite. Not like I'm requesting a list of names and addresses."

"This program is a last chance for these boys. I'm committed—and so are other graduates of this program—to making sure nothing interferes with their recovery. Rewrite Interventions saved my life. It's going to get a chance to save theirs, too. Now that's all you are getting out of me. Move."

When I didn't move fast enough, he plucked the radio off his belt, bringing it to his mouth, static hissing back.

A voice crackled. "What's up?"

"Tell Sean, Malcolm, and Ryan to get down here. We have a situation."

I waved him off. "Never mind. I'm leaving."

If Phillip Crowder was here, which was a long shot anyway, I wasn't getting near him, not like this. I didn't know how they handled a "situation." But I wasn't sticking around to find out.

The escorted walk back to my truck was a long and humiliating one. I'd had my ass handed to me a lot over these past few years. Bowman, those dirty cops, assorted riffraff. I could stomach those beat-downs. They involved million-dollar projects, the high-stakes game of prisons-for-profit; they'd come at the hands of professionals, ex-bikers, rogue officers, mean mutherfuckers a lot tougher than me. You get whooped by men like that, you walk away with your head up high. Right now, I was hobbling past Slokey's Special, with my tail between my legs, bowels hammered so far back into my intestinal tract I felt like I had to take a shit. Knocked around by a pair of teenagers on a fucking maple syrup farm might've been a new personal best in terms of all-time low.

I was back on Billington Road less than a minute when Fisher rang me up.

"Please tell me you got some good news."

Fisher didn't answer. I figured the call dropped.

"Fisher?"

"Charlie's in the hospital. He collapsed at the Dubliner."

All I could think about was the injury sustained from the warehouse attack. He'd taken a blow to the knee. A good crack but not enough to warrant a hospital visit. I was fucked up far worse. Charlie had blown up like Brando, fat and bloated, but that added weight meant he should be able to take a crowbar to the knees. How fragile was the guy these days?

"Acute pancreatitis," Fisher said.

"Pancreatitis?"

This had nothing to do with the attack or my little world. There was no mystery to solve. This was me ignoring what had been right in front of my eyes the entire time. My best friend was killing himself.

"If he doesn't quit drinking, Porter, he's gonna die. That's what the doctor said. It's fucking serious, man."

"Pittsfield?" That was the closest ER.

"Just got off the phone with the hospital. I'm about to drive down to see him."

I told Fisher to hang tight. I'd swing by Charlie's and pick him up and we could go together.

CHAPTER SEVENTEEN

CHARLIE FINN WAS the closest thing to family I had left. Even when Chris was alive, Charlie and I were closer than he and I ever were. Blood complicates, a lifetime of bad choices implicates, and the guilt I felt over my brother's death twisted the blade deeper. Wasn't a day went by I didn't think about my brother and what I could've done differently to save him. But my relationship was with a ghost—Chris had been lost for a long, long time. My obsession with fixing him, my failure to do so, helped drive the wedge between me and my wife and son. Even after my brother's suicide, I lived in the past, rehashing, fretting about rewriting an irreversible script. I ached for a second try. The opportunity for salvation had been right in front of me. And I hadn't done a damn thing about it.

I knew Charlie drank too much. I saw the wear on his body. His memory had suffered—I'd have to repeat myself five times for him to get the point. He had grown increasingly sullen. Charlie used to be a fun guy. We could joke, talk pop culture, movies. Now he fucking moped. The only time I saw my friend was that first drink. After that, he slipped away, sliding somewhere between cheerless and inaccessible. And Charlie never stopped after just one. I'd stopped going to the Dubliner a while ago. I almost never met him out anymore. Too depressing. When I picked him up on Thanksgiving for that auction, I hadn't seen him for at least a month, maybe longer. And the only reason I picked him up that night was out of obligation, holiday blues, a sadness in his voice. Earlier today? I'd needed backup, and there was no one else to ask.

I'd endured a lot of lows in my life. I'd lost my wife, my family, and had been subjected to the one fate I swore I'd avoid at all costs: I was a part-time, long-distance dad. Another man was raising my child. I'd come to accept Dr. Shapiro-Weiss' assessment of PTSD. Fine, I had some mental issues. Didn't like acknowledging it, but whatever. Also meant I was a survivor. I possessed an ability to keep going when times got rough. When I got knocked down, I'd always get back up. Charlie and I both loved *Rocky*, the original. The sequels suck. Except the last one when Rocky is, like, really old. We'd watched that movie together dozens of times since high school. I remembered debating the everlasting appeal over beers one night. Last call at the Dubliner, gesticulating, pontificating, throwing around other really big words you only use when you're shit-faced. Charlie tried saying Rocky was a superhero.

"Bullshit," I said. "That's the crappy later ones. The original? Proves all you need is heart. You can get the crap knocked out of you, and if you stay on your feet long enough, make it till the final bell, no matter how battered, bloodied, bruised, you still win. That's not superhero. That's *heroic*."

"What's the difference?" Charlie asked.

"Superhero is fantasy, the shit kids believe in. It's not real. Heroic is everyman. You. Me. No talent or skill required. Just a willingness to go toe-to-toe with the best, take the hits, not let the bastards keep you down. You fall, you get up, you keep fighting."

But that was a lie. It was a talent; it was a skill. I had it. Charlie did not. Might've been the one true talent I possessed. Call it stubbornness, pride, a propensity to cut off my nose to spite my face, which I'd do if it meant paying back some of the hurt. I could bang my head against a wall longer than you. It kept me going. I'd will myself to continue on if only to prove my detractors wrong. That fire burned inside me. It did not burn inside Charlie. He didn't have what I did. Maybe I was being arrogant, vain, overselling internal fortitude and puffing out my chest because I wasn't the one lying in a hospital bed right now following major organ failure, sipping apple juice through a straw. Maybe assigning fate this way made the regret I felt more palatable. I couldn't say. But if I had to mortgage the farm on one of us standing at the final bell, I wasn't picking Charlie.

* * *

Charlie was propped up on pillows. He already looked better. A few hours off the sauce, having some electrolytes and nutrients pumped in his body, his skin had returned to a healthier shade of pale.

"How you feeling, buddy?"

"Only hurts when I laugh."

Fisher slinked around me, waving sheepishly.

I averted my eyes, shuffled my feet, tried to find a clock even though I had the time.

"Guys, I'm not dead. I'll be fine. As long as I . . ."

"Quit drinking," I said.

"Yeah. That." Charlie glanced around the hospital room, searching for that lost time, too.

Fisher and I stayed till visiting hours were up. Watching our friend lying there was tough for both of us. Charlie tried making the same lame jokes. Fisher and I pretended to laugh. Nothing was funny.

On the way out, we caught the doctor. He reiterated what we already knew. "Your friend had an acute pancreatic attack. He needs to stop drinking. Completely. Even the occasional beer will kill him."

Before leaving the hospital, I stopped off on Tom's floor to see how he was holding up. Didn't go in. No point. Nothing had changed. I stared through the glass, at the machines, the wires and plugs, the green screens, listening to the low hum of technology simulating life.

I brought Fisher back to Charlie's, a long ride punctuated by extended periods of silence and inescapable sorrow. Then I stopped by the market and returned to my sad, dumpy one-room apartment, feeling as low as I had in a while. With my brother's death, Jenny divorcing me, taking our son with her, I wasn't ready for another loss. Felt like another chunk of my heart was being lopped off, cauterized, blackened, nerves numbed, deadened. Echoes of mortality, finality, the sound of windows closing forever. In other words, it brought up a lot of shit. For one, I needed to be a better friend to Charlie and make more of an effort than I had. And I would. Stopping drinking was going to be hard for the guy, but what choice did he have if he wanted to stay alive? Maybe I could quit with him, the way some people shave their heads when a friend gets cancer, a show of solidarity.

I cracked a beer and was in the middle of boiling pasta for dinner. Slather butter, sprinkle garlic powder, Parmesan cheese, you have a fucking feast. Someone gently rapped on my door. Might as well leave it unlocked for as often as people dropped by uninvited. Maybe Vin Biscoglio had returned. In which case, I planned to strap him to a chair and waterboard the fucker until he explained what was happening, because this sure as shit wasn't about any missing kid. I jerked open the door, brandishing a wooden spoon.

"How'd you know where I lived?"

"You left your card?" Alison Rodgers said. "Remember?"

"No, I don't." I crossed my eyes. "I was pretty doped up. So whacked on painkillers I don't remember anything." I stopped talking, fluttering lashes. "Wait. Who are you again?"

"Can I come in?"

I let the door fall open. "I should warn you accommodations aren't quite as nice as your posh digs. Guess being a junkman doesn't pay as well as kidnapping."

Alison looked embarrassed for me. I felt embarrassed for me. I didn't know why I still acted like this sometimes.

"Mind if I sit?"

"Sure. I'm about to have dinner. I can dump in more spaghetti if you'd like to join me?"

"I'm good, thanks."

I returned to stirring the pot.

"You visited one of our farms today."

"I did. I am trying to find Phillip Crowder. I've been clear about that."

"You are persistent."

"My ex-wife calls it pigheaded. But I like your take better. You want some coffee?"

"That would be nice. Thank you."

I thought about taking a poke at how all these ex-addicts love their caffeine. But I didn't. End of a long day, the fight had drained out of me. "You could've called, saved yourself the trip."

"I wanted to see you in person."

I dug the coffee out of the cupboard, measured the dose, flipped the switch. "We keep meeting like this, people are going to start talking." I looked at the clock on the microwave. "Especially at this hour."

"I stopped by earlier. There's a meeting I attend not far from here. You weren't home."

"Yeah, I was out and about, getting kicked around."

"Are you okay, Jay? You seem a little—"

"What?"

"Angry? I mean, angrier than usual."

I turned off the burner, leaving my spaghetti to cook on its own, and joined her at the table.

"Want to tell me about it?" Alison said.

"What's your deal? Are you just, like, super nice? One of these people who goes around trying to help everyone all the time?"

Alison laughed. "I used to be a bad person. I try to be a better person now. I am not a saint." The way she wrinkled her nose when she said that last bit was the cutest goddamn thing I'd ever seen.

"A good friend of mine. Charlie. He ended up in the hospital today. From drinking." I hopped up, checked the coffeemaker, fished the sugar from the shelf. "Threw me for a . . . loop. I guess that's the word I'm looking for. Do you want milk?" I'd already put sugar on the table.

The way she looked up at me, that mix of tenderness and empathy, was too much.

"Please, don't do that."

"What?"

"Look at me like I'm some wounded bird or wet kitten you found in the rain."

"It hurts me to see you hurting."

"Why? You don't know me. There are people hurting all over this world. I am a good-looking white man living in America. The world is made for people like me."

"But you're not happy."

"No one is happy after childhood. Just a fact of life. It's not a realistic, grown-up expectation to want to be happy all the time."

"How about some of the time?"

"You want to help make me happy?"

She knitted her eyebrows, but not in a good way. Another bad habit of mine. I acted like a bigger asshole when I was hurting.

"Tell me where I can find Phillip Crowder."

"You know I can't do that." She waited three ticks, exact. "Even if I knew who Phillip Crowder was."

"Okay," I said, transferring hot coffee from pot to mug. "How about you tell me what it is you *really* do at Rewrite Interventions? Can we start there?"

"Sure. Public information. And it is not illegal."

"That depends on what your definition of 'it' is."

"Rewrite Interventions is a last resort for many parents. They've tried everything to help their child, and nothing has worked. They see their sons and daughters heading toward a bad place, and they make the informed, conscientious decision to take drastic action before it's too late."

"Great. Now let's try it again. This time without the sales pitch?"

"Can I ask you something?"

"Are you asking if you can . . . ask a question?"

"Haven't you wondered if you could've done more to help your brother? Or how about this friend, Charlie? Let me rephrase. Knowing how your brother's life ended, if you could do it over again, would you do something different?"

"It's a bullshit question."

"Why?"

"Because of course the answer is yes."

"There you go."

"Because he's dead. I'd enlist him in the fucking Navy if I could go back in time. Chain him to the radiator and throw away the key until the dope sweated out of his system. There is, like, nothing I could've done to make it worse. So of course I'd do something different. But time doesn't work like that. Life doesn't work like that. It goes forward. You don't get do-overs."

"Sometimes you do." The way Alison said it, weighting the words, conveyed the double meaning. "I drove out to see you because after you visited the sugarbush today, Richard was upset."

"Richard? Your husband."

"Yes, my husband."

"I hate to break it to you, Alison, but I don't give a shit about your husband."

"I like you, Jay."

"Good. I like you, too. Maybe we can catch a movie sometime?"

"What we do at Rewrite is avant garde, radical even, I'll admit that. We sometimes have to take a child, who is addicted, against his or her will. With parental permission, of course. These kids are not in their right mind, nor are they old enough to give consent. It's a gray area."

"Gray area."

"Legally speaking. These are often children of affluent parents—"

"The dudes who jacked me up at the sugarbush this afternoon didn't look like they came from money. Seemed more like hoodrats."

"I said 'often.' Richard and I oversee a far-reaching operation, with many partnerships. The orchards, mills, farms, sugarbushes are just part of it. In the past, we've teamed up with the Salvation Army, Bridges and Hands, inner-city shelters. Addiction does not discriminate."

"Your point?"

"We can't go to the police."

"Who said anything about the cops?"

"When there is an instance of someone attempting to reach a client without permission, when they are trespassing, poking around—when they are causing trouble—we don't have the luxury of calling the authorities for help. We are left to our own devices."

"Causing trouble? You mean by trying to find Phillip Crowder, son of Ethan and Joanne Crowder, none of whom you can confirm nor deny exist?"

Alison stood up, collected her purse, done with my playful banter. "You're an intelligent guy, Jay. If you tried applying that intelligence to being something other than a smart-ass, you might find some of that happiness you say eludes you."

"Ouch."

"What I'm trying to say is Richard—"

"Your husband?"

"I think we've established that, yes. When Richard—my husband—feels our mission is being compromised—"

"Is that what you call it? A mission? Like from what? God?"

"Please listen."

"All ears."

"Those boys at the sugarbush? There are a lot of graduates like that from the program. They volunteer their time, services, and will do *whatever* necessary to protect our patients and assets."

"Are you seriously standing in my kitchen, admitting criminal behavior, and threatening to have me fucked up if I keep trying to find Phillip?"

"Don't take this the wrong way. But I can see why you had trouble in your marriage."

"I'm not sure there's a 'right' way to take that."

She winced a phony smile and buttoned up to face the cold night. "Be careful, okay?"

"Tell your husband the warning has been received, loud and clear."

"My *husband* doesn't know I'm here."

From the window, I watched her walk to her car. She knew I was watching her, too. Christ, she was beautiful.

I'd headed into the kitchen, dumping the flaccid noodles in a colander, then slid the slop on a plate, doctoring best I could. I sat down and tried to eat, poking and twirling. I emptied my bland dinner in the garbage. I didn't have the stomach to see it through. I needed another beer.

A text came in.

Blocked number.

A one-word.

Donuts.

CHAPTER EIGHTEEN

THREE YEARS AGO, in the midst of the Judge Roberts investigation, Erik Bowman had shown up at my house in Plasterville, tipping me off that a pair of dirty cops waited outside to cap my ass. Under normal circumstances, I'm not trusting ex-gang members with neck tattoos and lengthy prison records, but that night was anything but normal. I took a flyer. Mostly because I didn't have any other choice. I'd already had a run-in with the whole lot of them, and I liked the one-on-one odds better. Bowman drove us out to the Dunkin' Donuts on the Merrick Parkway, where he spilled the goods on Lombardi, Roberts, and shared a bunch of other secrets he'd learned while working construction security. I didn't consider the guy a friend, and I didn't trust him any more this time around—he made no bones about personal vendettas—but I also wasn't in any position to refuse the call.

Besides, what's the difference between facing mortal enemies and having your heart broken for the thousandth time? I slid on my tan winter coat and hit the night.

No one waited outside for me this time; there were no tangled briar patches to navigate. My shoulders didn't tense in anticipation of the sniper's slug. The streets were deserted. A smattering of lightless houses peppered the block, all the good people asleep. I was surprised Fisher had been able to relay a message to Bowman so quick. After our meeting at Dunkin' Donuts that night, I had no idea where Bowman had gone. He'd hinted he was leaving the state, maybe the country. I couldn't text back the blocked number. I knew the cryptic message was from him, though. No one else was inviting me for donuts at midnight.

I didn't know his angle yet, but I wasn't scared to meet him alone; this was as close to an upper hand as I was getting. I'd lived in this same apartment most of my life. Anyone wanted to find me, all they had to do was walk up the rickety old stairs and knock. There was a reason Bowman was texting using secret codes, selecting clandestine meeting spots, conversing via private language. I had no idea why he'd foregone a regular phone call, but the last time I'd seen him he'd been the one on the run, not me. I had nothing to lose. Unless of course Bowman simply wanted a powdered jelly before he shot me for the hell of it. With Bowman, you never could be too sure.

Soon as I sat in my Chevy, I tried to remember how to even get to the Merrick Parkway from Ashton. The seldom-used thoroughfare was closer to Plasterville. From Ashton, I'd have to go around the mountain. With all the snow, sections of Lamentation were no doubt closed off, and forget reliable GPS.

I snagged the road map from my glove compartment, trying to draw the fastest, most direct route, which soon dissolved into an endless series of intersecting, squiggly lines. I really wanted to avoid strapping on my chains if I could avoid it. My phone rang. Another blocked number. I answered. No one spoke, hollow winds echoing in the earpiece.

"Good," he said. "You're outside."

"Bowman?"

"What do you want?"

"You called me."

"Yeah, because you're trying to reach me. You got two minutes, Jay. Make it quick."

I fired up the engine, taking my time. It was going to take a while for the heat to kick in. I thought about how to handle the rare advantage. At least I thought I had the catbird seat.

"It's cold as fuck out here," I said. "Why couldn't we talk when I was inside my apartment?"

"Because it's bugged."

"What do you mean 'it's bugged'? Why would anyone bug my apartment?" The idea was laughable until the joke ceased being absurd. "You told Vin Biscoglio about me."

"Is that the name he gave you?"

"That's not his real name?"

"What do you care? You don't use my real name either. Call him Vinny B. I don't give a fuck. Won't make a difference. One minute."

"Why did you send him?"

"I thought you could help."

"Why would I want to help that guy? Or Ethan Crowder. They are no better than Lomb—"

"The mother and the boy."

"Joanne and Phillip?"

The voice echoed peculiar. The mouthpiece projected a particular timbre, tinny, like he was speaking underwater and from somewhere very far away. Then I remembered what the sound was. A pay phone. Who uses a pay phone these days?

"Forty-five seconds."

"Why do you want to help Joanne and Phillip?"

"Don't worry about the why."

"So this is, what, penance? You stopped clubbing people in the back of the head, and now go around assisting damsels in distress and orphan boys?"

"Let's say, I used to be a bad person. I try to be a better person now."

The midnight winds scurried along valley walls, sweeping tundra and tarmac, snaking between the rivets and bolts of my Chevy, infiltrating my truck, which was slow to warm, metal contracting, creaking steel, leaving me freezing balls. I missed that line at the time. It wouldn't hit me till later.

"I don't have much time left," Bowman said. "So let me give it to you straight, since you're asking all the wrong questions. Your buddy 'Vin' is what's known in the business as a fixer, the sort of man they send along to solve the real fucked-up shit. We are in touch because we work together. Or used to. I'm a bad man. He's worse."

"Thanks for turning him on to me."

"It was you or someone else. I had more faith in you."

"Thanks. I think."

"Don't fuck around with him. He's a man with a particular set of skills."

"Good to know, Liam—"

"Tours, ops, shadow shit. Crowder only uses him for the darkest and dirtiest deeds. Listen to me—and listen close—whatever you find out, you keep your streak of unsung hero status going, okay? Anonymous packet to the Boston papers. That's it. Then get the fuck out of the way."

"Um, okay. I have no idea what you're smoking—"

"Look at Crowder's other marriage, how much money his family paid out, the scandals, hush money, why if he had a prenup, he signed over custody of the boy. Why he couldn't bully this one."

"Why would I care?"

"Because you do. I gotta go."

"Wait. Whoa. What if I need to reach you again?"

"You won't be able to."

He clicked off. The heat came on.

By then, of course, it was too late.

* * *

For as long I could remember, the first thing I'd done upon waking was worry. Subject matter varied, of course. But the panic remained the same, the flooding part. It all came back. Every stupid, lousy thing I'd ever done or said. Used to be the minor, inconsequential shit, like not talking to Muriel Kacharzic when we had blackboard duty together in the second grade; a witty comeback I missed at a party; a clumsy come-on at the bar. Then people started dying, and the bigger stuff began creeping in. Like not getting to know my parents better before they were gone for good. The mistakes I made with Chris. Being too hard on him. Not being hard enough. Everything in between. For the past few years, when I wanted to feel bad about myself, Jenny had been my go-to. All the shit she put up with. Not knowing what I had until it was gone. How I'd blown the love of a good woman. Which evoked my son, and all that I was missing out on.

The new day's light seared its accusation through fish-eyed lids. Regret, guilt, shame, dread, hopelessness. Thirty-four years' worth of disaster and disappointment packed into a nanosecond. Like being woken up by a Taser gun on my balls. Today's hysteria came with the added bonus of paranoia.

Following my phone call with Bowman, I'd returned to the apartment, reaching for Jenny's *Italian Heritage* cookbook, the one Vin Biscoglio inspected during his visit. I flipped through and discovered a small, square, metallic object affixed to the back. Could've been an anti-theft device the bookstore had neglected to remove. Then again, how else was Bowman able to parrot back exactly what Alison Rodgers had told me mere minutes earlier? The "I used to be bad, I'm trying to be better" speech he'd nailed word for word. He must've spoken with Vin Biscoglio. Unless only Alison *or* Bowman had said it, déjà vu reverberating, a residual from the PTSD or whatever label modern psych wanted to slap on me. Not like it was a movie I could rewind, a book whose passage I could revisit. You leave a monkey in a room with a typewriter long enough, you're bound to encounter similar tales of fall and redemption.

Even if Bowman and Biscoglio hadn't just spoken, why was Bowman warning me to stay away from the same guy he'd sent to my apartment? Last week I'm supposed to help him, now he's the enemy? What was all that "unsung hero" crap about? A two-minute timed phone call—and it had been two minutes, to the second—I checked the dash clock. And why a pay phone? My brother, too broke-ass to afford a cell, used to call from pay phones at the truck stop all the time, collect of course. No one else used them anymore. If I had half a brain, I would've saved whatever I found stuck to the back of that cookbook instead of chucking it out the window into the snow. But I didn't want that thing anywhere near me.

I couldn't sit around all day waiting for magic solutions. I needed to get down to the warehouse, haul another load to Everything Under the Sun, if only to maintain my sanity. Or reel it back in. If I'd lost touch with reality again, it couldn't have wandered too far. I called the one guy who might be able to get answers. Either Fisher wasn't awake, or he was screening his calls, sick of me, too. He didn't pick up and I had to leave a message.

I showered, shaved, found my cleanest dirty tee shirt in the hamper, and put on some coffee. I was pouring an uninspiring mugful when Fisher rang me back.

"Guess you were able to get a message to Bowman?"

"What are you talking about, Porter?"

"He called me last night. Bizarre conversation. He was going on about—"

"I didn't relay any message to Bowman. But I can tell you this: the guy definitely *does not* work for Crowder Steel. Not anymore. He's serving four years in Mass Correctional."

"How do you know?"

"Did you even put his real name in Google, man? He was busted last summer, sentenced this fall, pled guilty to assault charges. Prosecution piled on a bunch of other charges, crimes he looked good for. Locked up snug as a bug in a rug."

"Are you sure? There was no 'you are getting a call from prison' or anything."

"Probably used a burner. They sneak those things in to prison all the time."

"Sounded like a pay phone."

"Calling card? That shit is like currency to convicts."

"He sent me a text first."

"Can't text from a pay phone."

"He sent a text to go outside, then called and told me my apartment was bugged."

"Plenty of ways to relay messages from prison. Was it?"

"Was what?"

"Your apartment. Was it bugged?"

"I don't know. Maybe."

"What did he say?"

"He warned me about Vin Biscoglio, which apparently isn't even his real name. Makes no sense since Bowman admitted sending him to me in the first place."

"I told you I didn't know that guy," Fisher said, vindicated. "What's his real name if it's not Biscoglio?"

"No idea. But I think Bowman wants me to help the boy."

"Phillip Crowder? Why?"

"I don't know."

"Did he tell you how you're supposed to help him? Assuming you can find him."

"That would be useful, wouldn't it?"

"Did he give you *any*thing concrete?"

"He said to look at Ethan's other marriage and relationships."

"We already did that. He smacked them around. What else?"

"Told me to be careful." I saw I had a call coming in on the other line. "I gotta go."

I switched over to Turley, who asked me to come down to the station. My first reaction was this had to be about Tom, and if Turley wanted to see me in person, the news couldn't be good.

"No, it's not about Tom," Turley said. "There's no change in his condition."

"Then why do you want to see me?"

"Can you just come down here?" Turley whined. "Please. Make things easy for once?"

"Should I call a lawyer?"

"Jesus, Jay. No, you don't need a lawyer. But I do need to talk to you."

"It's a weekday morning, man. I have to get to work. Just because Tom is laid up doesn't mean I get time off—"

"Please." That last *please* sounded so exhausted, exasperated, I gave in.

Even I knew how hard it had to be dealing with me sometimes.

* * *

Pulling into the Ashton PD parking lot, I spotted the long black, luxury car with Massachusetts plates. I didn't know what the play was, why my presence was required, but this wasn't shaking out in my favor, that much was for sure.

Sitting in my truck, I watched Vin Biscoglio, or whatever his name was, exit precinct doors first. He shielded a slight, silver-haired man, equally well dressed in a gray suit beneath black overcoat. Far from the monster I'd conjured in my mind's eye, the silver-haired man exuded class, elegance, like a latter-day Paul Newman. When you think domestic abuser, you didn't picture this guy.

I wasn't surprised when Vin Biscoglio barely glanced in my direction, and I didn't let it hurt my feelings that the slight, silver-haired man didn't look at me at all. Whatever was going down, my day was about to get a whole lot worse.

Biscoglio opened the back door, the man slipped behind tinted windows, and then both were gone. Leaving me with one question: What the fuck was Ethan Crowder doing in Ashton?

CHAPTER NINETEEN

I NODDED HELLO to Claire, the receptionist, who waved with one hand and plucked the phone with the other. A moment later Sheriff Rob Turley emerged from the back.

We shook hands with needless formality. Turley led me to a conference room where we each took opposite sides across a long, rectangular table. I'd been in this spot before. It reminded me of going down to the courthouse with Jenny, the day the divorce became final. A tape recorder sat between us. Turley pressed the red button.

"What's this about?" I said, recalling Crowder's slow, deliberate stroll to his town car.

"You've been investigating the disappearance of Ethan Crowder's son, Phillip?"

"Is that a question?"

Turley hit pause. "I need a formal response." Then record again. "Have you been investigating the disappearance of Ethan Crowder's son? Yes or no?"

"Not exactly."

Turley opened his folder, fanning chicken scratch notes. "I just met with Ethan Crowder, who maintains he solicited your help in the search for his son, Phillip. Is this true?"

"What the fuck is all this 'solicited' shit, Turley? Why are you talking to me like you're auditioning for a role on *CSI*?"

"But you *have* been looking into Phillip Crowder's whereabouts? I should point out, Jay, that conducting a private investigation without a license—"

"Screw you, Turley. I'm not conducting jack, all right? And if I were working as a private investigator, that would entail getting paid, right? And I haven't been paid a dime. So, no, I am not investigating the disappearance of Phillip Crowder or anyone else. I'm just trying to get Everything Under the Sun ready for when my boss wakes up."

"You've visited Rewrite Intervention facilities on several occasions—"

"So fucking what?"

"And I have it on good authority you've been out to Mrs. Crowder's—Joanne's—residence."

"Good authority?" I didn't have time for this community theater horseshit. "Listen, I don't know why you dragged me down here, but I have a job to get to. Our warehouse was broken into, remember? When I was assaulted in the dark? Shouldn't you be out there trying to catch whoever did it?" I nodded at the empty space previously occupied by Vin Biscoglio and Ethan Crowder. "Where were *they* yesterday?"

"You're not suggesting that little old man beat you up?"

"Nobody 'beat me up.' I got in my shots, too. And I'm not suggesting anything other than leave me alone." I stopped. "What was the name of the guy with Crowder?"

"Huh?"

"The man with Crowder. What name did he give you?"

"Vin Biscoglio. Why?"

I thought a moment. "He show you an ID?"

"No. That's not SOP." Turley turned off the recorder. "SOP stands for—"

"I know what SOP stands for. I'm not a moron. I've watched cop movies."

I should've known better than to believe Bowman. Unless Vin Biscoglio was playing Turley, too. Wouldn't be the first time an out-of-towner had their way with Mayberry's finest.

"Whatever fairy tale those two are spinning," I said, "I want you to think long and hard about the last time you bought bull-shit from a stranger." I started to get up.

Turley pointed to the chair. "We're not finished yet."

"Why were those two up from Boston?"

"I'm trying to tell you, Jay, if you'll stop being a pain in my ass. Please. Sit back down and let me finish my report."

I dropped back in my seat.

"Joanne Crowder's body was found this morning."

"Where?"

"Her garage."

"You don't think I had anything to do with that—"

"No," Turley said, "of course not. Please relax. Give me a break, man, okay? I'm just trying to do my job. I need a statement."

"What happened?"

"Suicide. Carbon monoxide. Hooked up a hose to the tailpipe, through the window."

I'd peeked in that garage. Seen the car. Didn't see any hose. Or body. I hadn't gone inside so I couldn't be sure. Might've been slumped over. Had she been dead the whole time?

"Was she found upright?" I asked.

"What?"

"Joanne Crowder's body. Was she found in an upright position, or had she slid to the floor?"

"I don't know."

"Did she leave a note?"

"I'm not at liberty to say."

I recalled Ethan Crowder's reaction outside, the blank expression. Which could have been numbness, a shutdown to avoid the pangs of loss. Or maybe he already knew and the bastard was one cold fish. Regardless of how unpleasant a marriage ends, however nasty a divorce gets, when there's a child involved, you'd expect *some* reaction. We're talking the mother of his only child.

"I'm sorry to hear about Joanne," I said.

"Jay, I need to know where the boy is."

"How the fuck should I know? Vin Biscoglio, the man who you just talked to? He's the one who told me Phillip was at Rewrite Interventions. Ask him. Where do you think I got that information? You know as much as I do."

"Mr. Crowder seems to think you know more than you're letting on."

"He can think whatever he wants."

"The boy needs to know about his mother."

"Then you fucking call them."

"Rewrite Interventions doesn't make it easy. Their methods invite unwanted scrutiny. They don't trust the police."

"Kidnapping kids in the night? Pillowcases over their heads? Whisked to secret locations in the back of a van? It's funny. No one gave a shit about those kids until a rich fuck like Ethan Crowder was affected."

I didn't mention Richard or Alison by name, or the fact that I had Alison's cell number. I couldn't care less about him, but I liked her, even if we didn't see eye-to-eye on RI's tactics. Despite Turley's grandstanding and the loaded words I used to combat them, I knew Alison's heart was in the right place. Their public profile was available to the Ashton PD, same as it had been to Fisher and me. Might take a little digging. I agreed Phillip needed to know about his mom, but I wasn't doing Turley's job for him. And I'd long ago resolved I wasn't lifting a goddamn finger to help Ethan Crowder.

"I'd think as a divorced father, you would—"

"Don't. Biscoglio already tried laying that guilt trip. My ex-wife and son have nothing to do with this. You can contact Rewrite same as me."

"You're right. I have Alison and Richard Rodgers' home address and business number. So does Middlesex PD. But you've been harassing them so much lately they've lawyered up, gone radio silent. They won't talk to the authorities. And they don't have to. Richard, in particular, does not seem very fond of you. We can't get them to divulge whereabouts without a court order."

"Then get one. They're not going to tell me either."

"When was the last time you visited Joanne's home?"

"Friday? Saturday?"

"Be specific. It's important, Jay."

"Saturday."

"Is there anything you can tell me?"

"Like what?"

"Did you look in the garage?"

"Peeked in the window. That's why I asked how her body was found. I didn't see the top of anyone's head. Biscoglio said he thought she was out of town. But he's probably full of shit. Who found the body?"

"Patrolman. Got a call from a neighbor. No one had seen Joanne for a few days. Sent a car out there. You know Coal Creek. It's no-man's land. Not Ashton's jurisdiction."

I thought about that response, a peculiar detail hitting me. Neighbors worried because they hadn't seen Joanne in a few days? More like a well-timed anonymous tip. The way houses spread out up there, I imagined entire seasons passed without glimpses of a neighbor. Crimson Peak was where you went when you didn't want to be disturbed.

"Have you been up to the house?" I asked.

"Yes, I was up there."

"Footprints in the snow?"

"Just the one set leading up to the garage door. What size boot do you wear?"

"Hey, Frank Cannon, I told you I was up there. Knock off the movie-of-the-week horseshit. Coroner have a time of death?"

"She'd been in that car for a while. At least a few days."

"What day was the last newspaper delivered?"

"What newspaper?"

"When I was there over the weekend, there were a bunch of financial newspapers that hadn't been picked up. Blue plastic sticking out of the snow."

"I don't recall seeing any newspapers." Turley scratched his head. "Probably buried. We've had so many storms."

"Maybe." Something wasn't sitting right.

Turley caught on. Sort of. "Right. Good point. Because then we'd know the last day Joanne left the house. I'll have one of my men check into that." He pointed his stubby finger. "You might have a future in investigations after all."

That wasn't where I was going but whatever. Let Turley conduct his own investigation. I'd handle mine. With all the violent weather on that mountain, drift fluctuated. But some of the papers should still be visible. Unless they'd been picked up. There are plenty of ways to kill a person. Plenty of places to do it, too, leaving the body to be discovered an afterthought.

Turley tried one last-ditch attempt. "Any additional information you'd like to share with me?" I knew he meant Alison's personal cell. I folded my arms and leaned back.

"With Joanne's death," he said, "Ethan will have his court order very soon."

"Works out well for him then that she's dead."

"Careful. That's a serious allegation."

"Try and remember that the next time you accuse someone of cutting a brake line. Or beating a man unconscious."

Turley glanced around the room, kneading the back of his thick steak neck, probing for deeper cuts in the police procedural handbook. But he'd exhausted options. Finally he said, "Thanks for coming in. Guess I'll leave a message for the Rodgers through their website. Terrible way for a boy to find out about his mother." He paused to catch my eye. "Or maybe you want to call. You know, the number you don't have?"

As I stood to leave, he said to hold on.

"Let me return this to you." He pulled a piece of paper from his back pocket. The list of items taken from the storage shed. "Nothing turned up in any of the pawnshops or furniture outlets. We'll keep checking."

"Thanks," I said, jamming the list in my jeans. I knew it was a dead end. Nothing was turning up.

Fisher rang me as I was walking to my truck.

"Where you at?"

"Police station. Cops found Joanne Crowder's body."

"Dead?"

"Suicide. Supposedly."

"You think otherwise?"

"I don't know what to think."

Angry skies menaced miles away, storm front rolling in fast. Tentacles snaked over mountaintops, slithering like beasts on a bender. This was shaping up to be another bitch of a blizzard. I'd already slid out my Marlboro, cancer stick jammed in my piehole, hands cupped to block out gusting winds. A nicotine rush would help hash out possibilities. One set of footprints? If it wasn't a suicide, there weren't a whole lot of suspects. Had Bowman been trying to warn me? Or was this, too, part of the setup? Was I meant to find Phillip? Or lead the enemy straight to him?

"Did you hear me, Porter?"

"Huh?"

"Stop daydreaming. I said I was able to hack into Tom's e-mail."

"And?"

"Nothing the morning of the crash."

"Maybe Charlie will have more luck—" I caught myself. Charlie wasn't tracing phone calls anytime soon.

"I did find an e-mail. Last-minute plea to hold the auction on Thanksgiving. Pretty desperate sounding. Think you might want to read this one."

"I know all about it. Keith Mortenson. Was in a rush to get out of town. Works down in Boston, accountant for Ethan Crowder. Too bizarre a coincidence, I agree." Wish I'd taken my time to talk to him that night. Never even got a contact for the guy. Tom had that. I thought for a moment. "Hey, did Mortenson leave a number? I haven't been able to track him down." I'd tried leaving messages on his work phone. Nada.

"Jay—"

"At least I have an e-mail address now, which is better than nothing. Good work. Thanks, Fisher."

"The e-mail about the sale isn't from Mortenson. It's from the wife."

"Wife?" I didn't know anything about Keith Mortenson's wife, except that she lived in North Carolina, and wanted him home as soon as possible. E-mailing to set up her husband's sales? Guess we knew who wore the pants in that family. "Okay. Give me the wife's e-mail. At least she'll be able to put me in touch with Keith."

"You're not listening," Fisher said. "Not Mortenson's wife."

The cell reception started to cut out. "I can't hear you, man."

"The e-mail," Fisher shouted across the bad connection. "I mean Ethan Crowder's wife." He waited for me to catch up. "The email is from Joanne."

"What does it say?"

"She asks for you to handle the sale. Personally. By name. Jay Porter."

"Me?" I didn't know the woman . . .

The paper Turley returned wadded up my ass. I pulled out the list of stolen items, written on the back a death certificate belonging to a foreign stranger. Maria Morales. Discovered in the pocket of a winter coat, a gift for overseeing a last-minute sale, moving tons of product for pennies on the dollar. Mother, father, place of birth, cause of death. Everything appeared in order, not that I knew what a Mexican death certificate was supposed to look like. Seemed officious enough. But something caught my eye. A second set of numbers. Lower left. Maybe it was the fresher ink, the unnatural shade of blue. Like the ten digits had been imprinted with a newer stamp, added after the fact. An abused wife calling out for help from beyond the grave.

"Fisher?"

"Yeah?"

"What's the area code for Wyoming?"

CHAPTER TWENTY

I SPENT THE afternoon packing up the warehouse until it was too late to haul another load south. My head wasn't in the right space anyway, consumed with why the dead woman, not Keith Mortenson, had been so adamant about holding an auction Thanksgiving night; a series of seemingly chance events suddenly turned calculated. Tom and I hadn't been chosen at random. Our auction house had been selected for a reason, and now I knew what that reason was: me.

Driving back to my place, I attempted to put it all together. At some point, Bowman and Biscoglio must've been charged with handling the wife. Monitoring, spying, bugging? Taxed with retrieving the death certificate dangled over Ethan's head. But how did the rest of it work? Bowman goes down for his other crimes, and, what? Has a crisis of conscience and thinks of me? Considering all Bowman and I had been through, irony lurked in there somewhere. The sacrifice was tougher to swallow. Was Bowman getting soft in his old age? Of course when you don't have all the facts—when all you have is conjecture and speculation—the best you can do is force a picture from the pieces you do have. Which leaves you with a potentially warped portrait. Was I guilty of wishful thinking? Self-fulfilling prophecy? I'd be the first to admit my theory stressed creativity. Unless someone returned my call from Wyoming and proved me right. I may never know why the wheels had been set in motion. But I was starting to get an idea of where this bus was headed. Because I was the one driving the damn thing.

The medication designed to calm the crazy was not working its magic, leaving me high strung, on edge, crawling out of my skin. When I got like this, I knew my head and reasoning couldn't be trusted. I had to take a break, get a good night's sleep. See how this looked in the morning light. But too much was going on to take a break now.

I couldn't wait for suspicions to be confirmed; I needed to call Alison, give her a heads-up about Joanne, let her know Ethan was coming for them. I doubted this news would force her to divulge Phillip's whereabouts, but she'd do a better job breaking the news to the boy than the police would. With enough warning, she might be able to find a safer haven. Sleep was a luxury I did not have.

Before Fisher and I ended our call, he said he'd talked to Charlie, and that he sounded good. Better than good, in fact. He sounded hopeful. Charlie had already gotten his hands on a copy of Alcoholics Anonymous, and was writing down all the meetings in the area, vouching to never touch another drop, done with the drink forever. Fisher said he thought this acute pancreatic attack might be the kick in the ass our friend needed to get his act together. I said I hoped he was right. Charlie needed a wake-up call. Sometimes those calls come in our darkest hour. Sometimes they come when we need them most. And sometimes those two are the same thing.

When I pulled onto my street, something felt off. An eerie premonition, the white streets too still, too silent, too white. I sensed I was being watched. Or rather my place was. Just because you're paranoid doesn't mean they're not out to get you.

I killed the lights, eased up slow, stopping a good half block short. Nothing rustled beneath the dark sky. But I felt it. Fuckers had been getting the jump on me too much lately. Time to sniff out the attack before it happened. I wasn't walking into another ambush. I stared up at my cold, unlit apartment.

I dug out my smartphone, clicking the icon for that high-tech lighting system Fisher installed. Hadn't used it yet, had no idea if it even worked. But we were about to find out. I opened the app. Turned out it wasn't a whole lot of guesswork. Press the big button marked "on." Just had to hope I was close enough to my router and in a pocket of cellular service for the instructions to register. I saw the lights switch on. In my upstairs window. From my truck, a hundred feet away. Like living in the future. Kicked on the heater too. Might as well make it nice and toasty for the bastards. Able to control the dimness for each room, I started in the kitchen, as if I were walking through my front door after a long day of work, adjusting the rest of the house, room by room, lingering in the can while I took a leak.

Sitting in my truck, in awe of progress—if not for mankind then at least for me—maybe I was evolving—I'd forgotten the purpose of the exercise.

Until I saw the two shadows slinking through Hank Miller's parking lot, opening the door to my well, creeping up the backstairs to my apartment.

I watched the thieves enter my home and made the call. Then I got out of my Chevy, walked around my bed, and wrenched free my tire iron from the undercarriage. Crossing the snowy road, I peered up to my second-floor window, observing stealth silhouettes canvassing my home.

The door to my apartment was ajar. There was no way out except through me. Probably not the smartest move, heading in on my own. *Wait for the cops, Jay.* There wasn't much worth stealing in my dumpy one-bedroom above the filling station. But it was my dumpy one-bedroom above the filling station, and *my* shit not worth stealing, this was where my kid slept when he visited, and I'd be damned if I was going to get pushed around in my own home. When you have so little left, you get protective of the scraps. Everyone knows you don't take bones from a junkyard dog.

Easing open my front door, I could hear them in the rear, sniffing, rooting around. Back when my brother was alive I'd caught him doing the same thing more than once. Skeezy junkie shit, pocketing trinkets to pawn. Except these two, whoever they were, had come in after the lights and heat switched on, which meant they hadn't been canvassing the place for a robbery; they were waiting for me to show up.

I had no way of knowing if the men were armed, and if so, with what; all I had was the element of surprise. And a tire iron. They'd already had time to go through my apartment—it wasn't big and there were only so many places to hide. I heard a muffled voice. Sounded like it came from the porch at the far end. I backtracked into the kitchen, slipping inside my bathroom, crouched behind the door. When they realized I wasn't out there on the porch hiding like a coward, they'd have to leave the way they'd come, and then I was going to bust some kneecaps.

The voices got louder as the men drew closer. When they passed, I saw neither was holding a gun, and I knew right away where they were from. A little older than the thugs at Prasch Sugarbush, these two were also graduates of the program. Same bodies forged from lifting steel in the juvie yard. One was taller, and the other, well, not as black. I had a good idea who'd sent them, too. I waited until they both passed, and then I hopped out, tire iron wrapped above my head.

"Hey, fuckos!"

They both practically jumped out of their kicks. When they saw the tire iron, they shot up their hands in surrender.

"Whoa! Calm down!"

They both outweighed me, and each looked like they'd been in more fights than I had. But their hands were in the air and empty; I was holding steel. If they lowered and charged, I was getting in one good crack.

"What the fuck are you doing in my apartment?"

"Relax, man. We just want to talk."

Alison had warned me Richard would be sending more leg-breakers if I didn't back off. When I'd been accosted at the sugarbush, I felt menace oozing out of their pores, the purport of malice. Those guys would just as soon have tossed me from the mountaintop as they would look at me. The vibe I was getting from these two was off. Where was the hate? The desire to do me harm? I couldn't find it. Then again it's hard to gauge emotions or intentions when your heart is jammed up in your throat.

"How did you get in?" I said.

"Door was open."

"Bullshit."

"I swear. It was unlocked."

I'd been so scatterbrained and stressed of late—had I forgotten to lock up?

"You just walk into people's houses uninvited? Start rifling through their shit?"

"Saw the lights flick on. Thought you was home."

"We was looking for a lighter, man." One of the boys held up a crushed pack of Newports. "Can smell the cigarette smoke in here, figured it was cool."

"Well, it's not 'cool.'"

"My name's Mal," the first one said. "That's Leone." He gestured for me to lower the tire iron.

"Mal . . . and Leone," I repeated.

"Short for Malcolm."

"Leone's my last name."

I didn't answer, keeping my distance. I wasn't putting down my tire iron.

"Hey, man, just want to talk," Mal repeated.

"Make it quick."

"We're friends of Phillip."

"Really? You two?" With their prison ink, gold teeth, and baggy jeans, these were the guys who sold the drugs to boys like Phillip Crowder; they didn't hang out with him.

"Addiction doesn't discriminate," Leone said.

"I've seen that bumper sticker, too. Let me guess. You want me to stop looking for Phillip?"

"Yeah," Mal said. "But it's not like you think, man."

"I don't scare easy."

"That's not what we're saying. *Phillip* wants you to stop looking for him."

"Phillip knows I'm looking for him?"

"You were at the Prasch Sugarbush this afternoon."

"Maybe. Why? Was Phillip there?"

Mal shook his head no.

"Then what? Rewrite has farms spread all over the place. How did Phillip even find out?" I set the tire iron on the stovetop and turned on a burner. I lit up and passed along my Marlboro. "I don't have a lighter."

"You were at the same sugarhouse as us," Mal said. "There's an AA meeting every night. Vans take busloads. We all meet up. We talked to Phillip. He asked us to relay the information. Can you respect that?"

"You guys can come and go as you please?"

"We're Level Three," Leone said.

"What level is Phillip?"

"A level that can't come and go like we can."

"Phillip wants me to stop looking for him? Why? He likes working on a farm that much? Rich kid like him, with his soft, ivory hands? Sure. Did Richard Rodgers send you?"

"Man, you're not listening. This ain't about Mr. Rodgers. And this ain't about you, yo. Phillip doesn't want his father to know where he is."

"Why?"

"Because the man is a monster."

"Why don't you tell me where Phillip is, and we can have this conversation in person. I hear it from his mouth, I'll leave him be, won't say a word. Scout's honor."

Malcolm seemed to be considering my offer, when fists pounded my door. "Police!"

I stepped around Mal and Leone, whose eyes widened in surprise—or maybe it was terror.

Two of Ashton's finest entered, guns drawn.

"Got a call about a break-in?"

I didn't know his name. I knew his partner's name was Ramone. He was Puerto Rican and seldom spoke.

"Dispatch reported you saw a couple men breaking into your apartment?"

I squinted to read his name tag. Miller.

Officer Miller looked over Mal and Leone, the obvious answer to his question. I did, too, weighing what I should do. Did I believe them? Maybe. Maybe not. But if this visit was supposed to be a threat, it was a pretty mild one. These guys seemed cool. Even if they *did* bust in my place, I wasn't jamming them up over walking in uninvited.

"Let's see some ID."

"I'm sorry, Officer Miller," I said. "I made a mistake. I didn't recognize them at first. It's been a while. These guys are old friends of my brother."

Miller glanced from me to the intruders, taking in their hip-hop attire, gold chains, and ass hanging out their pants, panning back to me. "You *know* these two?"

"Yes. Through my brother. Chris. Startled me is all. It was dark. I saw a couple dudes hanging outside my place. I panicked." I caught their eyes. "They were in the neighborhood. Stopped by to say hi."

"Yeah," Mal said. "We stopped by to say hi."

"They were just leaving, right, guys?"

Mal nodded. "About to head out, yup. Nice seeing you again, Jay."

I shook their hands with needless formality. "Don't be such strangers, okay?"

Ramone considered the stiff exchange. He knew something was up but couldn't say what. The new guy wasn't going to call me a liar. I had no idea about Malcolm or Leone's pasts, if they had a criminal record like my brother. But the last thing a guy like that needs is to get jacked up over some penny-ante bullshit. Cops run names, an old failure to appear pops up, and like that, he's back down in the hole, right when he was getting on his feet again, putting his life in order.

The two cops stood on my stoop, watching the boys leave, still not convinced, Miller poking his head back in to double-check with me, as if I were a battered housewife scared to speak in my abuser's presence.

"Sorry to call you out here on a false alarm."

"Those boys looked pretty tough. Not sure I should've just let them waltz—"

"I told you. We're all good. Call Turley."

Miller sent Ramone after Mal and Leone to make sure they stayed gone. Miller stepped to the stoop out of earshot. I didn't know if he was taking me up on my offer, but if he relayed my story, Turley would back me up. My brother Chris ran with a rough-and-tumble crowd. Plus police hated unnecessary paperwork. I didn't want any knuckleheaded boosting charge from five years ago biting them on the ass. Everyone deserves a second chance.

The two officers returned. Not wanting to be rude, I small-talked about random shit. The recent snowstorms. Whether the Ashton Redcoats fielded a quality squad this year—like I gave a flying fuck about high school football. Must be boring as hell working law enforcement in a town like Ashton, especially after they shut down the truck stop, which was where 90 percent of the crime took place. Then again in the last week we'd seen a murder attempt, suffered a slew of break-ins, robberies, assaults, and a possible kidnapping. So maybe our little town was getting as progressive as the big city.

Once they left, I slid the dead bolt, grabbed my landline, and called Alison. I liked that she took my calls. Despite her being married and our, at best, complicated relationship, these conversations were the highlight of miserable days. I was also willing to overlook the possibility that her husband had dispatched two thugs to rough me up—if that's what was even happening. Alison was the only friend I had right now who wasn't admitted to a hospital with blunt head trauma and/or major organ failure. No love story is perfect.

"Hello, Jay. This isn't a good time."

"Just got home. Found a couple guys from your program lurking in my apartment. Wouldn't know anything about that, would you?"

She didn't say anything.

"Did your husband send them?"

"Not that I know of." Long pause. "I mean, I don't think so."

"That doesn't sound very convincing. If he did, it was a tepid warning—"

"This isn't a good time—"

"Less a warning, more like a pleasant request."

"Request?"

"To stop looking for Phillip Crowder."

"I already told you that."

"Things have changed. Might not have that option anymore."

"Jay, this is getting old—"

"I need to see you. In person. I don't want to do this over the phone."

"Do what?"

"It's about the woman who retained your services? Who asked you to kidnap her son? It's about Joanne Crowder."

"I've been explicit. I cannot talk about—"

"She's dead. Joanne Crowder, the woman who hired you—or rather the woman you can't confirm hired you, can't admit knowing, can't admit what-the-fuck-ever she is to you—she's dead."

"Oh my God." Alison tripped over herself, still trying to maintain patient confidentiality, like it mattered in times like this. "That's what the police wanted," she added softly, as if to herself. Voices muffled on the other end, a dinner party bleeding through.

"Am I calling at a bad time?"

"It's fine," she said. It sounded like she'd moved to a quieter room with more privacy. I couldn't hear any more third-party conversation. "What happened?"

"You want the official version?"

"Sure. Start there."

"Suicide. Found the body in her car. In the garage. Carbon monoxide poisoning."

I went to the window, checked up and down the block. I didn't know what I was looking for.

"I appreciate you calling," she said.

"I think we should meet. Go over a plan."

"I can't right now."

"Listen, Ethan Crowder is going to petition the courts to get a court order. He's sole custodian of his son now. You have a day, two tops. Then the police will come with a warrant, whether you want to talk to them or not. You'll have to tell them where he is, and they will take him away."

"A couple days ago you wanted me to divulge a patient's where-abouts so you could return him to his father. Now you want to help me keep him hidden?"

"Let's meet for dinner?" I caught myself. "I mean, get together, go out?"

"I'm married, Jay."

"I am aware of that. But we need to talk about this. Maybe we can put our heads together, make a plan."

I heard her thinking on the other end of the line, relenting with a sigh. "You're going to have to give me time."

"I know just the place. Laid-back little joint."

"A bar?"

"Not a bar-bar. More like a café. But they serve alcohol. Most places do. Unless you want to come over to my apartment?"

When Alison didn't respond right away, I fantasized she was scared to be alone with me. Maybe I was imagining this thing be-tween us, this tension, which could've been nothing more than annoyance and a desire to get rid of me the quickest way possible. After my long-term, volatile relationship with Jenny, which had been filled with so many knockdown drag-out fights, I wasn't sure I could tell the difference anymore.

"No," she said, "public is better."

"The Blue Carousel. Torrington. Twenty minutes southeast of you. Very low key, mellow. Meet there in an hour?"

"Make it two. This is going to take some doing."

I didn't mind coming to her this time, and Torrington was still far enough out of the way that she'd be safe from prying eyes.

After we hung up, I hopped in the shower, shaved, and put on my nicest button-up. Found a pair of dress shoes buried in the back of the closet. I wanted to pretend this wasn't a date. But I had a hard time fighting the flutters. As uncertain and awkward as I felt, I was glad those parts still existed, that I still had a heart that could be crushed.

CHAPTER TWENTY-ONE

I ARRIVED AT the Blue Carousel early. Walking along the ice-slicked sidewalk to the bar, I saw the sandwich board sign. Performing Nightly: Stan the Magic Man. I instantly regretted my choice of venue. I could only imagine how bad Stan the Magic Man must suck.

A long-haired hippy dude sat at the piano, tickling the ivories, singing a song I never heard before, with his eyes closed. I wanted to hate Stan the Magic Man. And I tried. But, goddamn, he was good.

The low-lit bar drew a decent crowd for a weeknight. I'd been here with Jenny a long time ago. I remembered digging the laid-back, authentic vibe. Drinks were cheap, great pub food, darts, décor understated. Of course, like everything else, that had changed. The bar now possessed that hipster feel so many places get because any place that's cool can't stay cool for long because the dipshits and douchebags always find out about it and ruin everything by showing up.

Huge beer fermenters, obtrusive stainless steel tanks, occupied half the space, brewing pretentious craft beers they served with fruit wedges. I counted four men dressed like lumberjacks—flannels, suede work boots, with big, bushy beards but skinny as fuck—drinking these fruity craft beers. All four together didn't weigh half as much as a genuine mountain man like Tom Gable.

There was also one very sad-looking woman, who had to be in her late forties, maybe early fifties. I imagined her a former beauty queen in another life. If every face told a story, I didn't want to know how hers ended.

The Blue Carousel still retained enough old-school cred that it wasn't too far gone. Give it a few years. The saving grace was Stan the Magic Man. If I could choose one, true artistic talent, I'd pick a voice like that. Any time I tried to sing, I sounded like a seal getting clubbed by Gordon Gano.

I sat at the bar and ordered an IPA, wishing you could still smoke inside. Stan the Magic Man was cigarette-and-beer music. He launched into this old Tony Carey tune I hadn't heard in forever, "A Fine, Fine Day." When he got to the part about Uncle Sonny giving the cabbie twenty bucks to drive around Central Park, I got chills, choked up. I would've asked Stan the Magic Man what he was doing here if I didn't hate Billy Joel so goddamn much.

A short while later, Alison walked in. I wasn't imagining things. She'd taken the time to make herself look pretty. She was pretty anyway, but tonight she arrived the way a woman does a date. The subtle things—blush, lipstick reapplied, whatever they do to their hair to make your heart yearn. I felt like I was sixteen again.

I almost asked what she was drinking, before remembering the whole AA thing. I started feeling like an asshole for suggesting the place. I'd recalled the Blue Carousel as having more of an English pub vibe. But this was a straight-up bar, even if the addition of the piano was a nice touch.

"I'm sorry," I said. "We can go somewhere else."

"Not that big a deal." She nodded toward the Magic Man. "He's pretty good."

"Does it ever get to you?"

"What's that?"

"That you can't drink?"

"That's what you don't understand about recovery. It's not that I can't. It's that I choose not to. Not drinking is a choice. Not drugging is a choice. *My* choice. I used to get high off the drug. Now I get high on the self-control. Does that make sense?"

I shrugged before taking a swig of beer.

"How's your friend? Charlie?"

"Better. I think. He's gung-ho about turning his life around. Says he'll never touch a drop again. Sounds like he means it. I don't know. I can be cynical."

"No, really? You?"

"I want to believe him. He'll die otherwise. It's weird. Right now he's confined to a hospital bed, they're telling him he has to completely overhaul his life, and he seems happier than he has in years."

"Floating on the pink cloud."

"Pink cloud?"

"Do you really want to talk recovery?"

"Sure. Why not?" I didn't say I just liked the sound of her voice, or that being near her was, clichés aside, intoxicating. I would've sat there listening to her read the day's soup specials.

"When someone makes the decision to sober up, there's a brief period where they *do* embrace a promising future. They are buoyed by the possibilities of what this new, sober life offers, the chances they'll have. On some level we all know when we're fucking up. By admitting we are powerless, we make a decision to take the first step, turn our lives over to something greater than ourselves, which makes us feel powerful. We are reclaiming what we've lost. This produces waves of euphoria, and you float high in the rosy sky with no worries, optimistic and hopeful."

"Pink cloud. Got it."

"The problem isn't the first few days. It's the long haul."

I'd taken off my winter coat, and I saw her checking out my arms, which were covered in long sleeves to hide the bruises. "You look like you work out."

I didn't bother mentioning I hadn't seen the inside of a gym since high school. Working outdoors, lifting heavy shit has its perks. I'd take the compliment.

"You know how hard it is exercising? Keeping up a routine. All those people at the gym the first day of the new year? The revolutionaries? By week three they are gone. Same with staying sober. Racing out of the gate is great. But it's the turtle and the hare. Consistency is key. You need an answer to 'why not'? When it is four thirty on a Tuesday afternoon and you suddenly find yourself with forty dollars in your pocket. Why not call the man, get high? Why not head down to the liquor store or bar? The same intensity and drive you put into getting high, you need to put into staying clean."

I tried to pay attention but I'd drifted off, eyes glassing over, the way they do when your doctor tells you that you need to stop smoking.

"So what do you really want to talk about, Jay?"

I pointed at the bartender for another beer. "Were you having a dinner party?"

"It was a get-together. A few friends." She anticipated what I was going to ask next, namely how she escaped. "I told Richard a friend was having a crisis." When I didn't get what she meant, she added, "In recovery, being of service to other addicts and alcoholics is part of the program. Crisis means a free pass to leave dinner parties, no questions asked."

"So you lied?"

"Not exactly."

I tried not to be too sensitive. How much of that was true, at least in her mind? Did she seriously see me as having a problem? I wasn't asking that question. I'd already exposed myself more than I wanted to. I learned a long time ago that you never ask a question unless you are certain the answer is going to be in your favor.

"So Phillip Crowder's two buddies who stopped by?" I said, priming the conversation. "Malcolm and Leone?"

If this kidnapping and recovery business didn't pan out, Alison Rodgers had a real future in Texas Hold 'Em. She gave away nothing.

The bartender brought my beer. Alison ordered a club soda and lime. Stan the Magic Man was now covering Terry Reid, and I wanted to believe it would feel good to be back where I belonged. Soon as I figured out where that was.

"You okay?" she asked.

"Rough week. I know you can't tell me if Malcolm and Leone are clients—"

"At this point, does it matter? No, they're not. They were. Graduated a month ago. They're good kids."

"But they still work on the farm?"

"Service."

"Right."

"It's not uncommon for graduates to stay on, become full-time employees of whatever farm they'd been assigned during treatment."

"They said they were Level Three."

"That's what we call it. A paid probationary period with the business, contingent on passing urine tests, making meetings, doing their steps. But for all practical purposes, they are on their own. They can leave grounds after work, drive to meetings, enjoy weekend passes, that kind of thing."

"They're friends with Phillip?"

Alison nodded.

"Kinda weird, no?"

"What's that?"

"Phillip Crowder is the definition of silver spoon, born in a lap of luxury, and Malcolm and Leone struck me as more street."

"I told you. Addiction does not discriminate. A drug is a drug is a drug. Rewrite takes all comers."

"And you're sure they weren't sent by Richard."

"They weren't."

"You're the one who warned me to be on the lookout."

"My husband would like you to stop interfering with our business. Now we have your local sheriff bugging us, Middlesex PD threatening injunctions. Richard wanted to deliver the message to back off. And he seems willing to make an example of you. It's personal."

"Why am I such a threat?"

I could feel her cheeks blush.

"Come on, Alison, I can take it."

"He thinks you have a thing for me."

"A thing?"

"A crush."

"That's so cute. Like we're in high school or something. Can I slip you a note, ask you to check off a box, see if you 'like' me, too?"

Alison found the clock on the wall. "I have to go." She made ready to leave. "I know for a fact Richard didn't send anyone to your place, okay? Whatever else you got going on, that's on you."

"Are you happy with him?"

"My husband? That's none of your business." She narrowed her eyes. "Is this what you do now? Your wife left you, so you go around trying to break up other marriages?"

"I didn't mean it like that."

"How did you mean it then?"

"You seem . . . I don't know. You're right. It's none of my business. I thought . . . never mind."

"It doesn't matter, does it? I'm married."

She'd stood to go but hadn't left yet.

I reached out and touched her sleeve. "Sorry. I crossed the line. Please stay. I want to talk about how to help Phillip."

She had her sights fixed on the door but sat back down.

"I don't get you, Jay. You run around risking limb and neck to find this kid, are willing to get your ass kicked to get hold of him, and then soon as you get close, you're doing a one-eighty? Last week, Rewrite Interventions was this evil corporation that had to be stopped at all costs, and now you're on board, want to help?"

"A lot has changed since then. Starting with Joanne Crowder being dead."

Alison sighed, shoulders slagged, the reaction you get when you've exhausted someone to resignation. How many times had I seen Jenny do the same? "I've already violated half a dozen principles. I might as well tell you that Phillip didn't have a very good home life. People who resort to drugs seldom do."

"Malcolm and Leone said that he's scared of his father."

"The worst thing that can happen is being released into his father's custody. Phillip is seventeen—"

"I thought he was sixteen?"

"No, he's seventeen. In a few more months he's free of that man. I can't betray confidence. I mean, I can't get into specifics, but the things Ethan Crowder has done to that boy reserve a special place in hell. I assume you've researched online?"

"I read about domestic violence charges that never stuck."

"Against men like him they never do."

"What can we do?"

"*We?* Nothing. With Joanne dead, you're right, Ethan will go to the courts. Joanne was the good parent. We didn't have to 'kidnap' Phillip, as you put it. We were helping keep him safe."

"So you treat addiction. And harbor refugees?"

"Phillip was smoking too much pot to deal with the stress. But, yes, sometimes lines aren't so clear. Rehabs are confidential. Well, they're *supposed* to be. We won't have any sway to hold him against an injunction. And given Ethan's political pull, I'm guessing we'll see that court order sooner rather than later." Alison collected her handbag and jacket. "I really have to get going."

I stood up. "I'll walk you to your car."

"That's not necessary."

"I insist."

"So do I. Listen, Jay. I'm not going to pretend. Okay? I'm not sending you home thinking you are fucked up *and* delusional. You're not imagining it. But this isn't a once-in-a-lifetime feeling. I've felt it before. I used to feel it with Richard, and I'm sure I'll feel it with other men, too. It's nice. An urge. It's fleeting. No different than watching you drink those ice-cold beers, knowing how good they'd taste now, and how much they would cost me later. My life started getting better when I drew some lines, created boundaries for myself, and I began respecting them. I don't cross these lines." She took my hand. "Thank you for the heads-up. Take care of yourself."

Alison Rodgers left me alone in the bar.

I sat down and ordered another beer.

Stan the Magic Man played the opening notes to Springsteen's "The River." Just the piano and voice, stripped-down, soulful, aching. In the bone-chill of winter, with silver flakes floating down, dancing in a shivery sheet, that story cut deeper than usual, and it always cut deep.

You could write an entire book and not capture what Springsteen conveys in a few short lines. It's more than the tragedy of missed opportunity and wasted youth. Born into this life, cursed by a name from which there is no escape, you never had a chance. They'll tell you you're more than the subdivisions and street signs that box you in; that the world is bigger than the town limits that define you; that the ending isn't already written. The Boss knows better. Highways bypass small towns for a reason.

Once he gets the girl pregnant, it's all over. The joyless city hall ceremony, the soul-crushing job at the factory, the surrender to adult compromise. All that's left is the waiting. Car crash. Cirrhosis. Old-folks home, eaten away by cancer, saddled with Alzheimer's, whittling fucking sticks. What difference does it make?

Years later, when he's too used up to give a shit anymore, when his wife won't look him in the eye and he's tired of the lies mistaken for dreams, he reflects on being young again and driving in his brother's car, just him and his baby at the reservoir, lying on the shore, two naked bodies trembling in the moonlight. Like it really might've played out differently. These are the death knells. The ones that really hurt. The trust. The promise. The betrayal.

I'd heard the soft whimpers throughout the song, but caught up in the journey I hadn't allowed them to infiltrate my consciousness. I drank my beer, listened to the mourning, wondered what I was doing with my life. In other words, a Tuesday night. Now these cries had morphed into uncontrollable wailing, impossible to ignore. We all heard it.

I turned. The whole bar turned. At the end of the counter, the sad-looking former beauty queen had broken down, lost it. I'm talking chest-heaving, unable-to-breathe, inconsolable sobbing.

She was bawling so loud, in such torment, Stan the Magic Man had no choice but to stop playing the song.

CHAPTER TWENTY-TWO

I WAS DOWN at the warehouse, readying the next load. Power back on, the damage wasn't too bad. I still needed to get an inventory of what was missing. Never mind making a list for the cops. Tom would need one to file an insurance claim. In addition to the dressers and chests of drawers, we had plenty of expensive trinkets and baubles too. A pair of silver sconces could fetch as much as an eighteenth-century sleigh bed. I saw the sconces, which slipped inside a jacket easy enough, so that was good. But to know what was missing, I had to know what we had. I dealt with the day-to-day dirty work, the grunt labor; inventory was Tom's department. There was no single, definitive hard copy. Far as I knew, Tom stored all that information in his head. And right now his brain had powered down and was having a tough time rebooting.

All things considered, I wasn't feeling too bad. I'd long been at the mercy of my moods—good ones were pretty rare—but my day had started out with a surprise call from my son. Jenny got on the line and said Aiden had woken up insisting he talk to Daddy because he'd had a dream about me. Aiden tried to explain the dream, something about a ship on the lake. It was hard to understand. There was a hurricane and Indians, a witch, a cook, a church bell, y'know, a kid's dream. Didn't make sense. Didn't matter—I was still on my boy's mind. And it was nice hearing Jenny's voice, too. Reminded me there were better parts of me out there.

Charlie also called. He was being discharged from the hospital.

"How you feeling?"

"Better than I've felt in ages," Charlie said. "It was time to make some changes."

"That's good to hear."

"The doctor gave me a list of AA meetings in the area. There's like one every hour."

I asked him if he needed a ride, but he said Fisher was picking him up, since he was still staying at his house.

"Don't worry about me, Jay. I'm going to turn this thing around. I think I'm even going to start hitting the gym again. Start building some hurtin' bombs. Remember how good I used to look in high school, Jay? I'm getting back to that. I mean it. Gonna drop the extra weight, get back in fighting shape. You know what else? I'm thinking of applying to the post office. That'd be a good gig for me. Government job, good benefits. Outside a lot. Walking around. I'd be good at it."

After stopping for a Dunkin' Donuts coffee, I dug out my Springsteen *Live in NYC* disc. Smoking, listening to "The River" on my new stereo, tapping out a beat. When I got to the warehouse, I brought the double live album inside with me, blasting it out of a pair of Blaupunkts.

By noon, I'd picked up most of the mess, moving much faster than I'd anticipated. In lieu of a formal inventory, I eyeballed best I could. I didn't *see* anything missing.

I did not think about Ethan Crowder, Vin Biscoglio, or Owen Eaton. I did not think about my dead brother, my dead parents, or my failed marriage. I did not think about Phillip or his mom. I thought about my son's surprise phone call. And I thought about Alison Rodgers.

I was probably overanalyzing last night, reading more into what she'd said. You can see the good or bad in everything, depending on where you stand, on who you are. A lot of guys would've heard a strong, independent woman, firmly rooted in her recovery, someone who wasn't jeopardizing her new life over a fling. All I heard: there's a chance.

I hadn't heard anyone rattling the gate, music cranked so loud. Which was why Turley had resorted to bleating the air horn to catch my attention. I met him at the roll-up.

"Been trying to call you for the last half hour." Turley peered past my shoulder into the warehouse, Blaupunkt stereo on, shaking the walls. "Rocking out, eh?"

"What's up?"

"Come on," he said, suddenly turning stern. "Let's go."

"What for?"

"We're taking a ride."

"Where to?"

Turley cracked a grin, unable to keep the surprise going any longer. I could see now he'd been hamming up the heavy.

"Tom Gable woke up."

*　*　*

Even if I had answered the phone, I'd still be getting the personal escort. Turley wasn't missing this moment. I had to cut the guy some slack. Given our rocky history, that note had put him in a tough spot.

The room was packed with people who didn't like me. Murder charges aside, the affair accusation wasn't winning me any fans.

Freddie and her sisters huddled around the bed, skull-fucking me with serious stink eye.

But not Tom. Upon seeing me, he pushed himself up, beaming ear to ear. He scratched his wooly beard, then spread his lumberjack arms wide.

"Jay! Get over here." He wrapped me in a bear hug. The public embrace squashed any rumor I'd ever try to hurt him. "How's *our* business?" The way he said it, he was nipping that shit in the mutherfucking bud right now.

"Never better. Except for the break-in at the warehouse, our stuff being stolen from the storage pod, and someone trying to kill you."

"Besides that, Mrs. Lincoln?" He started laughing, then seized up, clutching his ribs, which were still heavily bandaged.

The nurse in the room urged him to remain calm.

He waved her off. "I feel like a million bucks. I got all my friends here." He made sure everyone saw he was looking at me when he said that.

"Tom," Turley said. "I need to ask you some questions. If you're up to it?"

Tom curled his fingers, a defiant "bring it on." "I'm famished." He turned to the nurse. "Can someone get me something to eat?" Tom Gable slapped his big belly. "You think this thing's gonna feed itself? I've been out almost a week."

"I'll see what I can do."

"Bring everything you got. Including the horse."

After she was gone, Tom leaned toward his wife, whispering, "Mind sneaking me up a coffee? They won't let me have anything but decaf."

Freddie and the harpies glowered as they took leave.

"Don't mind Freddie, Jay. She's been worried about me. This is all my fault."

"How's that, Tom?"

"The letter. I'm guessing that's what you want to talk about?"

"Among other things."

"Freddie told me." Tom turned my way. "Sorry. I was trying to help." Then back to Turley: "I got a call late Thanksgiving night. Like two in the morning. We'd been drinking most of the day. Party carried into night. I was pretty blotto, I'll admit."

"Who called?"

"Don't know. Didn't give his name. He wanted a list of all the items sold at auction that night, the one Jay handled."

"What'd this man say?"

"I told you. He wanted the list of all the merch that changed hands. He was adamant, rude, abrasive. I told him it was none of his fucking business. I got a little heated. Alcohol. I don't remember much of the conversation, only that it escalated quick. I don't take well to being pushed around. Especially in my own house. At some point the guy said he wanted that list and I'd better give it to him if I knew what was good for me, some macho bullshit, how that wasn't Joanne's stuff to sell, et cetera."

"Ethan," I said to Turley.

"Or Vin Biscoglio."

"I don't know who that is," Tom said.

"Don't worry about it. The letter?"

"Right. Ever hear the saying a drunk man's tongue is a sober man's mind? I'd been meaning to put something in writing, to protect Jay. In case something ever happened to me. My dad dropped dead of a heart attack at my age. I know how big I am, my heart, the cholesterol, the red meat. I remembered reading in a magazine how a dated letter in a sealed envelope was as good as a will. Save the lawyer costs. I hate giving those vultures a penny if I can avoid it. My heart was pounding so hard and fast when I hung up that phone. I guess I can get pretty sentimental when I'm hammered. Jay's always been like a son." He turned to me. "Don't mean to embarrass you. But you are. I had no idea this guy, who-ever he was, would make good on his threat. I'm sorry."

"Sorry? You wrote a note leaving me your company if you died. Why would you be sorry?"

"Because I almost died." He leered at Turley. "And apparently some people in this town still believe horseshit rumors and don't know what a stand-up guy you are."

Turley's face reddened.

"So," Tom said. "Jay's off the hook, right? For everything?"

"He was never on the hook. But someone *did* beat you senseless. Your brain hemorrhaged inside your skull. You were in a coma. I'd like to catch who did it. What happened that morning?"

"I'm not sure. Memory is hazy. It was the day after the storm. I'd met with Jay, run some errands, and was headed back up the mountain. I saw a car stuck in the snow. The driver was gunning metal, spinning tires, digging himself deeper."

"Make? Model?"

"Blue? Black? Sedan? Not sure." Tom shook his head. "I pulled behind them. Got out of my truck, and before I could even tell whoever it was to take their goddamn foot off the gas, they were only making it worse, that we needed to put down some two-by-fours for traction, I feel thunder strike at the base of my skull, and next thing I know, I wake up here."

"Someone snuck up behind you?"

"Whoever called me, I'd guess. Check the phone records." Tom's brow creased. "Where are my clothes?"

Tom buzzed a nurse into the room.

"Where are my clothes? The ones I was wearing when they brought me in here?"

The nurse, a fresh young thing just out of school, dolled-up and platinum as a candy striper, pointed at a locker.

"Mind getting my flannel for me, sugar?"

She retrieved the shirt. Tom fished the pockets. "It's not here."

"What?" Turley asked.

"The list from the sale. When I met Jay for breakfast, he'd given me a complete list of all the items sold that night. I had it in my pocket."

"You took a helluva beating," Turley said. "Could've gone flying out."

"Maybe."

"What was so important about that sale?"

I'd begun gathering my suspicions. Putting those suspicions into words right now wasn't going to help Turley.

Another nurse brought Tom his lunch. Nothing smells worse than the stench of warmed-up hospital food. You can smell the disappointment. Might be the one meal on earth worse than eating at Denny's. Not that Tom seemed to mind. He was scarfing ravenous, two-fisting slices of Wonder Bread and chicken legs, unwrapping plastic cutlery. He chomped down on the small, bruised apple.

"We do sales like that all the time," Tom said through a mouthful. "I can tell you everything that was bought and sold that night. You can run it through your systems, contact the buyers, however you want to handle it."

"Thought you said you lost the list?"

Tom tapped his head. "Better storage than the new iMac." He pointed a fork at me. "But I'm putting my money on that dresser Owen swindled."

"What dresser?" Turley said.

"French-carved, Chaucer antique," Tom said. "Sideboard, display. Owen Eaton got it for pennies on the dollar. Back-lot wheeling and dealing. Tried to do it off the books. Dirtbag move. Would've gone totally under the radar if not for our boy Jay here."

"Why didn't you mention this dresser sooner?" Turley asked me.

"I did. You weren't paying attention."

Freddie came back upstairs. At least she attempted a genuine smile this time. Turley said he'd be in touch.

Turley had to drive me back to the warehouse since we'd come together, which left us plenty of time to talk.

"What do you think any of that means?" he asked. "You know these Crowders better than I do."

"Not really. They were dealing with the fallout from a nasty breakup. I know Joanne arranged the sale." I was glad Turley didn't ask how I knew that. Confessing to hacking someone's email was not high on my priority list. "My guess? Joanne got rid of something Ethan didn't want gotten rid of. Something that painted him in a bad light or could prove something he didn't want proven. Have you talked to Keith Mortenson? He was on-site to oversee the auction."

"No one has seen Keith Mortenson since that sale. Never got on his flight. And divorced couples fight over personal possessions all the time. That doesn't equate to attempted murder. What about this dresser Tom was talking about? The one Owen low-balled on?"

"It was top-of-the-line, a once-in-a-lifetime find. But this isn't about the dresser."

"You ever hear the most logical answer is usually the correct one? It's how being a cop works. Moultonborough rang earlier.

Someone broke into the Clearing House last night. Tripped the security. Please tell me you weren't home alone with no one to verify your whereabouts?"

"You're kidding, right?"

"If someone's following that dresser, makes sense they'd hit up Owen next."

"Why didn't you check Tom's phone record?" I said. "See who called him that night? You know, you could've saved me a world of trouble."

"I fucked up, Jay. You're right. I should have. I apologize. I assumed it was you, and you were scared to admit it because it would make you look guilty. I was wrong." He peered over. "Now please give me an alibi for last night so I can report back to Moultonborough and tell them that it wasn't you. After all the aggravation you caused the guy, you know Owen was itching to drop your name."

"What time?"

"Eleven." Turley's expression conveyed eight degrees of pleading. I knew, after what happened with Tom, he didn't want to be having this conversation.

"Yes, someone can verify where I was. But don't bother her unless you have to."

He nodded.

"I was having a drink with Alison Rodgers. Down at the Blue Carousel. Torrington. About an hour from the lake. More than covers the time frame. I mean, I was having a drink. She had a club soda. But I'm serious, Turley. That will cause her a ton of aggravation if anyone finds out."

"Did you use a credit card for your drinks?"

"I had a couple beers. And no, I paid cash."

He dropped me off back at the warehouse, too preoccupied to ask why I was meeting with Alison Rodgers, or maybe he wasn't preoccupied at all and had class enough not to pry. No, this was Turley. He was distracted, hot on the trail of another lead. He was hung up on that dresser, and I might've been, too. It was the obvious solution. But nothing about this past week had been obvious. The most valuable item that evening hadn't been sold or swindled; it had been given away. And there was no record of it. I'd been walking around town with the answer on my back all along.

CHAPTER TWENTY-THREE

REVVING MY ENGINES, I headed into the plains. I hadn't been able to reach Fisher or Charlie on their cells, and no one was picking up the landline. I had spoken with the hospital and Charlie wasn't there anymore. Where else could they be? Now that Charlie wouldn't be frequenting the Dubliner, I expected the house to see a lot more action. I was only half right. Charlie wasn't there. Fisher was.

"What's up? Where's Charlie?"

"AA meeting at St. Paul's."

I dropped my Pats hat on top of the landline. "Can't pick up a phone?"

"I'm busy." Fisher had his laptop out, papers spread, tiny color-coded Post-It notes splitting sheaves, bookmarking God-knows-what. Charlie's place was always dark. Even with the lights on, in the middle of the day, the shadow of Lamentation Mountain loomed large, throwing shade across the whole valley. Another storm brewed, gathering fury over the summit.

"What are you working on?"

"Next issue of *Occam's Razor*. Electromagnetic pulses, Fukushima."

"Fuck you what?"

"Japan. Nuclear reactor meltdown. Don't worry about it, Porter. It's only going to impact the West Coast."

"My nephew lives on the West Coast."

"Tell him to avoid eating sushi for a while. What do you want?"

"Tom Gable woke up."

"Congratulations on being cleared of murder charges. I'd offer you a beer, but Charlie had me throw out all the alcohol."

"Even the beer?"

"Even the beer."

I pulled the list I'd copied for Turley, slapping the death certificate on the table.

"What's this?"

I spun around a wood chair, grabbed pine, and laid out what Tom had told Turley at the hospital, skipping past the dead-end dresser and getting to the heart of what we were dealing with.

"You think someone brained Tom on the side road . . . for a list of junk?"

"No. What that list of junk was written on." I pointed at the ten digits in the lower left-hand corner. "That's a phone number. Isabelle Crowder moved to Wyoming after the divorce."

"That's why you wanted the area code for Wyoming?" Fisher read the name on the death certificate. "Did we ever figure out who this Maria Morales is?"

"No clue. But I think Joanne Crowder was trying to get a message to me."

"Thought you didn't know her."

"I don't. I mean, I didn't." No one knew her anymore. "But I think she wanted me to call that number."

"Why didn't she just call you directly and tell you that? Better yet, why not tell you straight up what the fuck was going on, instead of opting for some whacky game of telephone?"

"I told you, I didn't know her."

"Let me get this straight, Porter. You think Joanne Crowder, a woman you never met, sent you a secret message with a phone number to call Ethan Crowder's ex-wife, on the back of a Mexican death certificate. And she did this because . . . ?"

When Fisher put it like that, it did sound a little out there.

"All I know is Keith Mortenson wanted me to have that winter coat, and that—" I pointed at the death certificate—"was in the pocket."

Fisher squinted elf-eyed, looking at me like I should be in Arkham.

"Joanne set up the sale. You sent me the e-mail. She must've given the coat to Mortenson. To give to me. What other explanation could there be? They're working together."

"Doesn't Mortenson work for Ethan?"

"I don't know. Yeah, he did. I mean, no one has seen him in days."

Fisher got up, went to the kitchen, came back with some water. "Drink this."

"I'm not crazy."

"No one said you were."

"This isn't like Judge Roberts or Chris, okay? This isn't stress. I'm not wigging out. I am thinking clearly."

"Let's say you're right. Joanne asks you to host a sale on Thanksgiving, tells Mortenson to give you a tip for doing her a solid—"

"The coat!"

"Fine. The coat. Maybe she bought the jacket used?"

"I don't think the Crowders do a lot of thrift store shopping. And whatever happened to 'there's no such thing as coincidence'?"

Fisher seemed to consider this as he sat back down and fingered his news about tainted fish. He spun around his laptop, dragging the death certificate in front of him, clacking away. He closed his computer. "I'm assuming you called the number?"

"Yup."

"No one answered?"

"Nope. No name. No outgoing message, either. I tried a reverse lookup on Google—"

"Google stopped doing that shit years ago."

"Can you find out if that number belongs to Isabelle Crowder?"

"Not if Isabelle doesn't want to be found. There's tons of ways to keep your number hidden these days. Call-forwarding, prepaid accounts, spoofcards. Fucking Freedom Voice. It's endless."

"If she didn't want to be found, why is her phone number on Maria Morales' death certificate?"

"How the hell should I know? You don't even know who this Maria Morales is. And we don't know if that *is* Isabelle Crowder's phone number."

"It's somebody's. Those numbers are not from the Mexican government. I checked online."

"Look at you, Porter. Getting all hi-tech with the e-research." He drummed his fingers on the laptop. "No shit. What do you think I was looking up?"

"Someone wanted to know what items changed hands from that sale—a sale Joanne, now dead, initiated. They broke into our warehouse looking for that list. They emptied our storage pod looking for that list. They almost killed Tom to get it. Keith Mortenson, the man who was on-site with the merchandise, has vanished. Someone broke into Owen Eaton's Clearing House last night. But no one cares about dressers or bedposts. No one cares about French-carved Chaucers. I'm telling you. They're searching for that specific piece of paper. There's no record of the coat. No one knows I have it."

"Didn't you suspect Owen of breaking into *your* warehouse?" Fisher circled back around to the beginning. "How would Joanne even know who you are?"

"Bowman."

"That psycho? Why?"

"Can you find out if that's her number?" I pointed at the laptop. "I thought you were good at that stuff."

"It's a computer, Porter. Not a gateway to another dimension, man."

I snatched the death certificate off the table. "Never mind."

He snatched it back out of my hand. "Don't get your panties in a bunch. I didn't say I wouldn't try. But it would help if I knew what I was looking for, beyond verifying phone numbers. Weren't Ethan and Isabelle married, like, two days? Even if that is her number, what do you think she's going to be able to tell you?"

"I don't know." I pointed at the death certificate. "But I have a feeling that's what everyone has been running around trying to find."

"I thought the goal was to find Phillip Crowder."

"I think those two might be the same thing."

*　*　*

I wasn't sitting around while Fisher worked cyber patrol. Like Baba O'Riley, I was better out in the fields. Except I couldn't reach out to Joanne, because she was dead. Keith Mortenson had disappeared from this mortal coil, too. I'd already called Wyoming, if that's where I was calling, and left a message after the beep, even though nothing had prompted me to do so. With no one having returned my call, my theory started to feel marooned between speculative fiction and Fantasy Island. The longer I thought about it, the more I empathized with Tattoo, jumping up and down trying to flag invisible planes. I had to make my move. Vin Biscoglio wasn't returning to my kitchen anytime soon. I'd been a tool used to set a plan in motion. Even if I didn't grasp all the particular parts, I knew the next step would be getting the boy.

Meaning I had to find Phillip Crowder first. There was only one way to do that, and with the courts about to intervene, it had to be tonight. I knew neither she—nor her husband—were going to be happy to see me.

Showing up on someone's doorstep unannounced is rude but it has its advantages. A phone call wasn't softening the blow. From what Alison told me last night at the Blue Carousel, the odds of Mr. Rodgers taking a swing at me were pretty high. That's what I'd do if I were in his shoes. There's a reason why I was divorced.

Alison answered the door. She didn't seem surprised to see me. She didn't seem particularly delighted either, more like worn down, broken, resigned. I had that effect on people. She left the door open.

The appeal of a house owes as much to an owner's individual tastes and decorative choices as it does any architectural layout. "You have a good eye for interior design." I doubted Richard's contribution to the cause. The nautical-themed artwork—wall hangings, stitching on sailor pillows, tapestries, paintings of harpoons, steamers, colonial advice typeset in tiny frames—tied the rooms together, all very New England.

"What are you doing here, Jay?"

"Is your husband home?"

"He went back out."

"For how long?"

"He went . . . back out." She stressed those last two words. "That's what they call it when an alcoholic falls off the wagon, relapses. Throws away twenty years of sobriety because he wants to act like a jealous lunatic."

I liked this woman and her warm, cozy home. Very much.
Outside it was cold, dark, and snowy. This kitchen was clean and
smelled nice, like orange blossoms and lavender water. Wasn't a
thing out of place. Not a single dirty dish. Not one unwashed
mug or spoon. My truck, on the other hand, was filthy and
smelled bad. Like old cheese and sad. But I wanted back in that
stinky truck, back on treacherous roads in a blizzard, far from the
pleasant company of this pretty woman. Because I knew nothing
about this conversation was going to work out in my favor.

Alison walked into the kitchen and sat at the island in the
middle, hands around a steaming cup of tea. She didn't look at
me. I had the chance to slip out, and considering the mess I'd just
stepped in, I knew I probably should. But I needed to talk to her
if I hoped to get to this kid before his dad did. That was, if Ethan
hadn't snatched him up already. I followed her to the island.

"Want to tell me what happened?" I braced for the blame. I
hadn't done anything, really, other than my job, and if the stress
of this situation had gotten to Richard, how was it *my* fault he'd
gone on a bender?

"Your sheriff called. Richard answered the phone."

This was my fault. In my rush to establish an alibi, I'd blown
hers. Even if I had warned Turley to leave her alone. Goddamn
cops. I sat down to accept my sentence. But she granted an unde-
served pardon.

"Things were falling apart before you got here. We were already
fighting. Richard and I have very different visions for Rewrite. A
lot of the practices you find questionable? I do, too. And if I'm
being honest, I used you, your involvement and coming around,
as an excuse to address that. It was convenient. And lousy of me.
One of those shitty things you do when you're married."

"I wouldn't be too hard on yourself."

"No, Jay, I don't imagine you would."

I didn't want to ask what she meant by that because I already had a good idea.

"But Richard was the one who decided to go back out. That was his choice. I didn't open that bottle for him. And neither did you. We got sober together. Met in rehab, actually. A long time ago. Wasn't always smooth sailing, but we stuck it out. Addicts substitute. Drug for a drug. Drug for a person. Person for a person. What I told you last night, about drawing lines and establishing boundaries, that was as much for my benefit as it was yours." She stood up and walked to the kitchen sink, cleaning her teacup on the spot.

I imagined when the moon was out, the light's reflection on her fair skin must be heavenly. But there was no moon out tonight. Just the darkness of an uncertain world.

She kept her back to me. Maybe it was easier that way. "For a long time, we were each other's drug. And believe it or not that worked for a while. Richard and I filled each other's empty parts. I think that's why we started Rewrite together, some unspoken belief that if we were always chasing a dream, we'd forever feed the high. But the road eventually ends. It always does. One way or the other."

I didn't know enough about addiction to offer advice, but I did know enough as a man to shut up and listen, which Alison clearly needed someone to do.

"That's the hard part about getting straight. The part no one tells you about. They try. But you can't hear it. Even after twenty years I couldn't hear it. All the problems that made you pick up in the first place are still there. They don't leave. You find other ways to fill the hole. Some healthy, like exercise, meetings, community. Some less so. But it's Band-Aids on a broken leg."

When Alison turned around, her eyes were rimmed with tears, and the suffering warred inside me, too. She took a step toward me, and I her, and in that moment I knew she would do anything to alleviate the pain. I could be that temporary fix. I wanted to be that reprieve, however fleeting, desperate, or wrong. And it was the last thing either of us needed right now.

So we both waited for the moment to pass.

"I'm guessing you didn't come here to listen to me complain about my marriage?"

There was no way to ease into what I needed.

"Has Phillip gone home?"

"We received the injunction today. Tomorrow morning."

"I need to see him, Alison. I don't think I'll get the chance once his father has custody. I have some questions only he can answer. You have to trust me."

"Answer me something."

I waited.

"These questions, do they help Phillip? I mean, if you get the answers you want, everything comes your way, best-case scenario, will his life be any better off?"

I wanted to lie. "Maybe."

"The Carlson Sugarhouse. Stuberville. Off the 3. Before the 16."

I made to go, but Alison caught my arm, turned me around.

"Now here's where I'll tell you not to head out to the sugar-house, that my husband may very well be there, waiting for you. He expects you to come. He knows you won't quit, and he hates to lose. Especially to someone like you. When he drinks, he be-comes a different man. It's been a long time since I've seen that man, but it didn't take more than a few minutes to remind me what that man is like. He is not a good man. That trailer those boys took you to? There's a hunting rifle under the desk. There is one at every sugarhouse. When I spoke to him on the phone, he was running hard, feeling indignant and righteous. That's a potent combination for a man like Richard. It's been a long time. I know what he'll do if he sees you. He'll kill you, and he'll be one hundred percent within his rights. You'll be trespassing on private property. If you have something concrete, go to your sheriff friend. Do this the right way. Otherwise this ends bad for you."

CHAPTER TWENTY-FOUR

IT WAS LATE and the skies had opened up, dumping snow by the bucketful. Stuberville wasn't like Ashton, or even Middlesex. There were no plows to ground out here. Thankfully I didn't have to go over the mountain and deal with pulling over and strapping on the chains, but that was about all I had to be thankful for. The terrain up here was steep and gnarled, rife with thicket, winding hills, and deep, dark wilderness. Without benefit of the occasional mailbox reflection, I enjoyed three-second lead-time of my headlights. Even if I'd wanted to take Alison's warning to heart and call Turley, I had no evidence to trade. Death certificates and winter coats didn't add up to squat. This wasn't Ashton's jurisdiction anyway. There was no crime being committed, other than the one I was guilty of, and for what? I wasn't working for Ethan Crowder or Vin Biscoglio, and now that Tom had woken up, I wasn't trying to clear my name. Was I as pigheaded as my wife said I was? Was I as bad as Richard, simply hating to lose? Lose what? I had nothing left.

I had my boy, a state over with his new, better dad. I had a nephew I barely knew. I didn't have a death wish like my brother. I wasn't looking to make some grand, dramatic statement and go out in a blaze. But I didn't turn around either.

Cranking gears up the hillside, I found no starlight, GPS, or celestial providence. After a while, I wasn't sure I had the right town anymore, my route a map I'd committed to memory in the flats. With the witches of November howling, the snow and ice piled fast. Every turn reckless, I risked rollover. When I saw the sign for Carlson Sugarbush, a minor miracle, I heaved a huge sigh of relief. Or that might've been my lungs catching up to the pack of Marlboros I'd inhaled.

The Carlson Sugarbush wasn't as big as the Prasch place. Less flash but more intimate. There wasn't any room for subterfuge, no tall trees in which to conceal cameras lining the driveway. This farm didn't cater to tourists, and there were no signs inviting the public to play pilgrim. Carlson was a regular, small working sugarbush. There were no cars in the parking lot, which granted my presence conspicuous cover. An American flag rippled proud atop a long pole in front of a tinderbox.

On my way in, I'd seen the outline of a large barn, the mill in which to produce the sugar, rising above the tree line on the horizon, miles away. Now in the valley, I no longer saw that barn, tormented by the knowledge of how far I had to go.

Tin buckets dangled from maple trunks, traps waiting for the extraction of spring. The sweet aroma of boiled sap saturated the air, drifting beyond hill and dale, cutting through the clean scent of freshly falling snow. The smell permanently steeped into the oxygen like fry grease into a waffle house apron.

I hadn't put my tire iron back, leaving little else in my truck to use as a weapon. What difference did it make? Nothing stops a bullet. I wasn't totally unprepared. I grabbed the biggest flathead I had from the toolbox. Stuck it in my back pocket for the quick draw. I also had a little flashlight, even if the dim shine didn't offer much more guidance than my cell across the foggy moor.

If Richard Rodgers lie in wait, he was flying blind, too. The heavy snowfall came down harder, swirling faster. Assuming the

dorms were on-site—I'd only glimpsed the barn—I had to hope
they were nearby. I wasn't lasting long in this weather. Stepping
over fallen branches, crackling bramble and kindling underfoot,
I headed deeper into the woods, trying to ignore Alison's question—was this really about helping Phillip? Or was I trying to
prove a point?

Maples, red, sugar, black, dotted the brae, obscured by dense
snowfall. Following this little light of mine, I forged my own path,
into parts unknown. The wet ground had already penetrated my
work boots, soaking through two pairs of socks. Alison told me
Phillip worked this farm but didn't mention where to actually
find him. More than once, I entertained notions of a setup, saying
Richard had gone back out a ruse to get me on their property,
provide probable cause to rid themselves of a pain in their ass. An
early sign of hypothermia: delusional thought.

I trekked forever though sticky powder, climbing over felled
logs and kicking through bramble and dead thorn bush. I stumbled, tripped on the slippery, shaky ground, which graded lower
and lower, sucking me farther into the valley. Even with gloves,
my hands were tender and raw. Grasping for tiny trees and limber
branches, hoping for bend but not break, the meat of my palms
shredded in the relentless search for higher ground. I had to pull
myself back up.

At the top of the hill, I passed a footbridge. A babbling brook
raced below the ice, cold waters gurgling through fissures. The
sugarhouse poked above the ridge, big square thing outlined
against the black. I heard footsteps behind me, and spun one-
eighty, screwdriver brandished, the Wild West's lamest gun-
slinger. I saw nothing but felt eyes studying my every move, like a
wild animal tracking me, the slow, precise menace of the hunt. I

holstered my weapon. Doubt I'd puncture the first layer of black bear fat.

When I turned back toward the barn, I saw a light flicker behind it. Maybe a hundred yards past the sugarhouse, up another hill. This had to be the dorms. I stuck the flashlight in my pocket, hands retreating into sleeves, bloody palms better served bunching my coat at the neck to stave off frostbite. I lowered my shoulders, bulling forward into slanting winds, fixed on the lighthouse in the squall.

Fighting uphill, I wasn't blazing any trail, and I had to stop and curl my body backwards, wait for the gales to break before I plowed on.

I came upon the modest, ramshackle dormitory, which reminded me of 1930 dustbowl photographs and sharecropper quarters. The only thing missing was the old-timer playing harmonica on the front steps without shoes. I liked Alison, but seeing where Rewrite housed their impoverished flock, I had a tough time buying earnest mission statements. Like a megachurch preacher begging for 10 percent of the welfare check while he bathes in champagne fountains. I'd seen how the Rodgers lived.

Tried the front door. Locked. Went around to the side and had better luck.

The dorm was as cold inside as it was out. Rodents and other woodland critters scurried beneath boards. Even if his mom sent him here, Phillip only had to find a pay phone, escape a collect call away. There were no chain-linked fences topped with barbed wire walling anyone in. Unless Malcolm and Leone had been telling the truth and Phillip Crowder didn't want to leave.

I pulled my flashlight. Slickers hung from pegs in a narrow mudroom, boots stashed beneath a bench, wood plank floor sloshed with dirty slush. In the next room, six cots lined against the wall like a youth hostel. I swept the flashlight over the space, which was no warmer than the entranceway. One of the boys shot up. Delicate, doe-eyed and trembling.

"Where's Phillip?" I said.

Another boy stirred. He was bigger, older, with arms chiseled from the hard life. "The fuck, man? I'm trying to sleep."

I didn't answer. He pulled the covers over his head.

The first boy pointed at an empty cot. Blankets tousled, sheets ripped to the floor, as if exit had been expedited.

"Where is he?"

"Someone came and got him."

"Fuck, I'm trying to sleep!"

"Who took him? Was it Richard? Do you know who Richard is?"

"Mr. Rodgers. But it wasn't him."

"Did Phillip go on his own? Did he seem scared?"

"Shut the fuck up!"

I spun around, screwdriver out. "Man, if you don't pull those covers back over your head and go to sleep, I swear to God I'm stabbing you in the fucking neck."

"This man came by, said to grab his things, that they were leaving. I never seen him before. Phillip grabbed his bag, and they left out the side door." He pointed the opposite way I'd come.

"How long ago?"

"Five, ten minutes?"

By now more boys had woken up, bitching about the noise. Someone muttered "mutherfucker," but I tried not to take it personally.

I crossed the floor. Door wide open. Panning my flickering flashlight over snowy ground, I saw the footprints, two sets, backtracking toward the sugarhouse. Couldn't have gotten far. I slapped the head of my flashlight, hoping for a sharper shaft.

The footprints stopped at the barn door, ajar and rocking with the wind. I aimed my light up the dusty ground, along creaking beams. A pair of giant tanks, steam stack top hats with vacuum gauges, split the difference. Vents rose past the crisscrossing walkways to the roof, where castoff released during the boil. This time of year, the traps remained closed.

Weaving past wheelbarrows and ladders, cords of split logs piled beside wood-burning stoves, I kept my searchlight roving over machines, scouring beneath stairs along the perimeter, settling on a table, a workstation in the corner. For a moment, I thought I'd hit the mother lode. Blocks of cash stacked high. What kind of illicit operation had I stumbled upon? I reached out for the money, only to discover wax-dipped cheddar cheese blocks, organized and labeled for shipment.

I caught a shadow twitch out of the corner of my eye, and swung the flashlight around. Two figures huddled behind an evaporator.

"Who are you?" a man called out, the voice so meek and apprehensive I stopped worrying about being shot.

"My name is Jay Porter. I'm looking for Phillip."

Footsteps shuffled out of the dust. I recognized Phillip from the pictures online. Older now, he sported the same shaggy yellow cut. The man with him was the bigger surprise. Keith Mortenson.

Took a moment for him to recognize me, too.

"You're that junkman? From Thanksgiving?"

I could see his brain twisting up. What fates had conspired to bring us together in the middle of this forest, surrounded by vats of maple syrup and stacks of cheese? I didn't have an answer to that one myself.

"Are you okay, Phillip?"

He nodded.

"Of course he's okay!" Keith Mortenson snapped. "You think I'd hurt him?"

"I don't know what to think. I've been trying very hard to find him."

"Why?"

"It's complicated. A man named Vin Biscoglio wanted to hire me—"

At the mention of Biscoglio's name, Keith Mortenson darted and grabbed the first weapon he could find, in this case a long power drill used to tap trees. I had a screwdriver in my back pocket. His firearm was unplugged. If this were headed toward a shootout, it would go down as the saddest in history.

"Relax. I'm not working for Biscoglio. Or anyone else. I just have a few questions."

That didn't set Mortenson at ease. The slender accountant's hand shook bad, limp wrist overpowered, like an old lady confronting an intruder with her dead husband's Colt 45.

I moved toward them. Keith Mortenson tucked Phillip Crowder behind him, jabbing the hand drill at me, unplugged cord smacking off the floor. "Stay back!"

Stashing my flathead, I showed my hands. Mortenson was terrified. I only had to get him to understand we were on the same side.

Looking into Phillip's eyes, I saw he knew about his mother. There's a spark that goes out when a boy loses his mom. It doesn't come back. I didn't want to make this situation any worse.

"Leave us alone, Mr. Porter," Mortenson said. "I'm honoring Joanne's wishes."

"Like overseeing that furniture sale on Thanksgiving? Giving me that coat?"

"Joanne was a good woman. I loved her. I love Phillip. Ethan is the one you should be worried about. I have to keep Phillip safe. They are coming for him. Like they came for her." Mortenson started groveling. "Let us go. Please. Let us go."

I looked down at my flashlight. "I'm not holding a gun on you, man."

The barn door swung open and shut with the gusting winds and vacuum effect. We were shouting at one another from fifteen feet away. "Tell me what you know. Maybe I can help—"

"You want to help? Help us get out of here, get a head start."

I remembered the empty parking lot. "A head start to where? In what?"

"My car is parked down the access road." Keith Mortenson froze. "You didn't park in the lot, did you? Oh, Christ. Are you stupid? They'll be here any—"

I heard the door kick open behind me, and I whipped around to find a very drunk Richard Rodgers staggering toward me, unsteady rifle aimed over my shoulder, vacillating between electric bellies and roof beams.

"Fucking cocksucker," he slurred.

I assumed he meant me, but he was looking at a push broom when he said it. I didn't know what he'd been drinking, but whatever it was, the liquor had packed a helluva punch. He could barely stand, let alone shoot straight. Not that I wanted to tempt fortunes or challenge theories about broken clocks. Caught in the crossfire, I was stuck between a man with a gun and another with an unplugged hand drill. Common sense dictated I move toward the latter, but I didn't want to give Richard Rodgers a bigger target, or put Phillip in the line of fire.

I held out my hand, opting to reason with Richard. Whatever his faults, the man wasn't a killer. "Why don't you put down the gun?" I gestured at the boy, who looked ready to piss himself. Keith Mortenson didn't seem to be holding up much better. "Come on, man. You're scaring the boy. Put the gun down. Let's talk about this."

Richard Rodgers hoisted the forestock to his shoulder. Odds were against him hitting the broad side of this place. The question was: How itchy was that trigger finger—and how lucky did I feel?

The barn door kept opening and shutting with the violent swirls, a jarring sound that makes jittery people jumpy. The metal stoppers scraped across the concrete floor. Then a hard wind sucked shut the door, slamming it with a thunderous clap, sealing us all inside.

A motor roared to life. The room filled with steam, a wall of smoke, and I couldn't see my hand in front of my face. As the engines thrummed, jacks began working double time, pistons chugging in sync. The smoke granted cover and the opportunity to make a run for it. I heard bodies shuffling but I had lost track of everyone—Richard, Keith, Phillip. Turned around in the steam and smoke, I stumbled past casters and valves opening and closing, searching for something to hold onto that wouldn't burn my hands. Running footsteps scuttled over the whirring candymakers. Someone screamed. Then I heard the blast. I ducked and dove in the direction of where I'd last seen Richard Rodgers. I crashed into him and he crumpled like a CPR practice dummy, damn near already passed out. I crawled around, feeling for the rifle that flew out of his hands. Richard lay in place, mumbling, "I'm sorry. I'm sorry."

My hands found the cold barrel, and I pulled the rifle to my chest, safe from enemy hands. I staggered to my feet, the loud report still ringing in my ears. Feeling around in the darkness, I located the switch to turn off the evaporator, then pushed open

the doors to clear the room. The ferocious storm sucked the
steam from the barn in seconds. The first thing I saw was Phillip
Crowder standing shell-shocked, staring at the spot on the floor
where Keith Mortenson lay, facedown, pool of blood seeping out
the giant hole in the side of his head.

After securing Richard Rodgers—it hadn't taken much effort
to restrain the guy, I'd barely touched him before he curled up,
drooling and sputtering, which made me wonder how, in his
inebriated state, he'd been able to get off such a precise shot—I
brought the kid outside to get him some air. Phillip didn't need to
see any more death. I heard sirens wailing in the distance. We had
a few minutes. This was what I'd been after for the past week, my
moment. And I had no idea what to say.

"I'm sorry about your mom."

The boy shirked off my condolence. With his fair skin and light
hair, he looked much more like his father than he did his mother.
His expression betrayed nothing. Like father like son. How could
I blame him? I still remembered the feeling when my folks died,
like a rusty spoon had been used to excavate chunks of my soul. I
hadn't been much younger than Phillip.

By now other inmates huddled inside the doorway. Six beds.
I counted three boys. Maybe the other two were heavy sleepers.
Squad cars raced up the drive, screeching to a stop. I knew it
would still take them several minutes to reach the sugarhouse and
barn. Intersecting shafts of light raked the forest, cut up by jagged, crooked branches, hillsides slapped with strips of blues and
reds. Against all that white snow, the moment felt pretty damned
patriotic.

"We're almost out of time. I have some questions."

The skinny seventeen-year-old boy peered up at me. He was
shivering. I draped my winter coat over his shoulders.

"Why did your mother send you here?"

"She thought I was partying too hard."

"Were you?"

"Sometimes."

"Did you want to come?"

"At first? No. But no one asked me."

"But you stayed?"

"I like it here. I don't have any brothers or sisters." He nodded at the other boys huddled together in the dormitory doorway. "They're like family."

Boots crunched crusted snow, snapping kindling. Flashlight streams fanned up the forest floor; next came the shouts for everyone to stay where they are, don't move. Usual cop bullshit.

"Do you want to go back to your father?"

"No."

The police were almost on us now.

"Is there anything you can tell me, Phillip? Anything that will help me keep you from him? Anything at all?"

He shrugged.

A cop ordered us to put our hands in the air where he could see them.

"Do you know Maria Morales?"

Phillip panned over.

That was it. The cops crashed the party, spinning me around, patting me down, and relieving me of my two dangerous weapons. The EMTs threw a blanket over Phillip's shoulders. As he was being led away, he glanced back, a haunting gaze that resurrected ghosts.

The police conducted their inquiry, determining I was one of the good guys, or at least a victim this time. I watched as officers placed a very drunk Richard Rodgers in the back of a squad car.

Practically had to carry him there, dead weight gouging trails in the snow. Medics wheeled away the lifeless body of Keith Mortenson, covered, like the rest of the countryside, in a sheet of white.

After my statement, which took a while—they had to suss out the exact nature of my relationship to the deceased and what I was doing there in the first place—they said I was free to leave. I got back in my truck and returned home.

Picking up my mail at midnight, I saw the large FedEx envelope from Wyoming.

CHAPTER TWENTY-FIVE

Dear Jay,

I hope this letter finds you well, whoever you are. Maria said if anyone called this number to pass along this information, no questions asked. Though I have plenty, I will honor my friend's request. Knowing the sort of man Ethan is, what he is capable of, I could not avoid a rudimentary background check. You seem like the kind of man Maria would trust. I realize this, you, might be a ploy on Ethan's part. I suppose I have to take that chance. Then again my ex-husband was never that smart, not in the cunning, scheming sense. I didn't need more than two days married to the son of a bitch to see that. Ethan was a petty, nasty little man who won the genetic lottery of being born a Crowder. Coddled and indulged as a child, Ethan grew up to be a temperamental, petulant adult, given to fits of violence, with the means to get away with murder. And that's what he did, and that's what this is, a confession. Or as close to one as you are going to get.

I know you have a lot of questions, and I wish I could take the chance of meeting face to face, or at least risk talking on the phone, explaining more, like how I met Ethan in a club when I was very young, the things he did to gain the trust of a scared, confused girl. The money his family paid to make a problem like me go away. If only scars disappeared so easily. The part you need to know is that

Joanne Crowder did not die last week as reported by your hometown paper. Joanne Crowder died June 17, 2000. I did not know her.

How I came to know Maria Morales is a far less interesting story. It started with a phone call from a scared new bride who'd found my name buried among the clutter of a new life. My mother relayed the message, I returned the call, and Maria and I struck up a friendship, a bond built around mutual pain and abuse, which lasted for years. Early on, I advised her to run, leave, get away by whatever means necessary. Of course Maria couldn't run. Since she was now Joanne, and not just in name. She loved that boy.

They say tigers don't change stripes, and I imagine the same goes for monsters. But I think Ethan was scared of Maria. I'm sure he thought he'd found another gullible girl—Ethan liked them young—but in the end Maria proved far stronger than I ever could, and she fought like hell. Maybe it was her love for the boy, a mission to protect the child from a man like Ethan that gave her such strength. I don't know what excuse Ethan used to get her aboard his private jet in 2000, to convince her to color her hair and answer to another name. But I know she did so willingly. Maria grew up one of several children in Coicoyan de las Flores, one of the most impoverished parts of Mexico. I don't think Ethan needed more than the promise of a better life. Believe it or not, once upon a time, my ex-husband could be charming. This was a chance for Maria to provide for her family, an opportunity to send home money and keep her brothers and sisters alive. Maria knew what she was doing, and more importantly she knew what Ethan had done. Any harm to her would expose his secret too.

Why everything fell apart now, I don't know. Maria and I had not spoken in a long time. My guess is Ethan grew sick of being under someone else's thumb. The humiliation of her leaving, forced to surrender custody of his possession, the tipping point. No matter what the papers say, I doubt Maria took her own life. Though seventeen years with that man could erode anyone's resolve.

As for definitive proof that Ethan killed his second wife, I can't give you that either. I can only tell you what Maria told me. While on vacation in Ixtapa, June 2000, Ethan, in a drunken rage, strangled the mother of his son. He dragged her body from his villa to the rough, choppy seas, and let the riptide carry his sins to a watery grave. Getting away with murder was the easy part. Ethan had the family jet, the resources to bribe corrupt officials and circumvent protocol. Back home, Phillip was an infant, left to the rotating care of nannies and assistants. If anyone noticed the new Mrs. Crowder looked or acted differently, no one brought it up. Joanne and Ethan had not been married long. Ethan traded in women like leases on cars, and the Crowders were notoriously reclusive. I am sure Dorothy and Victor, Ethan's parents, knew what their only son had done. They'd paid to cover up his transgressions before. They'd do so again.

I've enclosed the pictures. You will see the marked difference between the two versions, even with the bottled blonde hair. I am also including the names and numbers of her surviving family in Mexico. I don't know how you can convince authorities to look into this further or what the specific statutes are, but her family can provide all the proof you need that Maria Morales did not die in that car crash. You only have to get the American consultant to see that.

This is the information Ethan did not want to get out. Be careful. He has killed to keep his secrets before. He will surely do so again.

I'm sorry I didn't come forward earlier but this is what Maria wanted. She loved Phillip as her own. Everything Maria did was to make sure Phillip survived his eighteenth birthday, at which point he could hopefully be emancipated from that bastard and claim the inheritance that is rightfully his.

It looks like she almost made it to the finish line.
Maybe you can carry this home the rest of the way.
Warmly,
   Isabelle

PS Do not try to contact me again. By the time you get this letter,
I will be gone.

The sort of man Maria would trust? I never met Maria. Or Joanne. I tried the number again. Of course it was out of service.

*   *   *

Tom hadn't been cleared for work, and wouldn't be for a while. He and I had spoken first thing in the morning, because it was business as usual for me. Which began with shoveling Hank Miller's filling station. The latest sky dump had me wading knee deep in the fluffy white stuff. The plan was to head over to the warehouse, finish what I'd been doing yesterday, load up a U-Haul, and move the rest of our merchandise down to Everything Under the Sun. Then Tom wanted me to get started on clearing the old house on Worthington Ridge. At some point I knew I'd have to call Alison. As much as I enjoyed the sound of her voice, I wasn't looking forward to having that conversation. Even though her husband had fired the gun, in many ways I'd pulled the trigger.

I was filling up my gas-guzzler when Fisher pulled in the lot. I'd called him last night after I finished reading the letter.

"Don't you ever answer your phone, Porter?"

"I've been shoveling this shit for the past hour."

"The Crowder boy back with Dad?"

"I guess." I nodded at his car, which he'd left running, backseat packed with cardboard boxes, computer innards, and cord balls. "Going somewhere?"

"I've wasted enough time in this shitburg. I have to get home. Make sure to check in on Charlie. You haven't seen him since he's been released."

"Gee. I've been a little busy."

"I'm not busting your balls. Just saying you're his best friend, and if I'm not around, someone needs to check in on him."

"I thought you said he was doing well?" I pulled out the nozzle. "All gung-ho AA?"

"He is. He's at a meeting right now. Met a couple guys in the program. They pick him up, bring him home. He's a little insufferable with the sobriety stuff. The Big Book this. The Big Book that. He quotes verses like it's the Bible. But it's good for him. He's sober."

Fisher glanced around, hugging himself in the chill wind.

"What did you find out?"

Fisher pulled his phone, reading digital notes.

"Seventeen and a half years ago, Ethan and Joanne Crowder flew to Mexico. Phillip was two weeks old. He stayed home with the nanny."

"That's . . . of absolutely no help."

"That same year, same month, same week, Maria Morales died in a 'car accident' in Ixtapa. Over the cliff, into the water. No body recovered."

"I imagine there's a lot of Maria Moraleses down there."

"Same one. At least according to the information on the death certificate."

"How do you even verify this?"

"Everything is on the web, man. If you dig deep enough."

"So it's possible she's telling the truth?"

"The dates match up. June 2000. Ethan and Joanne flew back to the States a couple days later. On Crowder's private jet."

"I have to admit, Fisher. I'm almost impressed."

"That paper of mine you were making fun of?"

"The *Razor* Something."

"*Occam's Razor.* We have a lot of readers, from all over the globe, with various specialized fields, areas of interests. We are able to tap into the truths behind the lies."

"Great. A conspiracy paper sponsored by conspiracy nuts found evidence of a conspiracy."

"After 9/11, it's a different world. It was easier before."

"To do what? Kill somebody?"

"Get in and out of Mexico. You ever hear of ghosting?"

"Ghosting? Isn't that what kids call leaving a party without saying goodbye?"

"Ghosting is where you steal a dead person's identity. You read about the abuse allegations, the dismissed charges? Joanne was his second wife. His family paid a lot of cash to keep scandals out of the press. They'd only been married a few months before the trip to Mexico, during which time I uncovered documentation, hospital and police reports, of Joanne 'falling' down the stairs. While pregnant. Couldn't bury that lede. Is murder really that far-fetched?"

Neither of us answered the rhetorical. Instead we watched miniature snow tornadoes twirl across the permafrost in our own personal ballet.

"You send the information to Boston?"

"Not yet."

"What are you waiting for?"

"To hear what you found. I want ironclad proof."

"Not sure you're getting that."

"We've dealt with shaky photographic evidence before. How much is the word of a pissed-off ex-wife worth? That is, if we even believe her?"

"I believe her."

"She's in the wind now. Besides, you spend too much time with the crazies online."

"Life is a riddle, wrapped in a mystery, inside an enigma."

"Okay, Oliver. Don't forget to strap on your tinfoil hat when you get home."

"Har har. There was a reason you were meant to find that death certificate."

"Or, y'know, it was a discarded scrap of paper in an old winter coat someone donated."

"It's your dime, Porter. Till next time." Fisher stood at his open car door, gazing up at the peril of Lamentation Mountain. "I mean it, check in on Charlie."

I promised I would.

After loading up the U-Haul, which had taken all day, sweating balls in the subzero, I'd locked up and was sitting in my truck. Inside a brief pocket of reception, I pulled my cell and started to call Alison. But I stopped, and dialed my ex-wife instead. Jenny didn't pick up. I left a message to have Aiden call me later, and to tell him I loved him, and that I was looking forward to seeing him soon.

I'd just exited the parking lot, trailer burdened with a final, heavy load, when I saw the lights flashing and Turley waving behind the wheel. I glided to the shoulder of the long country road. Miles of nothing, in the middle of nowhere, with a long race still to run.

Through my side-view, I watched Turley stride up, hoisting britches around his big belly.

I left the engine idling and hopped out to meet him. Sooner we were done here, faster I got back on the road.

"What's up, Turley?" I gestured into the encroaching dusk. "Sort of in a hurry."

"Talked to Stuberville police. Had quite a night, eh?"

"Yeah. A fucking blast."

"I know you're interested in the boy. Thought you might like an update." He started back to his squad car, rolling his head for me to follow. It was freezing on the side of that road, gusts gathering down the range, a straight shot blowing through town.

"Got back ballistics," Turley said after we'd slipped into the front seat of his toasty sheriff's car. "Try and match the bullet to the gun that killed Mortenson."

"I was there when Richard Rodgers shot him."

"Wasn't Rodgers' gun."

"What are you talking about?"

"Besides the markings not matching his gun? Entry wound came from the back."

"But I saw Richard Rodgers. He had the hunting rifle in his hands. I heard the blast."

"Wasn't even loaded."

The news both relieved and depressed the shit out of me. Alison wouldn't hate me, which was cool. But now Richard wouldn't be shipped to jail and they'd stay married. Christ, I really was an asshole.

"Who fired the shot?"

"Good question. Park ranger found a body this afternoon. Bottom of a ravine. About half a mile from the Carlson place—you know the preserve over the hill? Some unforgiving geography up there. No gun. No face either. Dropped from on high. Skull caved in. Fingerprints revealed his identity though. Salvadore Bosco. Name ring any bells?"

I shook my head. "I'm guessing he wasn't some hiker who slipped and fell?"

"Salvadore Bosco was an Italian ex-military sharpshooter. And I don't think too many hikers are scaling rockwall in a Dormeuil Vanquish suit."

My mind went beyond bullet holes, to warnings about trespassers thrown off cliffs, a bedtime headcount a couple members short.

"Didn't see the body myself," Turley said, "but the physical description—stocky, bald as a cue, the nice threads—certainly sounds like our boy Biscoglio."

How protective were those graduates of their sacred ground? Or had they merely been following orders?

"Phillip back with Ethan?"

Turley nodded.

I made for the handle but stopped. "You did the autopsy on Joanne Crowder?"

"Not me personally."

"I mean, can Ashton PD access the report?"

"What are you looking for?"

"Teeth."

CHAPTER TWENTY-SIX

"I WAS SURPRISED you agreed to meet me."

"I'll admit my first instinct was to say no. Considering what you were asking for." Alison glanced around the upscale dining room. Justine's Supper Club was the nicest restaurant I knew. I'd only been there once before, with Jenny. No entree less than thirty bucks on the menu. Crackling fireplace and soft lighting, the kind of place where waiters in black vests come by every six minutes to scrape away breadcrumbs from stiff, bleached tablecloths. Was a drive, too, all the way to Piedmont, but some things are worth the effort.

A waiter came by for our drinks. I bypassed beer for some fancy six-dollar Italian soda. Alison said she was fine with water.

"How's Richard?"

"In treatment, getting the help he needs."

"Inpatient?"

"If he was home, do you think I'd be here?" She attempted a smile. "Before I agree to do this, I need to know I'm helping create a solution and not causing more problems."

"We're on the same side here."

"Are we?" Alison plucked a warm roll from the breadbasket lined with linen. "How did you convince the cops to even look into this without comparable DNA?"

"Besides the letter? Dental records."

"If the girl grew up as poor as you say, shantytown in a foreign country, no one's keeping reliable dental records."

"She had gold crowns."

"People that poor don't get gold crowns."

"I know." I sipped my sparkling grapefruit soda. "Forensics found traces of mercury and chromium-cobalt beneath the expensive upgrades."

Alison started to come around. "And with all that money, the Crowders aren't skimping on dentistry."

"Each part of the globe carries unique markers. See it all the time in estate clearing. Different alloys, sheen, chemical compounds."

Alison smiled. "Very smart, Jay."

Another well-groomed waiter took our dinner order. Alison got the Chilean sea bass. I wanted to tell her that there's no such thing, that when you order Chilean sea bass you are actually getting Patagonian toothfish; it's a marketing scam, like baby carrots or organic produce, but I was riding high and didn't want to risk sounding like a know-it-all. I got the rib eye, cooked extra bloody.

"I told you Joanne stashed Phillip to keep him safe."

"In so many words."

"What happens now?"

"The letter and teeth were enough to bend Turley's ear. But without Phillip's DNA, this theory is DOA. Ethan isn't signing off on a sample, and if he catches wind, he's gone. Probably to a country without extradition. You provide the cops with the blood work, they match it against the autopsy results—"

"I mean what happens to Phillip?"

"He'll be eighteen in a few months. If I'm right about this, either Dad goes away for murder and the money's all Phillip's, or he has enough evidence for a civil suit, or—"

"Is this really about Phillip?"

"It's about a man who almost got away with murder. Twice. Lied to his own son. Terrorized his family." I paused. "It's about justice."

"Ethan Crowder is also a very rich man."

"And?"

"And don't you think I researched you, too? I read about the Lombardis and Judge Roberts. You seem to have a grudge against people with money."

"That's not true." What was it with the fucking Internet? Was nothing sacred? "I don't like people thinking their bankroll can buy their way out of trouble. You pull this shit when you're broke, you're in prison. For life. You're rich like Ethan Crowder—"

"Or the Lombardis."

"Wrong is wrong."

"Can I give you some advice, Jay?"

"What am I supposed to say? No?"

"Life isn't fair. You live life on life's terms."

"Isn't that a bumper sticker?"

"One of many. But things become clichés because they are true. I think it's honorable you say you want to do the right thing. I'm glad you still have passion stirring inside you to get outraged. But what you are chasing, this sense of vengeance, retribution, payback for perceived slights? It will run you down, destroy you, leave you heartbroken and alone."

"You wanted to help Phillip, right? This helps Phillip."

"This *might* help Phillip. But I'd also like to help you."

"Good. I can use that blood work."

"I don't mean sending along a sample nurses took when Phillip was admitted, which, against my better judgment, I've already done." She looked me in the eye, rapt. "You ever hear the saying, 'When you point a finger at someone else, you have four more pointing back at you'?"

"Yeah. And I've always hated it. I had a chance a few years ago to put away a very bad man. I didn't pursue the pedophile charges against Gerry Lombardi. Thought the evidence was too weak. Or maybe the mountain was too steep to climb. He walked. And it's eaten away at me since."

"Ethan Crowder is not Gerry Lombardi."

"I know that. But I'm still me. I want to do better. Does that make sense?"

"Yes," she said, "it does."

"Now can I ask you something?"

"Are you asking . . . if you can ask a question?" She grinned at the exact line I'd used on her the other day. She had a beautiful smile, lit up her whole face.

"What do you think would've happened? With us?"

"I don't know how to answer that."

"I mean, if things were different?"

"It's a pointless question."

"Why?"

"Because if things were different, *every*thing would be different. You. Me. We wouldn't be sitting here, about to eat a nice dinner. That's sort of the point."

"Life on life's terms."

Alison winked.

Our food came, and we ate like regular grown-ups, talking in between bites about shit that neither cared about, or at least that I didn't care about, the harsh onset of winter, the new Coos County Treatment Center. It was a nice meal. I insisted on picking up the tab, even though it seriously tapped into my reserves.

Afterwards, I walked with her through the lightly falling snow, waiting while the valet fetched her car. I'd given up on the idea that there could be anything more between us. When her Lexus LC arrived and I went in for a goodnight hug, Alison kissed me on the cheek. I felt like the kiss lingered a little longer, was a bit closer to the lips than normal. But that might've been wishful thinking.

Alison got in her car and drove away. I watched the taillights disappear, until every trace of her was gone.

* * *

For the next week, I worked twelve-hour days. I had my son this weekend, and wanted to make the most of our time together. I was glad to stay busy. When I was out in the fields, I was in my element. No time to worry or think too much.

I wasn't surprised when Turley called with the test results. In fact, I would've been shocked by any other outcome.

That was how my two crazy weeks ended. With vindication. The blood sample Alison supplied and the dental work of "Joanne" Crowder left Ethan with a lot of explaining to do. On my lunch break, I bundled the lab results and everything Isabelle had mailed me, letter, pictures, the death certificate, and shipped it off to Boston. I'd done my part. It was somebody else's problem now. Tomorrow, Saturday, I'd drive over to Burlington to get my son. No more Ethan Crowder or Maria Morales or even Alison Rodgers. This weekend I'd just be a dad. I'd take Aiden wherever he wanted to go, do whatever he wanted to do. Chuck E. Cheese. Bowling. Snowball fights. Donuts. His choice. If there's one perk of being a part-time dad, it's that in my limited time I could spoil the shit out of my son. And I planned to do just that.

But I still had Friday night to kill. Plus, I hadn't seen Charlie since he got out of the hospital. I knew I'd have to endure the AA Kool-Aid—that Higher Power shit irritated me. But, fuck it, if it was keeping him sober, God bless. Driving out to his house in the flats, I was looking forward to having a conversation sober. I tried to recall the last time we'd spoken without a bottle between us. Been a while, that's for sure.

I got to Charlie's house around dusk, pink clouds parting to reveal a beautiful setting sun.

The light was on in his living room, and I could see the soft glow of his television through the front window, so I knew he was home, even if I didn't see the bicycle.

The front door was unlocked, Charlie vegging out in front of his TV.

I stomped the snow from my boots and shut the door.

"Dude, you will never believe what happened." I went to the fridge for a beer without even thinking. Of course there was no beer. Wasn't much food either. "Man, you have to go to the grocery store." Who was I to criticize? Without Jenny to do the shopping and cooking, I ate a lot of take-out. Remembering he didn't have wheels anymore, I added, "I have Aiden this weekend, but maybe Monday we can make a run before I start work?" Even as I said it, I knew hitting the Price Chopper that early was impossible. I filled a glass of tap, peering up at the mountain. A bright white moon rose, perfectly balanced between peaks.

Charlie didn't answer. I curled around the doorframe to see what movie had my best friend so enthralled. The original *Rocky*. Nice. It was early in the film, the part where Mickey has come to Rocky's shithole apartment and offers to train him for his improbable title shot, and Rocky, still pissed Mickey gave away his locker, hides in the can till he leaves. Always cracked me up when

Rocky pops his head out, sees Mickey still there, and then ducks back inside. Always made Charlie laugh, too, but this time he didn't even offer a courtesy chuckle. I recalled what Alison said, how initial enthusiasm wears off. Addicts and alcoholics race out of the gate. Then reality sets in and people get depressed. The way Charlie's shoulders slumped and his head hung low, I saw he had the blues. We had to talk. I'd been putting it off too long.

Heading for the living room, I dropped in the sofa, ready to fill in my buddy on what may've been the weirdest two weeks of my life. Charlie didn't bother glancing over. Now Rocky was drinking raw eggs at the crack of dawn while Philly trains rumbled over track. Charlie and I both owned a copy of the film. I remembered buying the DVDs together, back when you used to have to go to a physical store to do those things. There was this one summer in particular where all we did was drive up and down the Turnpike, hitting vintage record shops, buying music and movies. Man, what were we then? Nineteen? Seemed like a lifetime ago.

"So, Ethan Crowder—well, let's back up." I wanted to spare him the boring stuff, get right to the juicy parts. "We found out Crowder's ex-wife was living in Wyoming—did Fisher tell you? Woman named Isabelle. Anyway, here's where it gets strange. Even before that I found that death certificate . . ." I couldn't remember if Charlie knew about the death certificate. Was he still in the hospital? Didn't matter. He was there the night I got the coat. "Long story short, Isabelle's number was on the death certificate."

I waited for a little acknowledgment. A show of mild interest wouldn't kill the guy. It was hard to hear over the TV. He had the volume blaring. I thought about asking him to turn it down, but I spoke louder.

"We run a DNA test, right? With samples from the autopsy and blood drawn at Rewrite, and you're never going to believe this, Charlie. Guess?" He didn't answer, in no mood for games. I went ahead with the big reveal anyway. "Dude, they aren't even re—"

That's when I noticed something was wrong with Charlie. He hadn't said a word since I walked in. He was sitting there, watching TV with his eyes wide open, but now I saw he wasn't blinking either. His skin was tinged the wrong color, purplish, sallow and washed-out. Even after noting all this, I refused to allow reality to set in.

I don't think I moved for ten minutes, sitting on the sofa, watching my friend's rigid, immovable body, trying to process this latest final cut.

When I pushed myself up and walked over, I now saw Charlie clutched a tall glass in his other hand. It was filled with a frothy brown liquid. Took me a moment to understand I wasn't staring at stout. I was looking at vomit. In a dark corner, I counted the empty bottles. How long had Charlie sat in that chair? Refusing to get up, even as his pancreas and organs failed him, puking from where he sat to speed up the process. A man on a mission with no time to waste, in such a hurry to get out of here that he couldn't delay departure long enough to throw up in the toilet. Like those bars where they put a drain in the floor, right beneath the stools, so men can whip out their dicks, piss on the spot, and keep drinking.

"You stupid sonofabitch, Charlie," I said to no one.

I knew I had to phone it in. Then I'd have to sit around and wait for the ambulance and coroner, the cops, Turley, answer some more stupid fucking questions. I didn't have the heart for that right now. I put my hand on his shoulder and felt the cold through the thin fabric of his tee shirt, the life that was no longer inside him. The pungent, sour bile of days'-old vomit rose up from the froth.

I rushed back in the kitchen, wishing Fisher had forgotten to toss one beer. All this booze, he couldn't save one beer? I searched the pantry, cupboards, broom closet. I didn't have my meds with me. Just one drink. I could feel myself cracking the tab, tasting the ice-cold hops gliding over my tongue, soothing the back of my throat, the relief that would come with the clean bubbles and crisp burn. Was that too much to ask?

No, not a panic attack. Not now. Why did I leave my apartment without my pills? Here it comes. I hyperventilated, heart racing, terror invading, fear overtaking my body, jamming up my limbs, seizing fingertips and toes, choking my neck, cutting off air supply and making it hard to breathe. No choice but to weather the storm. I reached for the edge of something reliable to hold onto.

At the sink, I shoveled water into my mouth. I looked out the window, back up at Lamentation Mountain. The moon no longer balanced atop those peaks; the earth had shifted, everything off center.

This world would keep spinning. I'd wait here for that ball to teeter, topple past the tipping point, and start to roll, gather speed with the force of an avalanche and flatten these frozen fields of wheat and chaff.

ACKNOWLEDGMENTS

FIRST AND FOREMOST, thanks to my lovely wife, Justine. Living with a writer isn't easy. I disappear for months at a time to craft and create, and even when I'm not hunkered down in the basement, I live in a fantasy world, carrying on imaginary conversations with make-believe people as I stare across the kitchen table with a blank, vacant gaze. Somehow the children survive, the lights and heat stay on, and you are still there in the morning. For this and more I am truly blessed.

Thanks to my boys, Holden and Jackson Kerouac. You guys are still too young to understand how your being born made my life worthwhile. I am lucky to be your dad.

To my remaining family—my brothers, Josh and Jason; and my sister, Melissa: Jay, thanks for letting me steal parts of your life to create Jay Porter. Josh, sorry I wasn't a better big brother; I did my best. And, Melissa, Mom would be very proud to see the woman you've become.

Thanks to "Big" Jim Petersen. Every boy needs a dad, and even though you were under no obligation to do so, you stepped up and showed me the way. I shudder to think where I might've ended up had you not taken on the job.

Thanks to Rich, Tom, and Jimmy. The older I get, the fewer people I feel comfortable burdening with my problems. I'm glad

I met you when I did, that you knew me when, and that after everything you still take my calls.

To my writing mentors and teachers—in no particular order, Steve Ostrowski, Tom Hazuka, David Cappella, Ravi Shankar, Lynne Barrett, Les Standiford, James W. Hall, John Dufresne, Dan Wakefield, and anyone else I may've missed: thank you for all you've taught me. You took a trembling, skinny kid fresh off the streets and kept him safe under your wings. I probably don't have a writing career without you; I definitely don't stay alive.

Thanks to my East Coast experts on drugs, alcohol, and firearms, Josh Karaczewski and Scott Hartan.

To the Berlin High Class of '88: thanks for the continued support, and liberal use of your names, albeit for fictional purposes: Jim Case, Alison Hodgson, Tracy Bartlett, Christopher Ludko, Jack Lotko, Ron Lamontagne and Marc Boucher, and of course Vin Biscoglio, who is much, much nicer in real life.

To all my mystery writing peers and contemporaries: I've said it before and I'll say it again, and I'll probably keep saying it with every book I publish. You will never find kinder, more giving and supportive folks than those who write about murder for a living. Up until now, I've avoided listing everyone by name because I could fill up an entire book, but having just returned from Bouchercon 2016 in New Orleans, seeing your smiling faces, it's hard not to feel the love. So here goes: Hilary Davidson, Brian Panowich, Rob Hart, Catriona McPherson, Angel Colon, Mike Creeden, Rob Brunet, Terrence McCauley, Rob Pierce, Danny Gardner, Renee "Brandy" Pickup, Thomas Pluck, Keith Rawson, Pam Stack, Mike McCrary, Erik Storey, Erik Arneson, Chris Irvin, Ron Earl Phillips, Hector Duarte, Jr., William E. Wallace, Mike Miner, Will Viharo, Eryk Pruitt, James R. Tuck, James Grady, Nik Korpon, Jen Conley, Sara J. Henry, Craig T. McNeely,

Jordan Harper, Benoit Lelièvre, Mike Monson, Rebecca Swope, Michelle Isler, Charles Salzberg, Eric Beetner, David James Keaton, Benjamin Whitmer, Christa Faust, Johnny Shaw, Allison Davis, S.W. Lauden, Chris Dewildt, Fawn Neun, Nanette Blake, Todd Robinson, David Corbett, Ro Cuzon, and though I've already thanked him, I'll do it again because I love him that much—an extra shout-out to my brother from another, Tom Pitts. Glad you made it out, too. I know I am missing someone. So let's leave it at if we've ever shared a drink at the bar or a late-night e-rap session, this one goes out to you. (And special thanks to David Ivester for sticking around after hours, and Timothy McKean for bringing Jay Porter to life in our audiobooks.)

Thank you to my agent, Liz Kracht, and the Kimberley Cameron Agency. Your job is not all that dissimilar to my wife's—you have to deal with my neurosis, impatience, and insecurities—for a fraction of the glory. You've sold five of my novels in five years. Can't ask for much more than that. (Except France. I'd like to go to France.) Most of all, thank you for being my friend.

Thanks to the Oceanview team. Pat, Bob, Lee, Emily, and Lisa, you've given Jay Porter a home, and for that I am forever grateful. You have been everything I could ask for in a publisher. Thank you for believing in me. I will continue to work tirelessly to reward that faith.

And, finally, a hearty, heartfelt thank-you to all my readers and fans. You are why I do what I do . . .

CPSIA information can be obtained
at www.ICGtesting.com
Printed in the USA
BVHW07s0225220618
519494BV00003B/5/P

9 781608 092963